AMATA

BOOK THREE
·THE FIRST VESTALS OF ROME·
TRILOGY

AMATA

DEBRA MAY MACLEOD
AND SCOTT MACLEOD

Cover design by ebooklaunch.com
Stylized V symbol designed by Jeanine Henning
Book design by Maureen Cutajar, gopublished.com

Paperback edition: ISBN 978-1-990640-06-3
Hardcover edition: ISBN 978-1-990640-07-0
Ebook edition: ISBN 978-1-990640-08-7

DebraMayMacleod.com

CHAPTER 1

Rome

716 BCE

The sun that had just started to rise over Rome cast a hazy orange glow over the homes, shrines and temples of the city by the Tiber. It was a strange haze, one that crept up from the Forum to shroud the tops of the Capitoline and Palatine Hills, and on another morning King Romulus might have headed straight to the Auguraculum to take the auspices and see what it all meant. But not this morning. This morning, he was preoccupied by more mundane, earthly matters. More irritating matters. Senatorial matters.

When he was a young man and a new king, Romulus had placed great faith in the wise men who had first comprised the *Senatus Romanus.* They had seemed to him like the revered fathers of Latium—experienced, and though unavoidably self-interested, nonetheless steadfastly devoted to the city's success. They had given him invaluable counsel over the years. But now that he was over a half-century old himself, Romulus often found the advisory assembly that he had created in his youth more vexing than valuable.

As he passed through the gauzy Forum on his way to the *Comitium,* he spotted the only vendor awake and ready to serve at this hour—an old baker who for years had made it his practice to open with the dawn, for the king. The man bowed in greeting and spoke with familiarity.

"Fine morning, Highness," he said. "Air's murky as a whore's bathwater, though."

"Indeed," replied the king. He accepted a round loaf of bread from the man's burn-scarred hands, tore off a piece, and stuffed it into his mouth. "How is your new granddaughter, Memmius?"

"Howls like Cerberus in a foot trap," replied the vendor. "The walls shake with each shriek. I'll die from the shock of it one night."

"I hope not. Who will serve me my breakfast?" Romulus ate another piece of warm bread and casually tossed the rest of the loaf to the red-cloaked captain of his bodyguard, Statius, who caught it.

Like most mornings, Romulus was scheduled to meet with several aggrieved senators before the official sitting of the assembly began. It was a practice that had always come easy to the early rising king, but which had taken the better part of a year for Statius to adjust to. As the king walked on, the guard ordered his men to stand down. Soldiers were forbidden from entering the Comitium whenever senators were meeting in the Curia. He rested his elbows on the vendor's wooden stall and ordered wine with water. The king would not re-emerge until mid-morning at least.

Passing the decorated speaker's platform, Romulus noted with approval the thick smoke coming from the altar fire at the Shrine of Vulcan. That was good. Twice in as many months he'd had to threaten the priests with a public lashing for making late sacrifice. The birds and the gods were up before dawn, and if they could do it, so could the damn priests.

He continued through the open-sky Comitium toward the columned portico of the Curia, a wry grin appearing on his face at the sight of a dead bull calf lying in its own blood at the base of a wide stone altar just outside the entrance. On top of the altar, the young animal's innards burned in Vesta's purifying fire. No doubt, the sacrifice had been carried out by the senators who awaited him inside the Curia: the mashed appearance of the animal's head, the incorrect entrails in the fire, and the leftover mess was clearly the work of politicians, not priests. He stepped through the animal's blood and entered the senatorial assembly space.

"*Salve*, Your Highness," welcomed one of the senators. "We offered to your health this morning."

"Yes, I have your offering on my sandals, Senator Naevius."

"Apologies, Highness. We missed the priests, and unfortunately the sanitation slaves have not yet arrived. They are helping to clear a blockage from the sewer line."

Romulus strode past the fire that burned on another altar, this one smaller, in the center of the temple. He sat heavily in his carved wooden senatorial chair, unfastening his purple cloak and letting it fall over the backrest as the senators sat in the first row of seats in front of him. It was only then that he realized one of the senators, a hopelessly dismal and bloated man by the name of Calvisius, had brought his adult son to the meeting.

"Senator Calvisius," said Romulus, "I do not recall granting permission—"

The senator stood and put his hand on his chest, bowing to the king.

"Your Highness, Senator Oppius approved my request yesterday." He held a chest fold of his toga as he spoke, a posture that struck Romulus as pretentious. "Perhaps he forgot to mention it?"

"Perhaps," said Romulus. It was likely. At nearly ninety years old, Oppius seemed to forget more than he remembered these days. Still, as one of the first men to have sat in Rome's Senate— and one of the more useful, despite his age and infirmity—Romulus would not disrespect him by removing him from his position. "Make no mention of the oversight to Oppius," he said to Calvisius.

"Understood, Highness."

Romulus sat forward in his chair. "What is the matter you wish to discuss?"

Calvisius glanced at his colleagues, gripped his toga tighter, and held up his chin as he addressed the king. "It is the matter of the land appropriations that Your Highness has recently made in Etruria. My esteemed colleagues and I speak for many in the Senate who believe this is an unlawful"—he rethought the last word and softened it—"an *inappropriate* reallocation of property." He gestured to his son. "I had recently bestowed a fine villa with excellent pasture to my son Lucius as a wedding present. Imagine his offense, and my surprise, to receive armed soldiers on that land, claiming it for themselves."

"It should have been no surprise, Calvisius," said Romulus. "Had you spent more time in Rome attending the Senate and less time in the countryside with your mistress, you would have expected the company. I put the matter to a vote months before the land was redistributed."

Calvisius cast his companions an unhappy look. It was time someone else stood against the king, or at least backed him up. Reluctantly, a senator named Carteius stood and lowered his head to Romulus.

"Your Highness," he said cautiously, "you are correct that the matter was put to a vote. But as you will remember, the Senate voted overwhelmingly against the appropriations."

Romulus bristled. "It was my soldiers who fought alongside me in Etruria, not my senators." He made a show of inspecting the faces of the men before him. "I do not recall seeing any of you there. My men purchased that land with their blood and they deserve to retire on it."

"Our king and our brave soldiers deserve all honors and blessings," agreed Calvisius. "We all remember well the victory you achieved in Etruria. Every one of us celebrated the defeat of King Velsos." The senator's lips lifted into an adulating smile. "You marched him through the streets of Rome, beaten and dressed in a boy's tunica. It was fitting dress for a ruler who behaved with such puerility."

The king stood abruptly, causing Calvisius to take an involuntary step back. "If you have sewn an insult toward me into that statement, Senator, I will pull the string right now."

"Your Highness," said Carteius. "He means no insult, I can assure you." He raised his hands, petitioning for calm. "We only wish to inquire whether Your Highness plans to redistribute more of our land to your retiring soldiers. We have heard rumors that our properties in Caenina and—"

"You have heard rumors? You command a private audience with your king before Sol has fully risen because of rumors?" Romulus snorted. "I will hear no more of this." He took two long strides across the floor to leave when the beseeching face of Calvisius appeared before him.

"Your Highness, I beg your forgiveness, please allow us to—"

The senator's words ended in a gasp as he felt the sharp blade of the king's dagger press threateningly into the fatty folds of flesh on his neck.

Holding his blade against Calvisius's throat, Romulus watched a rivulet of blood disappear under the neckline of the senator's toga. He brought his face close. "You are a step away from sedition, sir. I should—"

A sudden searing pain in the center of his back made the king grunt and frown in confusion. He lowered his blade and twisted around to find Calvisius's son, Lucius, standing behind him, his eyes wide and his dagger clutched in one hand. The blade was dripping with fresh blood.

Romulus reached around to touch the wound on his back, and then brought his hand before his face. Warm blood coated his fingers. He could feel more blood running down his back, soaking his tunica. "*Quid ita?*" he asked in disbelief.

Calvisius clapped his hands to his face. "Lucius, you fool! What have you done?"

The young man gaped at his father. "He was going to kill you!"

Senator Naevius rushed forward and ripped the dagger out of Lucius's hand. He tossed it aside and it slid across the floor. He put his hands on Romulus's shoulders. "Your Highness, can you walk?"

"Of course I can walk," Romulus muttered through clenched teeth. He did not want to show how badly it hurt...or how disturbed he was by the strange numbness cascading down both legs like an immobilizing waterfall. He took a step forward, and found himself falling into Naevius's arms. He rested there, willing his legs to support him.

"Help me carry him!" Naevius shouted to the other senators. None moved.

Naevius blinked at them. "What are you waiting for? Help me! We are all dead men if he dies!"

Calvisius surveyed the halting expressions of the other senators. He turned back to Naevius. "We are all dead men if he *lives*," he replied, his voice a strident whisper. "You think he will spare us? Last week he killed a merchant for splashing mud on his toga. How do you think we will fare?"

"We are not guilty," said Naevius, "only your son is."

"We will all fly from the Tarpeian Rock before the day is over," Carteius replied. He stared forebodingly at the faltering king. The rest of the men exchanged dismayed glances, and then followed his stricken gaze.

Romulus had been preoccupied with the frightening state of his legs, but something in the air catalyzed his survival instincts and he suddenly sensed the increasingly conspiratorial mood around him. The threat had spread, like a contagion, from one man to all six. He grasped the fabric of Naevius's toga and tried to stand, sucking in air through his nose. He opened his mouth to call out to his guard. "Stat—"

With what seemed to the king like impossible speed, Lucius scrambled for his dagger on the floor and brought it up fast, sinking the blade deep into his back a second time. Romulus grimaced, but his body responded with a self-preserving rush of adrenaline and a burst of strength. Using Naevius's body as a bolster, he propelled himself toward Lucius, swiping his blade across the younger man's midsection. Lucius shrieked and collapsed onto the floor, writhing in pain.

Romulus could not stop himself from joining him there. His strength faded and panic flared throughout his body as his legs gave out under him. He sank to the floor still gripping his dagger, desperately trying to twist his body so that he could hold the blade defensively above him.

"Statius!" he called out, but his voice was as powerless as his legs, and only the feeblest sound came out. That weakness, even more than the senators' sacrilegious attack, enraged him.

Father Mars, he prayed, even as he felt a blade sink into his chest. *Enter my veins and give me the strength to strike them down!*

Romulus closed his eyes against the blazing pain of the metal shank as it pierced his ribcage. When he opened them, the light was gone—for a moment, he feared the blackness was Hades, but then he realized it was only the crowd of senators above him, blocking the light. He tried to raise his arms to push them off, but his body no longer obeyed his commands. He felt something thick in his throat and reflexively swallowed, hearing his own muffled groan as the blade remained unmoving, lodged in his neck.

"He won't die! Stab his heart!"

The Roman king's heart pounded madly for a moment, then met metal, and stopped.

For several long moments, none of the senators moved. None spoke. Other than the sound of their panting, erratic breaths, the Curia was silent. One by one, they stood and stepped back.

On the floor before them lay the unmoving body of Romulus. His lifeless eyes were open. His thin lips were slightly parted as if in silent protest, and blood dribbled out one side of his mouth to coat his black-bearded cheek. The handle of Lucius's dagger still protruded from his neck: the handle of the king's own dagger, the killing blade, protruded from his chest.

"*Jovis nos servet,*" whispered the oldest among them, a droopy-eyed man named Pele. It was the first thing he had said all morning. He wiped his mouth with the back of a trembling hand. "What have we done?"

Lucius, who lay near the slain king, pushed himself to his knees, clutching his stomach. "We have saved my father's life."

"You idiot," seethed the senator Antonius. "He would not have killed a senator!" He rounded on Calvisius. "Your son had no business being here. He doesn't know how the king is! Now look what has happened!"

"We don't have time to argue," replied Calvisius. "People will begin arriving soon." He looked down at the king's corpse. "We have to get rid of it."

"Get rid of it?" Antonius asked incredulously. He pointed at the body. "And how do you propose we get rid of *that* without being seen?"

Naevius stepped forward. "We can carry it out through the slave's entrance," he said, distress forcing his normally deep voice to rise. "We can put it in Pele's lectica."

Pele shook his head. "I didn't come in my lectica. I rode my horse today, as you did."

The brief rise of hope fell.

"We can cut him up."

They all turned to face the man who had spoken. Lucius. He was on his feet now, pressing a palm against the bloodstain over his belly. He reached down and withdrew his dagger from the king's neck. Blood came up with the blade.

"If we cut him up..." he licked his lips in revolt, but continued, "...if we take his arms and legs off first, and his head...the pieces would be small enough to..."

"Small enough to what?" his father prodded.

"To carry out under our togas," said Lucius. His breathing was short and shaky. Ignoring the horrified expressions of the senators, he pressed on. "We wouldn't have to make it far. Just to our horses." He took several steps toward the portico and listened intently. "I only hear a few voices coming from the *senaculum*," he said, referring to the area beyond the Comitium where senators gathered before entering the Curia. "Hardly any of the other senators have arrived yet, and the guards won't be able to see us from where they are in the Forum."

"And you don't think our colleagues will notice us limping through the Comitium with lumps of the king under our clothing?" asked Carteius.

"Not if we act normally," Lucius insisted. "They're politicians, not soldiers. They're busy gossiping or rehearsing what they will say in the Senate today, they won't give us a second glance. They aren't looking for anything out of the ordinary." He raked his fingers through his hair. "We just have to make it to our horses," he stressed again, "and then we'll have the cover of the stable. We can stuff the pieces in our horse pouches and ride away like nothing happened."

"And how do we explain the king's absence?" asked Naevius. "Everyone knows we had an early audience with him this morning. His guards will interrogate us."

Lucius held out his arms in a gesture of mock innocence. "We say he left after our meeting. We play stupid. We blame his guards for their laxity. As long as each of us sticks to the plan, as long as no one breaks under interrogation and confesses, they will have no grounds to convict us." He turned to his father. "You said it is the king's practice to meet with senators before session, correct? There is no reason for this morning to be any different."

It was an absurd plan. It would never work. Yet it was the only plan anyone had come up with in the midst of their grievous predicament. That was enough to give it authority.

"What about the blood?" asked Antonius. "It will look like we slaughtered ten goats in here!"

Lucius gestured to the wide stone altar just outside the portico where the sacrificial bull calf was still lying in a wide pool of its own blood. Bloody tracks made by the king's sandals made a path to where they all stood.

"You can say the sacrifice made a run for it and things got messy," he said, though unable to conceal the doubt in his voice.

"Anyway, the slaves will probably come and clean it up before anyone else arrives. It is still early." When no one moved, he spoke more emphatically. "We cannot waste more time talking about it." He looked at the dagger in his hand. "This won't do." Passing the dagger to Carteius, he rushed to the altar outside the portico, snatched the weightier sacrificial knife and axe off the top, and dashed back into the Curia. He set the instruments on the floor beside Romulus's body and cast the men a grim look. "Help me out of my toga."

Moved to action by sheer desperation and the momentum of Lucius's frantic lead—wasn't a bad plan better than no plan?—Naevius and Calvisius removed Lucius's toga, leaving the young man in his tunica. He pulled that off over his head and tossed it into Pele's arms before kneeling, wearing only his loincloth, next to the dead king. After stripping the king of his clothing and spreading his legs and arms open, Lucius picked up the axe and raised it over Romulus's shoulder joint.

An accomplished hunter who had butchered hundreds of large animals, Lucius knew it would take strength to dismember a human body, especially a man's body and one that had gained the bulk of middle age. And then there was the divinity. Would the son of Mars come apart as predictably as a wild boar? A deer?

He swung the axe down. The blade sank into the king's left shoulder and dislocated the ball from its bony socket with a mushy thud. Blood splattered onto Lucius's naked skin. He lifted the axe and chopped the shoulder a second time. Setting down the axe, he used the sacrificial blade to saw through the thick, fleshy strings that stubbornly clung to the limb. Romulus's arm came free from his body. Lucius lifted the limb, disregarding the grotesque weight, and held it up to the senators as blood flowed out of the king's body.

They gawked at each other in horror.

Lucius gritted his teeth. "Take it," he said, "or we will die much worse."

"Take it and do what with it?" asked Naevius.

"Wrap it in your tunica."

Naevius closed his eyes for a long moment. Accepting there was no other way, he allowed Pele and Antonius to hastily help him out of his toga and tunica. Setting his toga aside and holding the fabric of his tunica out, he used it to accept the dismembered arm, bending the limb at the elbow and wrapping it tightly. The morbid swaddling tamped the worst of the blood that streamed out of the severed end. He flashed the other senators a meaningful look and they began to help each other disrobe until they stood only in their loincloths, looking every bit as vulnerable and exposed as they felt.

Lucius looked down at the king's left leg. He raised the axe blade over Romulus's thigh and brought it down hard, chopping at the resistant bone as if it were a defiant limb of a tree that had to go. The blood splatter was worse here and he could feel blood splash onto his face, into his eyes and mouth, each time he chopped. The blood began to pool around him. As he dropped the axe to saw through the stringy ligaments, Antonius appeared at his side and began to mop up the worst of the blood with Romulus's tunica.

The king's left leg separated from his body. Lucius stared down at it, blinking the blood off his eyelashes. The limb was too big, too long, to manage. He picked up the axe and hacked at the knee twice. It hung on by a sinew. Lucius looked up at his father. "Pull the foot."

Obeying his son's order, Calvisius quickly squatted and gripped Romulus's sandaled foot. He pulled. The king's lower leg broke away at the knee so easily that the senator nearly fell onto his backside. He stood and accepted both parts of the leg from Lucius, placing them side by side onto a tunica that Carteius had laid on the floor and bundling the bloody package tightly.

Pushing himself to his feet, Lucius stepped over the king's torso to kneel at his other side. He repeated the macabre dismemberment process on the king's right arm and leg, handing the butchered cuts of bone and flesh to the senators who wrapped them in their tunicas.

When the limbs were off the corpse, Lucius sat back on his heels and looked down at his handiwork. The shocking sight of the king's armless and legless body made the bile rise from his gut, and he swallowed hard, feeling the dryness in his throat. His eyes inched toward Romulus's head. Yes, he would have to do it.

Inhaling a great breath—it was as much for courage as for strength—he raised the axe blade, aimed it at the king's neck, and swung downward. Romulus's throat collapsed under the first strike. With the second, his head came off. Blood surged out of the headless torso as Lucius clutched the black hair and lifted the head, setting it on the king's own outstretched loincloth. Even as he wrapped Romulus's head in the fabric, even as his hands shook with terror and panic, Lucius knew that Rome's founder deserved better. But it was done, and there was no point in him and his father chasing the king to the underworld.

The king's limbs and head now wrapped in blood-soaked clothing, the men stared at the remains. Romulus's torso lay on the floor, blood flowing out of the voids where his arms, legs and head used to be. Lucius grabbed the remaining tunicas, but even combined, the fabric was not substantial enough to wrap the trunk.

"Get his cloak," directed Lucius.

Naevius grabbed the king's purple cloak off the back of his chair and tossed it to Lucius. The younger man spread it out on the floor and rolled the torso on top, wrapping the stump of the king's body as best he could in the fine cloth as the blood slowly seeped through. He stood, his chest heaving from the effort.

Peeking out the portico and seeing no one there, Lucius sprinted past the stone altar to the large oval fountain that stood nearby, the one used by the priests, and occasionally the senators, to wash themselves after making sacrifice. He thrust his hands into the water and began to scrub the worst of the blood off his face and body. Antonius joined him. He plunged Romulus's blood-drenched tunica below the surface, turning the already red water even redder, then wrung out the fabric and raced back to the scene of the dismemberment to clean up more of the king's blood. He had repeated the trip twice by the time Lucius's body was relatively blood free.

Lucius returned to the Curia to find it as clean as it was going to get. Streaks of blood were still everywhere, but their story—the sacrifice had gotten away from them—could still work. After all, these men were senators, not *victimarii*.

By now, Pele and Carteius had finished re-dressing Antonius in his toga—the others were already dressed—and were arranging the folds in a way that covered his chest, minimizing the fact he wore no tunica underneath. That in itself was not suspect. Some senators clung to the original custom of wearing only a toga and, with the unusual heat Rome had been experiencing lately, even more were doing so. Yet with the others now dressed, Lucius had little choice—it would fall to him to don Romulus's blood and water-soaked tunica himself. He struggled into the woolen garment, the fabric clinging to his skin and amplifying the chill of panic. Finally, he held out his arms as his father and Naevius wrapped him in his toga.

Wordlessly, they all did what needed to be done. One by one, they each picked a piece of the king off the floor and stuffed it under the folds of their togas: Naevius and Pele each took an arm, while Antonius and Carteius struggled with the larger leg bundles.

That left the head and the larger, more problematic, torso.

"I will take the head," said Lucius. He spun to face his father. "You are the fattest, Father. We will put the torso under your toga...when we walk out to the stable make sure to double over, as if you are unwell."

"Son, I cannot carry that much weight. It will fall out and—"

"I will help you. It is our only chance."

His face drained of blood, Calvisius lifted the drapery of his toga as his son shoved the torso underneath. Lucius pulled the toga back down, frantically arranging the folds to cover the purple and red-stained package hidden below.

He shot anxious glances at all of the men. "We must move quickly, before the blood soaks through any further." His anxiousness hardened to admonishment. "We will be interrogated," he said warningly, "and possibly tortured. No matter what they do, no matter what reassurances they offer, do not confess. Stick to the story and we live."

"Don't speak to us like we're the fools," chastised Naevius. "It is your idiocy that has brought us to this."

Lucius nodded, accepting the rebuke. Placing the king's head under his own toga and supporting it with a forearm, he put his other arm around his father. Calvisius supported the torso with his hands—like a pregnant woman holding her belly—and bent over in feigned pain. As long as he moved fast, as long as no one looked too closely and Lucius shielded him, it would do. It would have to.

And then they all walked out of the Curia.

By now, the few voices that Lucius had heard earlier from the area of the senaculum had increased to several. Laughter and strident words of debate floated across the space of the Comitium, but the tremulous senators ignored them and hobbled as casually as they could toward the senatorial stable to the north.

As they passed by the entrance to the senaculum, two senators—Sertorius and Claudius—saw them and took a moment to offer an obligatory wave. Claudius rolled his eyes at the sight of the doubled-over Calvisius. The latter man's propensity for shirking his duties in the Senate by feigning some malady or other was common knowledge.

Clearing the senaculum, the parade of guilty men finally reached the stable. Each man proceeded quickly to his horse and stuffed his piece of the king into his horse's pouch before splashing his hands into his horse's water bucket to wash away the blood. With clean hands, they arranged each other's togas to hide any telltale blood spots.

Lucius and Calvisius were the last to arrive at their horses. Lucius shoved Romulus's head into his horse's pouch and then helped his father step up onto a mounting block to awkwardly straddle his horse. Calvisius balanced the torso in front of his stomach and leaned forward, holding the torso in place with one arm and gripping the reins with his free hand. Without a word of parting, he rode out of the stable. Lucius watched him go, fully expecting to see him stopped by a soldier and amazed when it did not happen.

Lucius mounted his horse and walked it out of the stable after his father. He could see Antonius, Naevius, Carteius and the elderly Pele strolling with forced nonchalance toward the senaculum to mingle with the other senators before session. Considering what they had all just been through, what they had done—and what could still await them—their collective composure was an impressive feat. He did not acknowledge them and they did not look at him.

He picked up his pace to ride at his father's side, both of them heading toward their home on the Esquiline Hill, the sun now fully risen over the kingless city behind them, and the hazy orange glow of dawn erased from the sky.

CHAPTER II

Alba Longa

Priestess Amata Silvia was in the middle of evening prayers at the shrine to Vesta in her courtyard when a flurry of activity from within the palace pierced her communion with the goddess. A door opened and a slave skittered into the rectangular garden space.

"*Domina*," said the slave. "King Sextus Julius and Queen Penelope are here."

"Now? At this hour?"

Amata had not fully risen to her feet and straightened the folds of her white *stola* when the royal couple of Alba Longa entered her courtyard. The queen, a pleasantly round woman a few years her senior, walked ahead of her husband and took both of Amata's hands in her own. The gesture of comfort only intensified the priestess's rush of anxiety.

"Penelope," said Amata, "what is wrong?"

When the queen hesitated, Amata looked to the king. A serious man, his face was even more serious than usual. He turned to two adjacent couches under a purple canopy.

"Come sit."

"*Dei mei,*" said Amata, as the three of them sat on the couches. "This cannot be good."

"We cannot assume the worst," Sextus began, although in a tone that suggested he already had. He glanced at his wife, and then spoke to Amata. "We just received a messenger from Proculus in Rome. We wanted to deliver the news to you personally..."

"Tell me," she said.

The queen spoke. "Romulus is missing."

Amata looked quizzically at the king and queen, two of her closest friends. A king could fall ill. A king could be killed or usurped. But a king could not go *missing.*

"Missing?" she asked. "What do you mean, missing?"

"He was last seen three days ago," said Sextus. "He had an early morning meeting with some senators, and sometime between then and when session actually began, he just..." the king shook his head, baffled, "disappeared."

"Which senators did he meet with?"

"Naevius, Antonius, Calvisius...I forget the other two names."

"I know Senator Naevius. I am good friends with his wife, Sellia. I know the others, too. They have had their grievances with Romulus, but they would not harm him."

"We don't know that he has suffered harm."

Amata shot Sextus a direful look. "Of course he has," she said. "You know it as well as I do, and Proculus knows it, too. He should have sent us a messenger the moment he realized that Romulus was missing."

Penelope looked away and scoffed. "You know Proculus."

"I should go to Rome," Amata muttered to herself, then looked at the Alban king and spoke more clearly. "Priestess Cloanthia can manage the temple in my absence. Do I have your permission to go?"

"Of course," Sextus replied.

The question was a polite formality. As cousin to the Roman king Romulus Silvius, and descendant of the Trojan hero Aeneas and his son Ascanius—the latter being the founder of Alba Longa—Amata did not need to seek permission for much. How could Sextus deny her anything? It was Romulus who had put him on the Alban throne all those years ago.

And if that weren't enough to grant her some liberties, Amata's circumstance as a lifelong virginal priestess of Vesta—a punitive consequence of her late father Nemeois's coup over Numitor—had given her a certain celebrity status in Latium. Although the appointment had been thrust upon her as a child, she had excelled in the role and had eventually been made High Priestess of the esteemed *Virgines Vestales Albanae*. Even those who were unimpressed by her Silvian lineage had to respect her unwavering religiousness and the sacrifice she had been forced to make for her father's crime. For while most women only served a tenure of six months in the temple and then went on to marry, Amata had spent over thirty years in service to the goddess.

Yet while Romulus had initially relegated her to strict temple life for her father's crime, Amata was his only surviving blood relative and he had soon shown her mercy. Although she would always remain an active Vestal within the temple, he had allowed her to move out of the *sacerdotes'* convent on Mount Albanus and into the Silvian palace in the city. In fact, he had given her full ownership of the palace. Eventually, he had even permitted her to travel at will between Alba Longa and Rome, building her a fine home on the Palatine Hill for her many visits to his city.

"When will you leave?" asked Sextus.

"At daybreak," replied Amata.

"Good. Send me at least one messenger a day, even if there is nothing new to report. Then I'll know you haven't gone missing as well. The gods know Proculus wouldn't inform me until the *Nemoralia*, and even then he'd send his slowest horse." His attempt at dry levity failing to distract the priestess from her worry, Sextus patted her knee. "You will be in Rome tomorrow. You will know more then."

"Our minds go to the worst place," added Penelope, "but there may be another reason for his absence."

Amata kicked off the covers and slipped out of bed. She crossed her bedchamber to reach the altar that stood on the far side of the expansive room and knelt before it, gazing into the high orange flame of the oil lamp that burned on top. She dipped her fingers into a shallow bowl of milk and dripped the liquid into the flame.

"*Vesta Mater*," she prayed. "Savior goddess of the Silvii, may your eternal flame protect your subject king, Romulus." She dripped more milk into the flame, noting how it burned straight and steady, without responding to the offering.

That is not a good sign, she thought gloomily. And then she returned to her bed to begin a long and sleepless night.

CHAPTER III

Rome

S tatius was not sure what had roused him from his stupor, but he blinked twice before the agony returned. He smelled something pungent—straw, manure—and knew he was still in the stable. Another odor—the stench of something vile cooking—perforated the smell of animals to fill his nostrils, and he groaned with the realization it was his own feet.

The groan swelled to a shouted, pain-filled profanity as Statius frantically struggled against the ropes that bound him to the chair, hoping that would be enough to overturn the bowl of fiery embers that his bare feet had been buried in. It was not. He threw his head back and sucked in a breath, calling upon his years of training to manage the searing pain...to think through it. When he righted his head, he found himself staring into the face of General Proculus Julius.

"I don't know where he is," grunted Statius. "I swear to the gods, the last I saw him, the last any of my men saw him, he was walking into the Comitium. He never came out."

"So then where did he go?" Proculus asked for what seemed like the thousandth time. "Into thin air?"

"I don't know, General." A lightning bolt of blazing pain burned through the bottom of his soles, and Statius tucked his chin to his chest, trying to breathe through it. "I mean, he didn't go anywhere. He never left the Comitium. Whatever happened to him, the senators—"

"Jove give me fucking patience!" exclaimed Proculus. "The guards blame the senators, and the senators blame the guards! The bloody baker is the only one I believe right now."

"Memmius," said Statius. "What did he say?"

Proculus kicked away the bowl at Statius's feet, and the king's guard nearly wept openly as his pain level dropped from unbearable to merely agonizing. The general gripped the seat of a nearby stool and pulled it toward Statius, sitting down in front of him. His interrogative demeanor dissolved, replaced by a more collegial tone. "He said the same as you. That he never left the Comitium." He withdrew the dagger at his side and leaned forward, cutting the ropes that bound Statius. "I never thought it was you, Statius, but you know how it is. We had to be sure."

The guard shook the ropes free and brought his hands to his face, wiping the blood out of his eyes. He had withstood three solid days of beatings and half a day of having his feet roasted, interrogation techniques that he knew could have been much worse. He looked down at his feet. The skin was peeled and black along the bottom, and swaths of blisters glistened up to his ankles. "I understand, sir." He spat out a mouthful of blood and looked at Proculus. "Have you learned anything at all?"

"Not a bloody thing." The general slumped forward, not bothering to hide the blush of emotion on his face. "Nothing but death could keep him away. But how? Where? The not knowing, it's driving me mad."

"General, my men..."

It took a moment for Proculus to break free of his thoughts and take Statius's meaning. "All but one survived interrogation," he said. "It was that new kid"—he tapped a front tooth—"the one with the gap between his teeth. We used half-hanging to see if we could get any information out of them, but unfortunately one of the ropes was too long. His neck snapped when he dropped."

"And the senators?"

"They all survived, but we had to go easier on the bastards."

"It had to be them," said Statius. He gingerly straightened his throbbing legs as a slave approached with a bucket of water to clean his burned feet, aid that Statius suspected would be as excruciating as the injury. "It's the only explanation. One of them knows something."

"They've been cleared," Proculus replied, and stood. "They bitch like women, but none had serious conflict with the king, nothing worth killing for at least, and none of them have the balls even if they did have cause."

"With respect, sir, I think that—"

A shrill scream interrupted Statius's assertion, which was just as well considering the impatience that had begun to cross Proculus's face, and both men eyed the adjacent stall: the interrogations were being carried out in one of the horse stables in the Campus Martius—one subject per stall—and weren't quite over yet.

"The baker," said Proculus. He took two steps over the straw and manure-covered floor and stuck his head over the partition, speaking to the soldier on the other side. "Leave off, already. He doesn't know anything."

"Yes, General," came the reply.

Proculus looked back at Statius, forcing the soldier to bite his bottom lip to prevent himself from uttering his own shrill scream as the man at his marred feet began to smear the charred skin with some kind of stomach-turning ointment. Statius was correct. The aid was as bad as the injury. He forced himself to maintain eye contact with the general, a man not known for his sympathetic nature. As if challenging him to do so, Proculus held his gaze, and Statius breathed a sigh of relief as one of the senior man's personal slaves rushed into the stable and bowed.

"What is it?" Proculus demanded of him.

"*Domine*, your wife sends word that Priestess Amata is due to arrive in Rome soon. She asks that you return home to prepare."

"Of course she does. Can't have the illustrious Lady Amata smelling the shit on my sandals, can we?" He grinned sardonically at Statius.

The soldier tried to offer a smirk of solidarity in response, but the mind-shattering anguish of his burns made it impossible to form any expression other than strained endurance. Mercifully, the general turned on his heel and followed the slave out of the stable, leaving Statius free, at long last, to scream in pain.

It was late afternoon by the time Amata arrived in Rome. Despite his façade that all would be well, Sextus had sent a small army of soldiers to accompany her on the journey and had ordered them to remain at her side at all times. It had taken a vocal argument with a frustratingly literalist officer before she had been allowed to enter the king's hut, located atop the Palatine Hill not far from her own home, without escort. She wasn't sure what she was looking for, if anything, but she felt compelled to enter anyway.

It had not been that long since she had been inside, no more than two months, but it was still long enough for cobwebs to have formed in a crevice in the thatched roof. As she did whenever she visited, Amata swept them down. In days gone by, she had hoped the king would marry or take a regular mistress, or even allow a slave to clean his hut once in a while, but those hopes had gone unrealized. She glanced around, her eyes lingering on the cool ashy remains of a fire in the hearth. Only recently, she and Romulus had sat by the flames and eaten together. Now, he seemed as much a ghost to her as the rest of her family.

She had only been inside a few moments when her solitude was broken. The wood-planked door opened and Proculus's wife, Valia, stepped inside. She gave Amata a sympathetic look— the red eyes, the pallid, drawn face—and embraced her.

"You look exhausted," she said. "How was the trip?"

"Bumpy," replied Amata, "and longer than usual."

"Worry slows down time, my dear."

"You sound like Nikandros," she cast her eyes around the hut as she spoke. "He says that only fear can shackle Cronus."

"How poetic."

"He has his moments." She turned to Valia. "I am afraid...for Romulus, I mean. I fear for his safety."

"We all do, Amata." Noticing the way the king's cousin was scrutinizing the hut's interior, she put a hand on her shoulder. "Proculus and the others have searched everything and everywhere," she said. "I promise, they have left nothing unexamined."

Amata nodded. Her eyes settled on a purple cloak draped over the back of a chair before they moved upward to study a number of items that hung from nails on the wall. Tools and weapons, mostly, but also Romulus's gold crown—it hung next to the collar that his dog Cerva had once worn—and the one artifact that always struck her as unsettling: a metal stake, dangling by a rope. It was the very stake that the former Vestal Tarpeia had been tied to at the foot of the Capitoline Hill. As punishment for her betrayal to Rome, Romulus had ordered shields thrown down from above, crushing her to death. Even though Tarpeia had briefly been his wife, Romulus had forbidden anyone from mentioning her in that capacity. She was referred to only as *the traitor.*

"You knew her," said Amata. "What was she like?"

"She was a traitor and an infanticide," Valia replied flatly. "Before that...well, before that, she was pleasant enough. At least from what I can remember. I was just a girl myself."

The two women fell into introspective silence for several long moments. Amata broke it. "I know Romulus has always valued you, Valia. Many times he has said how you were there for Rome after Hersilia left. You have always done for his city what a queen might have done." She smiled fondly. "That included playing surrogate mother to the king's little cousin when I first came to Rome. You were very much like a mother to me."

"It was an easy task. You were an obedient child."

"I was a terrified orphan," said Amata.

"My introduction to Rome was terrifying in its own way," said Valia, referring to her past as the one of the original Sabine women seized by Romulus. "Perhaps that is why I had such softness for you."

"I was lucky you did. Hersilia certainly did not. She hated me."

"Hersilia hated everyone after the death of little Avilius and Prima," replied Valia. "I have never seen anyone so changed."

"I have heard people say the same thing about you," smiled Amata. "You were quite the wild one in your youth, from what I hear—"

Valia blew a puff of air out of her lips. "Fama whispers nonsense in your ears. You should stuff wool in them before you go to sleep. Come, let's go to my house. Everyone will be there by now, and you must be starving."

Amata would have liked to remain a little longer, but Valia was already halfway out the door so she followed behind. She could return later. She picked up her pace to walk alongside Valia, guards trailing behind, and noted with irritation how the fire in the *Aedicula Vestae*—the shrine to Vesta that stood near the king's hut—was nearly out.

"A sacerdos should be tending to the sacred flames," she said to Valia, "especially now. This is unacceptable." She stopped in mid-stride, compelling Valia to do the same, and locked eyes with the soldier closest to her. "You," she ordered, "go straight to the *Aedes Vestae* in the Forum and tell the first sacerdos you see to get up here. Now."

"As you say, Priestess Amata," said the guard. He ran off.

The two women continued on, past Amata's house, soon reaching the expansive and well-guarded home of Proculus and Valia. A pair of red-cloaked soldiers bowed and parted to allow them entry and they stepped inside, at once immersed in the din of serious conversation and the smell of baked pheasant. Faces familiar to Amata—Gellius, Paeon, Appius and Acrisius—were already there, and greeted her with distracted smiles. They were too preoccupied with matters of state, with worry and speculation, to afford her any pleasantries.

Amata had known these men, Romulus's closest advisers, for most of her life. She was only a child when Romulus had first brought her to Rome to meet them, and although they had only been some ten years older than her—children themselves, as Valia had said—they had seemed so much older to her. After all, they had already built a city and conquered many others. Yet as the years went on, as her friendship with each of them had matured and solidified in its own way, the years between them disappeared. Yet another way that Cronus, the great Titan of time, slipped into the lives of men.

Valia waited for Amata to choose a couch first and sat beside her. More familiar faces met her with compassionate smiles, including Safinia and Rufina, wives of Gellius and Acrisius respectively, as well as Hostus Hostilius the younger and Gaius Julius. The latter was the only son of Valia and Proculus. Gaius had always struck Amata as resembling Romulus more than his father—the dark hair, dark eyes, and especially the serious nature. Perhaps that was not surprising. The Silvii and the Julii were related bloodlines.

It was Gaius who spoke to her first. "Priestess Amata," he said, "what do *you* think has happened to the king?"

Everyone, including the king's advisers, stopped talking. They all turned to Amata.

Amata adopted a sad but resigned expression. "I don't know what happened to him," she said to Gaius, "but Aule met me at the gate when I arrived. He said he's taken the auspices three times a day, every day, since Romulus disappeared. He feels the same as I do"—she spoke to them all—"the king is surely dead."

Hostus stood. "How can you say that?"

"It is the gods who say so," replied Amata. "The signs are clear."

"The signs have been wrong before," he said.

"They have been misinterpreted," said Amata, "but never wrong."

"Romulus is the son of Mars. The gods would not forsake him."

Amata folded her hands on her lap. "Such talk is not helpful, Hostus."

Hostus leaned against the wall and put his hands on his hips, shaking his head in frustration and avoiding looking at the older men. He knew better than to engage the king's cousin. "Forgive me, Lady Amata."

"There is nothing to forgive. Romulus was like a father to you, and I know he loved you as a son. I share your grief."

"Well, I am not yet ready to grieve," said Acrisius. He stared at the floor and scratched his bald head. He had worn it that way—shaved to the skin—for years, ever since having suffered a particularly treacherous case of lice on campaign as a younger man. "There is no proof he is dead."

"Where is he then?" challenged Acrisius's wife, Rufina. "Taken captive? There has been no ransom, no demand for gold from the Volsci, no whispers of a hostage king in the countryside."

"I've heard some people say he has ascended," said Gellius, "and gone to take his place with the gods."

The room fell silent as everyone absorbed his words. Amata waited for the silence to pass. It always surprised her how willing the Romans were to accept—or at least not outright reject—Romulus's claims of divinity. His subjects revered him with a maniacal religiousness: in fact, had it not been for her cynical tutor Nikandros keeping her in check and reminding her of his true history, she might have fallen into such reverence herself. After all, a man who believes what he says is the most believable of all.

"I saw him go from a peasant boy to a king," said Acrisius. He gripped his wine cup, thinking fondly of his childhood friend. "Who knows? Maybe a king to a god is the next step. If anyone could do it, Romulus could."

"Perhaps he is wounded somewhere," suggested Appius. "He often slips away to pray by himself, whether by the river or by one of the springs beyond the walls. He might have fallen down an embankment or something...he might have struck his head..."

"My men would have found him," countered Hostus. "They've strained every fish from the Tiber and turned over every rock in the country." He chuckled humorlessly. "They've found twelve corpses, eight stolen horses, and two buried stashes of silver, but no trace of the king."

"It is a similar story in the stable," said Proculus. He sauntered into the room, deliberately avoiding eye contact with Valia—he was later than expected and still reeked of manure—and leaned against the wall next to Hostus. "I've had men confess to theft, adultery and every conceivable manner of vice against man and the gods." His eyes met Amata's, and his tone grew less cavalier. "Not a word of the king, though."

"Priestess Amata fears he is already dead," said Valia.

"Nonsense," replied Proculus. "He lives and we will not give up until we find him. You will see. Fear not, we will all dine together again soon."

An almost imperceptible grin, a contemptuous grin, formed on Amata's face. Only Proculus saw it. He could hear the words she was thinking: *I believed your words of comfort once before.* Pushing himself away from the wall with his elbows, he moved to a carved wooden table and poured himself a cup of wine, the red liquid splashing over the rim.

"I'll die of thirst before the bloody slaves get around to it," he muttered.

An awkward silence hung in the air. Everyone knew the slaves were not being negligent. They were simply following their mistress's orders. The last thing Valia needed right now, the last thing Rome needed, was Proculus losing himself in drink.

Gellius glanced at his colleagues and sighed irritably at Proculus. "It's been chaos in the Senate since the king's disappearance," he said. "We need a plan. The city needs to be governed."

"We could appoint a magistrate until he returns," said Appius. "One of the older senators, perhaps even one of us."

Proculus refilled his cup. "There are too many Sabines in the Senate for that," he said. "They'll say it's an unlawful appointment."

"I agree," said Appius. "I already broached the subject with Senator Sertorius. He asked, 'What's to stop one of you Romans from keeping power once we give it to you?' They already distrust us."

Realizing she had not eaten since the previous day's supper, Amata accepted a plate of bread, nuts and pheasant from a slave. She forced herself to chew and swallow a piece of the warm meat. "A long time ago," she said, "before the Latium Confederation, the first kings of Alba Longa had a private council of elders. To fill the power void between the death of one king and the vows of the next, each elder would be granted sole power for just one day. This way, all of their ambitions were kept in check."

"That will work as well as anything," said Proculus. "Any objections?" When none were noted, he moved to pour himself a third cup of wine, rethought it, and sat next to Valia. "We'll move that Senator Oppius be the first, and then proceed according to age."

"Why age?" asked Hostus. As one of the younger senators in the assembly, he could potentially be waiting months for his turn. "Everyone knows I am the king's choice to succeed him."

That much was true. Hostus was the son of the elder Hostus Hostilius, one of Romulus's first soldiers, who had been killed in battle when Rome was in its infancy. After the man's death, Romulus had not just married his widow, Hersilia, but taken the younger Hostus under his care. That care had expanded upon the death of Hersilia. In many ways, the orphaned Hostus was something of a communal son, having been raised by all of Romulus's old guard. That included Acrisius.

"We are not talking about succession yet," said Acrisius, an edge of *Calm down, boy,* in his voice. "The king always bestows senatorial privileges according to age. This will be no different."

Hostus looked at Proculus and the others for support, but seeing none, conceded to Acrisius. "I understand, sir."

Gaius laughed. "Your concern for the king's safety lasts as long as my father's wine," he said.

"I am as concerned as you, Gaius," replied Hostus. "I am only voicing the king's wishes."

"Oh, my mistake, then," said Gaius, putting his hand to his chest. "Piety and ambition are so closely related, it is sometimes impossible to tell the difference. Either way, your poor wife Lucia will have to wait a while longer to be queen."

"Stop it," chided Valia, wagging a finger first at her son and then at Hostus. "You shame yourselves with this pettiness when Rome is in crisis."

The chastising landed as intended, and the two men offered each other conciliatory looks. Around them, having grown accustomed and apathetic to the rivalry between the two men, Proculus and the other generals and senators of Rome fell into a heated discussion of exactly how the *interregnum* period would proceed.

Valia leaned in to speak softly to Amata. "I am always surprised. They seem as though they will tear out each other's throats, and yet Rome survives."

"I pray to holy Vesta it will continue to do so," said Amata. Yet no matter how hard she tried to fight it, she could not help feeling that Romulus's beloved city, his eternal city, was dying before her eyes.

CHAPTER IV

The Vestal sacerdos Petronia had a reputation of being a creature—albeit a pretty one—of habit. As soon as she woke in the morning, even before her slave had warmed the water in her washbasin or set out her clothing, she sat up in bed and reached for her hairbrush. After twenty meticulous strokes, she set down the brush and picked up the bracelet her mother had given her shortly before her death. She kissed the garnet stone set in the gold band and slid it on her right wrist, simultaneously getting out of bed and thanking Apollo for the sunrise. Her mother had died in her sleep. Such things, at least as far as Petronia was concerned, made one more grateful for the dawn.

As her slave Malla approached her bedside with a cup of honey water—warm, not hot—Petronia looked up, her mind immediately turning to the subject that was on everyone's mind.

"Any news about the king?"

"Nothing, Domina."

Petronia set her feet on the floor and pressed her palms into the mattress on either side of her legs in thought. "It's definitely been too long now. He must be dead."

"When I was a girl, my father's favorite sheepdog went missing," said Malla, a young woman the same age as Petronia, though with a worn face that betrayed the difference in their lifestyle. "On the twenty-first day of his disappearance, my sister and I buried his leash and prayed Cerebus would admit him to the afterlife. But the very next morning, as if to spite our lack of faith in him, he showed up at the door. He was all bones, but he was alive, and my father had him working in the fields by midday."

Petronia nodded soberly. "I will speak with General Proculus," she said, "and ask that we bury the king's leash immediately. He will be back in the Comitium by midday tomorrow, and all of Rome will have me to thank for it."

Malla laughed and Petronia smiled, standing.

"I overheard some soldiers this morning," said the slave. "Priestess Amata arrived in Rome yesterday." She turned to stoke the hearthfire and then returned to help her mistress dress. "No doubt she'll be inspecting the Aedes Vestae."

"She won't find any mouse droppings or torn *strophia* on the floor," said Petronia, still grinning. "Lollia is on watch. Anyway, Priestess Amata—don't get me wrong, I like her—but she's kind of a snob. All the Vestals in Alba Longa are. They worship the old Trojan Vesta, and their temple is apparently quite the sight. The priestess probably thinks we let the fire go out every evening and scramble to relight it in the morning before anyone finds out. It's pointless trying to impress her."

"Don't be so sure. She has important friends, and you are in the market for a husband."

"You are self-serving wench, Malla," said Petronia. "You want to make sure I marry rich so that you can sleep in and order other slaves to help me dress."

The slave shrugged, but did not deny it.

As Malla smoothed a perfumed ointment over her mistress's arms, the grin slowly faded from Petronia's face. The truth was, the Petronii had at one time been one of the wealthiest and most respected families in Cures. Their star had fallen before Petronia's birth, however, when her uncle Petronius had become embroiled in scandal in Rome. Although the details of his downfall were lost to time, the general consensus was that he had in some way tried to corrupt the Vestal Tarpeia and had afterward been hunted down and killed by King Romulus. Being thus associated with Rome's most notorious traitor, and crossing its tempestuous king, had not been good for the family name, nor its trading business.

Yet after years of making reparations of gold and property to Rome—which had grown just as powerful as Cures—the Petronii had recently managed to regain much of their resources and status. Enough, at least, that Petronia had been permitted to complete her six-month tenure as a maiden sacerdos to Vesta in the Roman Aedes. For a woman "in the market for a husband," as Malla had said, it was the perfect way to fulfill one's duty to the goddess and catch the eye of an upscale suitor at the same time. No, Rome did not possess the history or affluence of a city like Alba Longa, but it attracted enough enterprising merchants, hot-blooded soldier types, and well-to-do young priests that a woman could do very well for herself.

"Perhaps you're right about Priestess Amata," said Petronia. "It doesn't hurt to be a little extra friendly. She must be very worried right now."

"That's the spirit," said Malla. She twisted a lock of her mistress's long, light brown hair around a finger and tugged gently. "Pretty as a primrose."

"Give me my wrap. It's a bit chilly this morning, isn't it?"

"It's a nice break from the heat," said Malla, as she placed the wool fabric around Petronia's shoulders.

The sacerdos slipped out of her home, into the stark brightness of morning and the sounds, smells and bustling activity of the Forum. Reaching the nearby Aedes Vestae, she spoke to the two soldiers who stood on either side of the closed door.

"Has Priestess Amata been by this morning?" she asked.

"Yes, my lady," replied one, his chest visibly puffing at the sight of the striking Petronia. She's not here anymore, though." He tilted his head in the direction of the Capitoline Hill. "She left with Sacerdos Aule."

Petronia rewarded the soldier with a friendly wink and turned, marching purposefully through the crowds and market, careful not to trip on the countless sacrifices—dead bull calves, piglets, dogs, chickens, and goats—that lined the streets, a spear protruding from the chest of each one. These were offerings to Mars, sacrifices given by the king's worried subjects for his safe return. They had sprung up all around the city and despite the flies and the smell, General Proculus had allowed it. In fact, he had instructed the sacerdotes of Vesta to purify each sacrifice where it lay. At the end of each day, the priests gathered them all up in a bloody cart and burned the lot of them by the Altar of Mars in the Campus Martius.

Petronia carried on until she reached what she knew was Aule's favorite vendor. As Rome's longest-serving holy man—he had come from Etruria in the city's earliest days—he was as much a creature of habit as she was. After accepting a cup of warm broth from the vendor, she continued on to the base of the citadel. Aule would be at the Auguraculum taking the auspices, as he had done every morning since the king's disappearance, so she lifted the bottom of her dress and ascended the staircase to the hilltop, careful not to spill the broth. Reaching the top step, she winked again at the soldiers who met her there.

"Sacerdos Aule is expecting me," she said. It wasn't an outright lie. She had brought Rome's elderly chief priest a cup of broth on two or three previous occasions, so he wouldn't *not* be expecting her. The soldiers let her pass—the boldest returned her wink with his own—and she brushed by them.

Petronia had never really liked the Auguraculum. Although it was a religious space and a well-ornamented one that allowed an unobstructed view of the Comitium and Forum below, not to mention the distant hills, the purpose of the roofless temple—to read the flight of birds and study the skies for signs from the gods—meant that the cypress and stone pine trees that had at one time decorated the hilltop as magnificently as any statue had long since been razed to the ground. There was always something disconcerting about this place to her...something exposed and vulnerable, as if the gods had a too-clear view of what the mortals far below them were up to. She shook off the feeling.

Arriving at the *templum*, Petronia lowered herself to her knees at the sight of Priestess Amata and the old priest Aule walking toward her. Aule was clutching his augur's *lituus* and waving it in the air, though he was doing so in animated conversation rather than ritual. When he saw Petronia, he grinned and spoke out the side of his mouth to Amata.

"Listen to this one," he said.

Petronia held out the cup of broth, which the priest accepted with slow-moving hands, and then lowered her head in deference to Amata. When the older priestess smiled back permissively, the young sacerdos stood and faced Aule with a playfully goading expression.

"Did you hear about the old Etruscan priest who asked his wine slave, 'How much wine can you put in a six-cup jug?'"

Aule did not react for a moment, but then the joke settled and he threw back his head with a laugh. It was a laugh that was hoarse with age, but nonetheless infectious, and Amata could not help but let out an involuntary giggle. The giggle turned into a strange chortle, then a sob, as Amata put a hand to her mouth.

"I am sorry," she said. "I do not mean to—"

Petronia took one of Amata's hands in her own. "Priestess, no one can fault you for crying," she said. Her voice was sincere, even protective. "He is our king, but he is your blood. You can raise the Tiber with your tears if you like."

"What good will that do?" asked Aule. "It will not bring him back."

"It will make her feel better," Petronia replied, careful to keep her tone respectful. "Perhaps that is good enough for now." She held her breath, worried the old priest might chastise her for contradicting him or for speaking so informally to the Alban high priestess, but no reproach came. Instead, Aule stared out absently over the Forum. He sighed sadly and gave the two women a cheerless smile as he departed.

"You must not speak to Aule that way again," Amata said when the priest was gone.

"I will not, Priestess," said Petronia. "Sometimes I don't think."

"I am the opposite these days. I think too much." She wiped her eyes with her wrap, regaining her composure. "I am surprised to see you are still in Rome, Petronia. I thought you would be long finished your tenure in the Aedes by now."

"I am in no hurry to leave."

"Perhaps you have no reason to leave."

Petronia avoided eye contact. "I was thinking that you might be able to...well, you have many friends..." She sensed Amata studying her. "I am sorry. See? I don't think before I speak. You have worries of your own right now."

Waving off the younger woman's discomfiture, Amata smiled indulgently. "You are well-liked, Petronia, and you have the benefit of a pretty face. I will see what I can do. Now if you'll excuse me," she set her eyes on the Temple of Jupiter, the tallest structure atop the Capitoline, "I am to meet with the priests." She took a single step, then stopped and glanced back at Petronia. "Thank you for your kind words."

"You are welcome, Priestess."

Petronia waited until Amata was several paces away before turning herself to descend the Capitoline, back to the Forum. She was not on watch in the temple until evening, so the day was her own. She knew exactly what she would do with it.

She lifted her wrap until it covered her head, and joined the diffuse gathering of people—some on foot, others on horseback, several pulling carts—that were lined up to leave the city through the gates. The guards waved her through without looking twice and she emerged onto the road beyond the wall, heading in the direction of the Viminal Hill where a decent-sized suburban settlement of modest huts and even a few fancier villas had sprung up in recent years. The walk was long enough to transform the slight chill of the morning into a warmth that spread over and through her. Her thoughts also warmed her. Thoughts that filled her with pleasant anticipation.

When she reached the Viminal, she veered off the main road and onto a footpath, trekking over the long grasses and yanking the bottom of her dress free from the thistles that snagged it. Swatting at a wasp that had insisted on tormenting her for the better part of a hundred paces, she finally arrived at an open field that boasted nothing but a small hut and a wooden tethering post. A young man was leading a goat to the post.

Petronia stopped and quietly watched him as he tethered the animal and squatted down to milk it. Although Theo was a few years younger than her, his gender afforded him bulk and height and it seemed to her that he looked stronger, more man-like and less boyish, every day.

She whistled, and he jumped, falling off his low stool and spilling what little milk he had collected. Seeing her, he lay back on the ground and laughed.

"I definitely won't get any work done now," he said.

"From what I can tell, it is the goat that does the work," replied Petronia. Chuckling at her own cleverness, she stepped over him and strolled into his hut, knowing full well that he would follow.

CHAPTER V

The black sky was boundless above her. The night air was warm. Humid. Low chants slipped into her ears. Prayers. Sobs. All around her, people made promises to the gods, bartered with the gods, begged the gods, all petitioning for the same thing: *Return King Romulus to his city!*

The bellow of a white bull was cut short by the blade of a sacrificial knife, and in the silence that followed, Amata could hear the drizzle of blood on the peperino stone surface of the great Altar of Mars in the Campus Martius as a priest placed the beast's hefty innards in a wide bronze firebowl on top. The drizzle was drowned out by the snaps and crackles of Vesta's purifying flames as they consumed the entrails. The pungent smoke rose up to the gods, but especially to Mars before whose altar the sacrifice had been made. If any god would be moved to save the king, would it not be Mars, the king's own divine father?

The sacrifices, the prayers, the offerings—they were all starting to wear thin on Amata. She knew Romulus was not coming back. Aule knew it, too. They had seen the signs in the sacred flames of Vesta and on the wings of the birds the gods sent across the sky. There was no need to petition the gods further. Yet they were not in charge of Rome and it was not their place to declare the king dead. Officially, that dark duty would fall upon whatever senator was playing the part of king for a day during the interregnum period. Unofficially, and far more likely, the decision would be made by Proculus Julius. Regardless of which senator sat upon the throne, he was the man in charge of Rome and everyone knew it.

With the sacrifice over and much of the somber gathering now departing, Amata raised her eyes to peer into the limitless blackness above. There was no moon, but swaths of silver stars decorated the high dark curtain that separated mortal from god. On the ground, torches encircled the war god's altar, the flames having been lit by fire from Vesta's temple. They burned silently, in deference to the altar fire that still snapped and crackled. Standing as she was inside the circle of torches gave Amata a sense of peace. She could imagine that she was inside the flames of the sacred hearthfire, like a blessed sacrifice, embraced but not enkindled.

By the light of the torches, she could see blood running down the altar, and she wondered how many sacrifices Romulus had offered over the years to the bellicose god. To him, there had been no more sacred place in his city. Even the Aedes Vestae in the Forum, even the temple to mighty Jupiter on the Capitoline, those did not seem to fill his heart with passion for the gods in the same way this altar did.

She remembered the first time Romulus had brought her to Rome as a child. He had spent the entire day with her, showing her his temples and shrines, his marketplace and the Comitium, and he had given her a fine home next to his on the Palatine. As the sun had begun to set, he had led her here, to the Altar of Mars. Having heard of his religiousness, she had expected an evening sacrifice, but instead, he had surprised her with a spread of food—fish, venison, fruit, cake, and wine—and pulled her on top of the altar where they had sat cross-legged together.

We will eat at my father's table, he had said.

After sunset, they had lain on their backs atop the altar and gazed up at the stars. Amata had pointed to the constellations that Nikandros had taught her, and they had made their own, too: constellations for their ancestors, Aeneas, Ascanius and Silvius, and the figures of the Trojan War: Priam, Hector, Achilles, Odysseus, and even the great wooden horse. Sometime during the night, they had fallen asleep together, less like a king and his captive, and more like true cousins.

Aule interrupted her thoughts. With his eyes on Proculus, who was in deep discussion with Gellius and Acrisius, the old priest folded his arms in front of his chest. "I don't know why he still prays to Father Mars. He should pray to the *ultima dea*," he said, referring to Spes, the goddess of last hopes. "The king has been gone for fourteen days."

Amata did not respond to that, but instead pointed her chin in the direction of her friend Sellia who was standing beside her husband, Senator Naevius. "Aule, is it my imagination or is Lady Sellia showing? I first noticed yesterday when I was dining with her. I hinted at it, but she didn't say anything."

"If she is with child, perhaps it will stave off the divorce."

"Divorce? I knew they were strained, but she has not mentioned divorce to me."

"She probably doesn't want to add to your worries," said the priest, "but Naevius came to me a few weeks ago, asking me to take the auspices for him. He wanted to know if he should divorce her."

"And?"

"The signs were unclear. I told him to come back in a few days, but then the king went missing and other matters took over."

"Hmm." Amata patted Aule on the elbow. "I am going to speak with her."

Leaving the priest's side, she exited the torchlit circle and caught the eye of Sellia, who seemed to be in the middle of discreetly reprimanding her husband. Sellia greeted her warmly, but

and urine, the smell strong enough to pulse through the pungent stench of manure. She was either unconscious or dead.

Naevius exhaled a loud, trembling moan of shock and fear. "Merciful Jove," he said softly.

General Proculus glanced at the only other person in the stable—Priestess Amata—and laughed at the senator. "You choose the wrong god to invoke, Naevius. Jove is a king himself. He will find no mercy in his heart for a regicide." Seeing the way the senator stared horrifically at his wife's limp and blood-drenched body, he adopted a reassuring tone. "Look on the bright side. She isn't pregnant with a slave's grub anymore."

Naevius dropped to his knees and clasped his hands in front of him. "General, my children are innocent. Spare them..."

"Start talking, and I'll think about it."

Naevius swallowed. "I tried to stop them, I swear it! It was Calvisius's son, Lucius! He stabbed the king...and it was his idea to..." He wrung his hands.

Proculus stepped toward Naevius and pointed the bloody tip of his dagger at him. "No point stopping now," he said. "Keep talking."

Even through Naevius's stark terror, a remnant of self-preservation remained. He suddenly realized that Sellia may have implicated him, but she didn't know the details of the murder. Perhaps he could buy himself some time. Some clemency.

"I tried to call for help," he said, his words tumbling out over one another, "after Lucius stabbed him the first time." He reached around to touch his back. "Lucius stabbed him here. Then the king stumbled and I caught him. I begged them to help me carry him outside, to call for help, but they were afraid. They said we were dead men if he lives. Then Lucius stabbed him again. The king fought for his life, but then Carteius said, 'Stab his heart!' and—"

His words were interrupted by a gasping sob as Amata put her hands on her midsection, bending over slightly as she began to weep. Proculus turned to her. His own eyes were wet with the vision of his oldest friend fighting in vain for his life, slaughtered by the very men he had trusted to place in his Senate.

Proculus glared at Naevius. "Where is his body?" The words came out with a certain finality that stabbed at Proculus's own heart. Despite it all, until this moment, he had truly believed the king would be found alive.

The muscles in Naevius's face twitched, as if unseen insects were scurrying over his skin. "It was not my idea"—he placed his palms on chest—"that was Lucius as well. It was his idea to..." he swallowed, and said with a grunt, "*to cut him up.*"

Amata stopped crying. The tears in Proculus's eyes dried. They both gaped at Naevius, still kneeling on the stable floor. The senator let his arms drop to his sides. No, he would not survive this. The best he could hope for now was to tell all and pray to Hades for a quick death, quicker at least than Sellia's, whose suspended body had begun to weakly convulse in front of him. In spite of her transgression, he had hoped she had already slipped into the mercy of death. He noted with horror and unexpected sympathy that one of her arms was longer than the other, having been dislocated from its socket. He looked away and vowed to never look again.

Appalled into silence by Naevius's confession, it took Proculus several long moments to speak. When he did, it was through gritted teeth. "What did you fucking say?"

"We cut him up," said Naevius. "It was Lucius's idea. He dismembered the king's body...his arms and legs first, and then"—he raised his bandaged fingers to his neck—"and then his head."

"How did you leave the Comitium unnoticed?"

"That was Lucius's—"

Proculus rushed at Naevius and struck his head with the hilt of his dagger. "How?" he shouted.

The senator fell over with a shriek. "We wrapped him in our tunicas!" he shouted. "And Lucius...he wrapped the king's head in his own loincloth!" He pushed himself back onto his knees as the memory of the assassination and the proximity of his impending death settled upon him, heavy as a lead cloak. "We all carried a piece of him out under our togas. The senators in the senaculum saw us heading to the stable, but didn't think twice. We put the packages in our horse pouches." A stream of blood gushed out one nostril. He wiped it away. "We swore an oath of secrecy and agreed that each of us would dispose of our part."

Amata moved slowly across the straw-covered floor to stand beside Proculus. "Do you know where we can find him?" she asked Naevius. "The pieces of him, I mean."

Naevius knew the question would come, and he forced himself to answer fully the first time. It would be much worse for him if she had to ask again. "I burned the flesh off his arm and buried the bones in the dead pit in my back field, where the slaves put the animal carcasses. Pele took his other arm and did the same on his land. Carteius and Antonius took his legs to their country villas south of the city, by the lake they call Diana's Mirror, and buried them behind a fishing shack on the shore." He paused to take in a deep breath, closing his eyes as he exhaled. "His torso and his head...Calvisius and Lucius said they buried them under an abandoned shrine to Vulcan somewhere around Vulsini."

The anger seemed to drain out of Proculus. He gripped the handle of his dagger and turned, reaching up to slice open Sellia's throat as if the act were a mere afterthought. Naevius leaned over and sobbed as his wife's blood rained down from above.

"*Dis Pater*," he prayed, pressing his head to the ground. "I come to—"

Naevius didn't have time to finish the prayer as Proculus stepped toward him and jabbed the unyielding blade of his knife into the side of the senator's neck. His body teetered for a moment, and then collapsed to the side in a heap.

Proculus broke the long silence that followed. He had been inwardly debating what to say to the priestess, whether to comfort her or somehow try to shoulder the burden of their shared grief, but he could not find the words. Their relationship, their complicated history, made such softness as impossible for him to give as it was for her to receive. "I'll have the other senators arrested immediately," he said.

He went to leave, but Amata gripped his arm. "Wait."

"What is it?"

She raked the fingers of both hands through her hair, dislodging the hairpins that held a tight bun in place. "Torn apart by his own senators," she said. "Is that how we want Romulus to be remembered?" She looked around the dimly lit stable until she spotted a cut section of a tree trunk that served as a makeshift stool, and sat dejectedly on top. "The son of Mars, birthed by a Vestal virgin and nursed by a she-wolf, led to Rome by Mars's spear and Vesta's *ignis mirabilis*, the living Quirinus..." she dug her sandals into the straw at her feet, "...dismembered like a pig that was barely fit for market. Is that to be his legacy?"

"The son of Mars," said Proculus. He shuffled tiredly across the stable floor and lowered himself onto one knee beside her. "I am surprised to hear you speak like that."

"Romulus was the last of the Silvian kings," she said. "He was the last with Trojan blood. His death should be as legendary as his birth."

Proculus nodded thoughtfully. "You are right," he said. "We will make sure he is remembered as he deserves to be." He stared hatefully at Naevius's body. "Then we'll figure out how to kill the rest of these bastards."

CHAPTER VI

Over the past thirty years—closer to forty, now—Proculus Julius had ascended the steps of the great speaker's platform near the Comitium more times than he could hope to remember. Whether it was to stand behind the king while he delivered a speech or a new law, or whether it was to ornament the stage-like *tribune* with some glittering spoil of war taken from a conquered city, his mind always flew back to the very first time he had stood upon it.

It was shortly after the abduction of the Sabine women in the Circus. During the violence and chaos of it all, and no doubt driven by the impetuousness of youth, Proculus had killed one of the more resistant Sabines. To punish him for his crime and to prove to their captives that no further violence would befall them, Romulus had ordered Proculus to stand on the tribune and strip down to his loincloth. After that, he had lashed him to the breaking point. It had taken ages for the wounds to heal, though the scars remained, as raised and unforgettable as the memory itself. The real wound had been inflicted upon his pride. Romulus had every right to do it. Proculus understood why he had done it. But even after the years of friendship between them, even now as he stood on the platform to tell the people of Rome that their king would never walk the streets of his beloved city again, Proculus felt the pain of the betrayal inch up his spine.

And yet something good had come out of it. Valia. As the crowds gathered in a spirit of grave expectation before him, his saw his wife sitting beside their son, Gaius, and he found himself contemplating their long marriage. They had met only days after her abduction and his lashing, and had immediately fallen in love. Never mind that he had still been mostly bedridden. Never mind that talk of his humbling public beating had still been on everyone's lips. She had been taken with him. In public, she had made light of the lashing to help him preserve his dignity. In private, she had tended to his wounds with diligence and good humor. When he looked at her now, he could see that much of that humor was gone from her eyes. He knew why, and he made a private vow: *Bacchus, keep your wine for yourself. I will have no more.*

He watched Valia say something to Gaius before twisting in her seat to speak to the wives of the other generals, women whose husbands also stood on the tribune. She turned to face the platform again and smiled feebly at him. Proculus saw she was crying and he looked away, finding strength in the grim but steadfast faces of Gellius, Acrisius, Paeon and Appius. Standing with Rome's "old guard" as they were known, were younger faces, including Hostus Hostilius, Romulus's stepson. Also on the platform was an old and respected Sabine senator by the name of Canuleius. According to the interregnum period, it his was day to be regent: he would represent the king and the Senate.

Finally, there was Priestess Amata. As Romulus's only living relative and the high priestess of the revered Alban order of Vestal sacerdotes, her presence was required. She held a flaming torch in one hand and it struck Proculus as ironic that of all those present on the tribune today, of all Romulus's friends and advisers, it was only the two of them who truly knew what had happened to the king. The only others who shared their secret were the assassin senators who sat among their distinguished colleagues in front of the tribune. Proculus did not look at them. He did not trust himself to.

With the crowd now silent in anticipation, Proculus stepped to the front of the speaker's platform, raising his arms in a dramatic posture.

"Esteemed senators, blessed priests and priestesses, friends and fellow Romans," he began. "I swear on Jove's stone that what I tell you here today, in the shadow of the great temple"—he gestured to the temple of Jupiter on the Capitoline and then turned back to the crowd—"is the truth. Our king and founder, the son of Mars, has transformed and risen to the heavens! I have seen that transformation myself, as witness to the holy apotheosis." He let a sudden rise of murmurs fall, and continued. "Yesterday, on the *nones* of Quintilis, after I had made sacrifice at the Altar of Mars in the Campus Martius, I walked alone along the river to the very spot where Father Tiber brought our king's basket to shore. There, as I gazed in reverence at the place, I heard a strange voice from the clouds. Looking up, I saw King Romulus, although no longer our earthly king, but now the god Quirinus, dressed in shining armor and ascending upward as though riding in an invisible chariot pulled by Apollo." More murmurs and another pause. "Overawed, I fell back on the grassy shore and beheld the holy sight until the voice came again, this time stronger and clearer. It was the voice of the king I knew in life, now tinged with the silver tones of immortality. Overcome with grief, I tried to speak, but could not. And yet the new god knew my mind. He said, 'These are divine matters, Roman. Tell my people that their destiny is to conquer the whole world with warfare and piety, and to thus be the *Caput Mundi*, the head of the world! Tell them also that I will forever be their deity, the living and immortal Quirinus!' This said, beams of light burst from his eyes and he ascended to the heavens before mine!"

The murmurs grew louder, more emotional, until a man in a worn toga thrust his arms skyward and cried out, "Bless us, Father

Quirinus!" A wave of excitement spread out from where he stood until others joined the cry and the crowd of men, women, and children became a sea of chanting devout, fervently praying to their newest god. He was the only god they had known in his mortality: they had seen him walk through the Forum and speak from the Capitoline. And if he could ascend to the heavens, could he not raise Rome and each of them to the greatest of heights?

Proculus lowered his arms and looked out over them. Their eyes were filled with awe. Well, mostly. A few of the more cynical among them frowned uncertainly, not quite convinced. He disregarded them—they would come around—and glanced at the men on the platform with him. Gellius and Acrisius, along with Romulus's other top generals, were exchanging looks of astonishment. Hostus Hostilius was grinning madly. The old senator Canuleius wore an almost comical look of surprise. In fact, the only person who did not look surprised by the proclamation was also the only woman on the tribune. Amata met his eyes with an emotionless face. His words had come as no shock to her. She had helped him choose every one.

"Romans!" said Proculus, shouting louder to be heard over the sobs and chants. "Do not grieve the loss of your king or fear that you will never lay eyes upon him again. For from this day forward, his form will be as visible to you as the skies overhead!"

At that, the general marched off the platform toward a towering structure draped by a heavy purple fabric. He gripped the edge of the unveiling cloth and pulled hard, revealing a dazzling larger-than-life statue of Quirinus. The bearded god's face was thoughtful and severe, and he was dressed in full shining armor. In one hand, he held the spear of Mars, and in the other, an orb representing the cosmos. The crowd erupted in awe at the sight.

Again, Proculus looked at Amata. For the first time, he noticed the edges of her mouth move up in the prelude to a smile. It was pure luck—and perhaps a bitter irony—that such a magnificent statue could be ready for today. Romulus had commissioned the work months earlier to be a statue of Mars, but with some minor reworking, its destiny was to be Quirinus instead.

With the awestruck crowd now consumed with religious fervor and swarming the statue to pray at its base, Proculus returned to the speaker's platform to stand alongside Senator Canuleius. It was the latter man's duty to deliver the latest news from the Senate. Now that the king was officially gone, the Senate's focus would be on naming a successor as soon as possible. Until then, the senator announced, the interregnum period would continue. But like any second-rate performer who has the misfortune to follow a much better act, the old man's shrill voice and administrative ramblings faded into the background.

Avoiding his fellow generals—he was not ready for their questions yet—Proculus found Amata on the tribune and stood beside her. She offered him a rare nod of approval, but stepped away. Proculus was not someone she enjoyed having any proximity to. As the passionate prayers and chants at the base of Romulus's statue intensified, she weaved through the generals on the platform to get a better look. People were now stripping what modest valuables they had—a bronze bracelet, a silver ring, a beaded necklace—and burying them in the earth at the statue's feet, offerings to their deified king.

Despite the somber occasion, Amata felt pleased with herself. Romulus would have wanted to be remembered like this. Was he not larger than life himself? Yet she knew it would never have worked in Alba Longa. King Sextus Julius was respected and admired, but if he were to die, the Alban people would never believe he had become a god. But then, Rome had always been its own creature. She hoped, for Romulus's sake, it always would be.

Proculus had picked his share of body parts off the ground. The first time was as a young man during Rome's fledgling but victorious battle against the Caeninenses. He had gathered the severed arms and legs of his fallen colleagues, also young men, and done his best to match the dismembered limbs with the right bodies. He had then helped burn the bodies, thus releasing the men's souls and properly sending them to the gods. Many more battles and many more bodies had followed. He remembered some of their faces and names. Men—friends—like Hostus Hostilius were hard to forget. Others were hard to remember. It wasn't that he didn't care. There were just too damn many of them.

Since Romulus's disappearance, and especially since learning of the certainty of his death, Proculus had found himself reminiscing about the many firsts in his life. That included the first time he met the man who would become his most cherished, most complicated, friend.

Proculus had been on the road returning to Alba Longa after visiting a friend's villa in the countryside when he had been attacked by, of all things, a bear. A young man dressed in a patched, ill-fitting tunica had chased the animal off, saving his life. That young man had been named Caelus, and with his swaybacked horse and humble manner, Proculus had immediately assumed he was a slave. The general could still hear the reply.

I have no master, sir. I am a free man.

A free man indeed. A king, too, though neither of them knew it at the time. Proculus had no way of knowing that the gold crown of a Silvian king lay sewn inside the young man's rough waterskin, and Caelus—though he knew he was a prince—had no way of knowing he was the crown prince. They would learn his true identity, King Romulus Silvius, together in the necropolis, directly from the lips of his real mother, Princess Rhea Silvia. Proculus had been the first to say the words: *Ave, Romulus Rex!* Yes, another first.

All those firsts were converging in the foreground of his memory as he dug through the mud at the base of a neglected shrine to Vulcan atop a rolling hill at Vulsini. The shrine had been one of the earliest ones in the region, although it had fallen into disuse long ago and been replaced by a larger, more accessible one in the nearby village. No doubt, most who remembered it was there were now too old to make the trek to reach it. Senator Calvisius had remembered, though, and had been motivated enough to travel there. Perhaps leaving the king's body parts in such a sanctified yet silent spot was his pathetic way of trying to atone for his sins.

As Proculus shoveled the wet earth, a chunk of ground gave way and he slipped, falling onto his left knee and barely avoiding a face-first landing in the mud. It had been a long, rainy ride north of Rome and the stumble chafed his already raw nerves.

"Bloody gods!" he shouted to no one.

Clutching the long handle of the shovel for support, he fought for purchase in the sloppy ground and managed to get both feet under him again. The activity stirred up a muddy soup of votive offerings left by long-gone worshippers—oil lamps, as well as terracotta figures of fish and blacksmith hammers. He felt something larger and solid against his left foot and thrust his arm deep into the mud, finding the unseen thing, exploring its smooth, domed surface with his fingers and searching for a place to grip until his middle finger found a depression. Bracing himself, he slid his finger inside and pulled the skull out of the heavy muck.

Except it wasn't a skull. It was a bronze helmet, another votive offering. He swore, tossed it aside, and kept searching. Only a step ahead, he saw the dome of another mud-covered helmet. This one looked different, though. Smaller. Reaching forward as far as he could, he scooped it toward himself, instantly recognizing the feel of bone against his fingertips as he took hold of it.

The sight of the skull made his stomach sink. He held it to his chest and clambered through the thick mire to a dry patch of ground where the bones he had already unearthed—the king's ribs, spine and hipbones—were drying in the feeble sunlight that was only now breaking through the clouds. He slumped onto the ground and wiped the worst of the mud off the skull, digging sludge out of the eye sockets with his fingers and flicking it to the side.

Of course it was Romulus. Like all the bones he had spent the last several days tracking down and stealthily digging up, it was exactly where Naevius said it would be. And if that weren't proof enough of its identity, the teeth were. The skull was missing two teeth on the bottom left side and, although it looked grim and macabre without the flesh of lips around it, Proculus would recognize the cracked front tooth anywhere. It was he who had given it to the king while training at swords. Romulus's jaw had swollen to twice its size, but he had only laughed: *You are finally prettier than me, Proculus!*

Proculus stared into the empty eye sockets. "I am sorry, my friend."

His horse, tied to a nearby tree, neighed restlessly and pawed at the ground. Proculus looked at the animal and it sneezed, as if commenting on the miserable weather and urging its master to move. The beast was correct; it was time to go. Like Hercules completing his last labor, Proculus had found the last of the king's bones. He had done it alone, too. Never mind the hundreds of men under his command, it had come down to him to do it. He took a final look at the skull. It was mostly free of flesh, but bits of soft meat still stubbornly clung to it in spots. It struck Proculus that Remus's skull, which long ago had also been left to the elements, hadn't looked all that much different.

Proculus's horse sneezed again and the general regarded it. "All right, you impatient bastard." He stood up, put the skull and bones in a sack, and mounted his horse for the long journey back to Rome.

CHAPTER VII

Now in his late thirties, Hostus Hostilius was no longer the youngest man in the Roman Senate. Nonetheless, he still held the distinction of being the youngest man to have been appointed as a senator. He had only been nineteen years old at the time, yet since the appointment had come directly from the king, those senators who disagreed with it had chosen to forgo the usual opposition process and instead content themselves with grumbling about it in private to their wives over supper.

Yet as the Senate erupted into shouted arguments and heated debates all around him, Hostus knew this second nomination—as king of Rome—would not be nearly as easy to achieve. Romulus was not here to compel it. Rather, it would go to a vote in the Senate. Even worse, some of the men who had quietly opposed his initial senatorial appointment were still alive, still sore about it. That included a number of Sabine senators. Hostus held up his arms to address them directly.

"Esteemed colleagues," he said, putting a hand to his chest. "Why do you oppose my accession? You know it was the king's wish. And do we not share Sabine blood? Am I not the son of a Sabine princess?"

"Lady Hersilia was an illegitimate daughter of an idiot king," said a meticulously groomed senator named Terentilius. "And you are more Roman than Sabine."

Gellius stood. "Are we not all Romans here, Senator Terentilius? Have we not sat on this council for years together, for the greater good of Rome?"

Another man, a respected senator by the name of Claudius, stood. "Then let's discuss the greater good of Rome," he said. He gestured to Hostus. "No one can deny this man has proven himself both on the battlefield and in the Senate. He has led our troops to victory and our city to glory on many occasions. Four times he has hung the armor of defeated kings on the branches of the *arbor felix* by the Temple of Jupiter Feretrius. Do not forget his accomplishments, my friends, or how his courage has expanded your own wealth." When a collective murmur of agreement settled, he continued. "Hostus was taught how to fight, how to win, and how to rule, by the king himself. Like King Romulus, he is a man of war." Here, his voice leveled. "But I ask you—is that what Rome needs right now?"

"Who would you prefer we elect?" asked Acrisius, standing. The question was probing, but not aggressive. "Members of this council have done an adequate job with their regency appointments, but Rome has lacked fearsome leadership since the king disappeared, and it's starting to show. If I didn't know any better, I'd think even the city slaves are slacking off, seeing what they can get away with. The sewers need repair, the herds go unfed, and the temples are unwashed. The locusts tend to the crops instead of the slaves. There are open brawls on the streets, and a thief on every corner. And we've all heard the latest excitement," he said dryly, "gold going missing from the treasury. So, with respect, Senator Claudius, Rome does need a man of war. Who else could rule such a place?"

"The matters of which you speak are civic matters," said Claudius. "Our most urgent problems come from within. They have nothing to do with a foreign enemy. If we elect a warlike king, he will act according to his nature. He will wage war. Our sons and grandsons will leave the city for the battlefield, and when they do, Rome will fall into further neglect." He pivoted, speaking to the entire assembly. "Every man on this council knows that I loved our king, but I love his city even more. That is why I cannot support the accession of Hostus Hostilius. Rome is no longer a child. We must let it grow and mature. We have won enough wars, taken enough spoils and terrified enough of our enemies and allies. What we need now is infrastructure. Better roads and drainage, finer temples, more extensive trading networks. Innovation. Culture." He shook his head. "Not war."

As bursts of agreement sounded around him, Hostus sat, irked. He wished Proculus were here. While Gellius, Acrisius and all of Rome's old guard spoke on his behalf and supported his accession, it was Proculus in particular who held sway over the Senate. As Romulus's right-hand man, he had learned how to manage the often conflicting opinions and interests of the various Romans, Sabines and Etruscans who comprised the Senate. Why he had chosen this politically pressing time to retreat to the countryside for an unscheduled vacation was beyond him. Couldn't he wait a few more days to rest?

Acrisius scowled—he didn't like where this was going either—but he had little choice. The Senate functioned in a certain way, and unless he and other like-minded senators were willing to resort to military pressure, something that would shatter the already thin trust between the Roman and Sabine senators, he would have to adhere to the process. "Hostus has my support and the support of many others," he said to Claudius. "The names of Senators Sertorius, Occius, and Rasinius have also been put forward. Do you have another name to propose, Senator Claudius?"

"I do, Senator Acrisius," replied Claudius. "There is a man in Cures by the name of Numa Pompilius. He has spent most of his life in Athens with his mother, but has recently returned to Sabinum. He is an educated man, a diplomatic one, and very pious."

"A foreigner?" decried Acrisius. "You would propose that a man who has never even sat among us in this Senate be our king?"

"Yes," said Claudius, "and for that very reason. His upbringing in Greece means that he is no more loyal to Sabinum than to Rome. He will be unbiased and progressive. That is what Rome needs right now."

"We will agree to disagree," said Acrisius, "and let our votes decide."

Claudius nodded to Acrisius in a conciliatory manner. "Then we will dispatch an emissary to speak with Pompilius. If he consents, his name will be added to the list of candidates."

As Claudius sat down, the aged Senator Oppius stood. "All senatorial matters have thus been concluded for this day," he said. "With the permission of all present, and under the eyes of the divine Quirinus, we will set the regal vote for the kalends of Sextilis. Until then, Senate is adjourned."

It had stopped raining the day before, but the great oval track of the Circus hadn't had nearly enough time to dry in the sun before the day's horserace. The powers that be in Rome had nonetheless ordered the event to proceed in honor of Neptune and Furina, whose respective festivals were well underway. As many had predicted, the race had seen a disaster—a champion horse had stumbled and fallen in the mud, breaking a leg and needing to be bludgeoned to death on the track. Its rider had fared slightly better: he had fallen so violently that his elbow had bent the wrong way and fractured, leaving his lower arm to dangle like a piece of loose fabric at his side. The crowd had loved it.

Theo was unimpressed. Wasn't the point of the races to celebrate the speed of the beast and the skill of the rider? Since when did accidents and grotesque injuries become more entertaining than the actual race? Yet as Petronia had foretold, it was good for his business. Despite his youth, he had inherited the position of

Circus *vulnerarius* after his predecessor had died, leaving him with the responsibility of treating injured chariot drivers, riders and horses on the track—or more accurately, getting them off the track as swiftly as possible, so the race could proceed without further delay. He was paid an *aes rude* for each body he could expeditiously remove, and another for any life, man or horse, he could be credited with saving. It was good work that paid well, and he didn't even have to do much of the work himself, thanks to the team of city slaves now under his direct supervision.

Yet it was those very city slaves who now had him scouring the inside track of the deserted Circus under a setting sun, sticking the point of a spear into the earth and striking—as he suspected—a virtual field of fist-sized rocks hidden in the ground. He threw the spear aside angrily, then turned at the sound of a laugh to see General Appius approaching from behind.

"What has you so riled up, boy?" asked Appius.

"I'll show you, sir," replied Theo. He thrust his hand into the dirt at his feet and withdrew a large, jagged rock. He held it in front of him. "This."

Appius frowned. "Sabotage."

"Unless it fell from the clouds in the last rainfall, yes." He corrected his tone. "I mean, yes, General. Sabotage."

"And you suspect the slaves?"

"I know it's them. They've been acting strange lately." He pointed to the ground ahead of him. "The fall happened on the most inside track, which is where all the rocks are. When I arrived this morning—and I got here well before dawn—three of the men on my team were already here walking the track. I assumed the sacks on their backs were to pick up any stones, not plant them."

"We'll have them tortured for a name," said Appius. "I'm sure it'll be that merchant from Fidenae. He won the last two pots, didn't he?" He huffed and absently looked around. "Bribery, indolence, theft...it's the same throughout the whole city. Everybody thinks that because the king is gone, they're safe to pull a fast one."

"I've heard about the treasury gold..."

"You'll get paid, boy. Don't worry."

"Thank you, General."

Appius departed, leaving Theo to walk the track for the rest of the fading afternoon and then into the night by torchlight, picking rocks until he could not take another step. Exhausted, he mounted a city-owned horse and rode out through the gates, reaching his humble and isolated home on the Viminal with the moon shining high overhead.

He tethered the horse to a post, left his muddy boots and tunica outside, and stepped into his hut wearing only a loincloth. He grinned at what greeted him inside. Petronia was curled up in a chair in front of the hearthfire, sleeping contentedly. His goat was sleeping on its side on the floor beneath her, with Petronia's bare feet tucked under its body for warmth. She woke when he neared the fire to stoke it. The animal did not stir.

"It's about time," she said sleepily. "Your goat is poor company."

"She never complains," he replied. "That's the best kind of company."

She yawned. "Why do you insist on keeping it inside at night?"

Theo poured himself a cup of wine and sat on the floor, leaning his bare back against Petronia's legs and scratching the sleeping goat's head. "She is made of gold and I don't want anyone to steal her." Petronia scoffed, and he looked up affectionately at her. "I am serious. Last month, I overheard two shepherds talking about the riches they were making selling a type of tooth paste made from goat's milk and urine to the women in their village." He rubbed his front teeth with a finger. "It whitens the teeth. I've been experimenting for weeks with the ratio and getting some of the neighborhood girls to try it. I think I finally have it right. When I take this to Rome, I'll be a rich man." He tapped the goat's head. "And it's all because of her."

"Does it really work?"

"It does."

"So the girls have white teeth," said Petronia, "but do their lovers not feel like they're kissing a goat?"

"A goat with white teeth."

"But still a goat."

"Some men are not fussy," said Theo, and beamed as Petronia laughed. She leaned over to place a quick kiss on his lips, but he reached up to hold the back of her head and kissed her deeper.

"I am on watch in the Aedes at dawn," said Petronia.

"Then we'd better not waste any more time," replied Theo. He rose and moved to the small straw-filled bed on the other side of the hut.

Petronia watched him climb under the blankets. *I should stop this*, she thought to herself. *No matter what he says, I know he loves me.*

Their secret affair had begun during her second week in Rome as a sacerdos of Vesta. They had met eyes at a race in the Circus and cast flirtatious looks at each other all day. His eyes had followed her into the evening, and when she finally slipped away under some false pretense, he had whistled to her from the trees. His mischievous yet innocent smile had drawn her in.

It was an easy liaison to begin and an even easier one to continue. Sacerdotes of her humble status did not warrant their own guard, so getting away was not difficult. And then there was Theo's status as an orphan—both his parents had died of a fever year earlier—and his secluded hut which he shared with no one but his golden goat. The only difficult part had been keeping his growing feelings for her at bay. The Petronii were middling nobles at best, but her family name nonetheless required her to marry better. Much better. A poor boy who picked body parts off the racetrack and lived with a goat would not do.

She resolved to resist him. If it were discovered that she was coupling with him during her tenure to the virgin Vesta, she would be expelled from the order and banished from Rome. She would have no choice but to return to her family and beg for charity. Instead of bringing honor upon the Petronii from her

position in Rome, she would bring disgrace. As bad, it was unlikely that she would ever find a noble husband. Petronia knew
of two sacerdotes who had coupled with men during their service
to the goddess: one had been left with no better option than to
marry a creepy old fisherman, and the other was still a spinster.
Neither outcome appealed to her.

"We cannot do this much longer, Theo," she said from her
chair. "I hope to be betrothed soon."

Theo sat up in bed and leaned back on his arms. "I know that,"
he said. He looked away from her. "I still don't know why we
can't—"

"Because we can't," she interrupted. She tried, but couldn't
find the words to finish without sounding cruel, so said nothing.
Instead, she got up and joined him under the blankets, swearing
to herself—yet again—that it would be the last time.

The Aedes Vestae in the Roman Forum had been rebuilt three
times over the past thirty-five years. The first time was after the
traitor Tarpeia had deliberately set it ablaze, causing it to burn to
the ground. The second and third rebuildings also followed dev-
astating fires, although these latter fires were not due to
treasonous sacerdotes, but merely negligent ones. Yet to Amata,
there was no difference. Dishonoring Vesta by failing to dili-
gently honor her sacred flame was treason even if there was no
intent to do harm. The goddess had no patience for idleness or
idiocy among her sacerdotes, and as the high priestess of the Vestales Albanae, Amata had even less.

She strode along the cobblestone street that led to the Aedes
and watched trails of thin smoke escape from the circular oculus
in the roof. After the last conflagration some ten years ago, she
had pleaded with Romulus to rebuild the structure in stone, following the model of the much finer Temple of Vesta in Alba
Longa. He had briefly considered it, but ultimately decided to

copy the original design approved by his mother, Priestess Rhea Silvia: a round hut-like structure with wattle and daub walls and a thatched roof. Amata suspected the decision had less to do with respecting his mother's vision and more to do with his own reluctance to really think about it.

The truth was, the Vestal order in Rome had never recovered from the treachery of Tarpeia, and neither had Romulus. Amata, along with the priestesses of Ceres and the other priesthoods of Rome, had tried to improve the order's reputation and the discipline of its sacerdotes many times over the years, but Romulus had always dismissed their suggestions. He just didn't want to talk about it. Other than the annual renewal of the sacred flame in the Aedes Vestae each spring, he rarely even visited the site but rather chose to honor the goddess at the smaller shine to Vesta on the Palatine Hill, the one next to his and Amata's respective homes.

The fragmentary foundation of the order thus meant that sacerdotes who served their six-month tenure to Vesta in Rome were essentially left to manage themselves under the supervision of whichever one of them happened to be the most senior at the time. The priest Aule did his best to manage things from arm's length and with the limited time he had, always repeating the same complaint about the sacerdotes: *They are too focused on finding a rich husband, and not focused enough on tending to the sacred flame.*

Amata shared his frustration. Yet she could not entirely blame the sacerdotes for their impiety. For those young women who served as priestesses in Rome, finding a good husband while they were still in the virginal blush of youth was a matter of survival. It was different in Alba Longa. There, women did not begin their tenure until after they were already betrothed. The hunt was over, so to speak, so they could concentrate on honoring the goddess. That rule was one of many customs that contributed to the enduring success of the Alban order.

Amata had nearly reached the Aedes when she heard a voice behind her.

"Good morning, High Priestess."

She stopped and turned to face Petronia, who was several paces behind her on the street.

"Good morning, Petronia," replied Amata. The young woman's cheeks were pink and her hair tousled. She had obviously slept in and was late for her morning watch. Amata made no comment, but did not bother to resist the slight frown of disapproval that formed on her face.

"I am glad I ran into you," said Petronia, doing her best to trim the edge of sheepishness from her voice. "I wanted to offer my condolences."

"We all grieve the king," said Amata.

"Yes, but I am actually speaking of your friend Lady Sellia. I heard what happened to her...murdered by her own husband, who then kills himself? Such a tragedy."

"Love affairs are complicated, Petronia." The frown on Amata's face deepened. Petronia's sympathy was sincere, but she was overreaching, even if she didn't know it. It was not her place to mention such matters. It reminded Amata of the overfamiliarity with which the young woman had spoken to Aule. She quickened her pace to reach the door of the Aedes.

Stepping inside the warmth of the circular sanctum, Amata found the sacred hearth snapping healthily. An auburn-haired sacerdos was in the middle of placing a stripped oak branch into the flames, but her sister sacerdos was leaning against the solid wall. Dozing. Amata cleared her throat, and the sleeping girl jerked awake.

The auburn-haired sacerdos looked suitably horrified. "Priestess Amata," she lowered her head. "Welcome."

"Thank you..." Amata struggled to remember her name.

"Lollia."

"Of course, Lollia," replied Amata. "Forgive me."

"Not at all, Priestess." Lollia raised her eyebrows at Petronia as she entered the Aedes after Amata. "Ah, Petronia. Were you able to find the kindling we were talking about?"

The young woman's attempt to cover for her friend's slackness was more entertaining than effective, and Amata's frown disappeared. "Never mind that," she said. "Carry on." She turned to go, but paused and faced the sacerdos who had been dozing. "I know it's only Rome's pact with the gods and the very survival of the city that is at stake," she said bitingly, "but if you could summon the vigor to stay awake during your watch, that would be stellar."

Amata exited the Aedes, conscious of the strained silence she left behind, and stepped back onto the street to make her way toward the Palatine Gate located at the base of the fortified hill. The guards opened the gate and she passed through, ascending the stone pathway to reach the hilltop and then strolling lazily along the *viae,* past the shrines of the gods and the homes of her friends. Ahead, she saw the familiar figure of Gellius emerge from his house.

"Amata," he said. "You're up early. Checking up on those girls in the Aedes?"

"Don't get me started."

He raised his eyebrows and laughed. "The other day you said you wanted to talk to me about something..."

Amata wrinkled her nose. "I thought I had a good match for your younger son, Paullus," she said, "but now I'm not sure."

"Too bad," replied Gellius. A soldier called to him from a small armament building tucked into a nearby cluster of trees, and he waved to say he was coming before turning back to Amata. "You look tired," he said. "Get some rest." He jogged off to join the soldier.

Amata watched him go. It seemed like everyone but she had somewhere to go and something to do. It was time for her to return to her priestly duties and her life in Alba Longa. Although Priestess Cloanthia had been expertly managing the Alban order while Amata was in Rome, King Sextus was already pressuring her to return. Just a few more days, a few more loose ends to tie up, and she would be able to leave the stench of Rome's open sewers and the irritation of its lackadaisical Vestal order behind her, and go home.

CHAPTER VIII

Amata had spent her last few days in Rome cleaning Romulus's hut and bestowing much of his property according to the directions he had left her. The bulk of his wealth and gold were, of course, left to Rome. His offspring. Many of his personal belongings were left to Amata, particularly those items that had belonged to the Silvii for ages. This included busts of Aeneas, Ascanius and Silvius, a tapestry of the great white sow—it had at one time hung in the palace at Alba Longa—his mother's jewelry, and even the gold oak-leaf crown that Rhea had, so long ago, frantically placed in the bottom of a laundry basket.

Yet Romulus had always made it clear to Amata that certain sentimental items were to be given to those people he had been closest to, and that was a task she had personally seen to. She brought his augur's lituus to Aule's home and presented it to him in a long box of rare carved ivory, telling him how often the king had spoken of his deep friendship with his city's first chief priest, the man who had taught him so much about the gods. She visited the home of Senator Oppius to deliver the king's own senatorial chair, the one he had sat on for nearly forty years. She then dispensed his regal armor, accoutrements, and weapons between his generals: Acrisius, Gellius, Paeon, and Appius were gifted fine breastplates and gold-hilted swords, while Proculus received the king's richest purple cloak, along with his entire personal stable of champion horses. To the first mothers of Rome, the Sabine women who Romulus had seized decades earlier in the Circus, she dutifully apportioned the splendid royal jewels that had been taken from the rooms of the Etruscan queen Tarquitia and the princess Laria after Romulus's defeat of Velsos.

Those tasks done, Amata returned home for a brief rest before rising again to prepare for the afternoon's outdoor banquet on the Palatine. She dressed without the aid of a slave, clipping two dangling gold earrings that once belonged to Rhea Silvia onto her earlobes. It was pleasant weather, but the emotional work had left her drained and chilled, so she wrapped a dark indigo mourning cloak around her sleeveless white dress and set out.

As soon as she was again outside, her spirit lifted with the pleasant music of *citharae* and the invigorating din of conversation that arose from the large gathering of her friends, almost all of whom were also her neighbors. She approached a table stocked with wine and delicacies, helped herself to a little of both, and eyed the rows of sumptuous suckling pigs roasting nearby. A number of food slaves were tending to them, though Gellius's wife, Safinia, was pointing to this pig and that one, chastising the head cook for skimping on the seasoning. If there was a brewing pestilence in Rome's crops, it was not affecting supper on the Palatine.

Amata chose an empty spot on a couch next to Valia. On an adjacent couch, Hostus was still lamenting the indignity of his succession challenges as heads bobbed in agreement all around him.

"Priestess Amata," he said. "What do you think?"

"You know what I think, Hostus," she said. "I am in favor of your succession. It was the king's intention, and that should be honored. But as you also know, I am a woman and cannot enter the Senate, never mind vote in it." She gestured to the wives around her, including Hostus's own wife, Lucia. "Perhaps if you are elected king, you will change that."

Everyone laughed. The laughter subsided, however, as Proculus appeared on the scene carrying a jug—not a cup—of wine. He walked past the couches to a nearby chair and dragged it back to sit closer to his reclining wife. Valia sat up, her change in position reflecting the rise in tension. Proculus had been absent from Rome for days, and his return was as unexpected as his departure had been.

"Women in the Senate," he said, slurring just a little. He looked at Hostus. "That's as unlikely as you getting elected king, my boy."

Gaius assessed his father before speaking. This was disappointing. Proculus had not taken any wine since the day he had stood on the speaker's platform and proclaimed Romulus a god, but that streak of sobriety was now clearly over. He broke the awkward silence.

"Senator Claudius tracked me down today," Gaius announced to everyone. "He wants me to travel to Cures as emissary and ask Numa Pompilius if he will accept the regal nomination."

"Why would he ask you?" questioned Hostus. "Why not send one of the usual emissaries?"

"Do you have a problem with me going?" challenged Gaius. "Or maybe you're afraid of the competition. Numa is gaining a lot of support in the Senate, and the man doesn't even know he's in the running."

"It's a fair question," Gellius said to Gaius. "Why is Claudius sending you?"

"I've met Numa before," Gaius replied. "Twice, actually. Once at his wedding to King Tatius's daughter, and the second time at her funeral. You may not remember, but Romulus ordered me to go because nobody else wanted to."

"That's because Numa is the son of a traitor," said Hostus.

This piqued Amata's curiosity. "What do you mean?"

It was Proculus who explained. "Numa's father was the Sabine general Pomponius. He was the one who overthrew Tatius and set the whole Tarpeia fiasco into motion. Romulus had him executed"—he smiled broadly at the memory—"he ordered Gellius here to cut off his head, and then he sent it back to Cures in a sack. That's how Tatius got his throne back, although the fool always answered to Rome afterward."

"Numa barely knew his father," said Gaius. "And he's no tyrant, I can promise you that. He's a pacifist. Kind of a strange one, too. Thinks he can talk to the gods."

"Anyone can talk to the gods," said Amata.

"Well, Numa thinks they talk back to him," Gaius replied.

"He sounds mad," Valia chimed in. It was the first she had spoken since her husband's inelegant arrival.

Proculus looked at her and grunted. "Actually, he sounds perfect," he said. Ignoring the scoffs that followed, he sat forward in his chair, his eyes suddenly shining with equal parts drink and shrewdness. "Who is in the lead right now?"

Gellius answered. "Senator Sertorius."

"Exactly," said Proculus, "and if he's elected, we're fucked." He shook his finger. "Sertorius has the staunch Sabine vote secured, but not necessarily the moderates. If we aligned with them and threw the Roman vote behind Numa..." he snapped his fingers "he'd be in. With the ratio of Sabine to Roman votes in the Senate right now, Hostus doesn't stand a chance. At this point, the best we can hope to have is a king we can manage. Someone pliable." He turned to Gaius. "You've met him. What do you think?"

"I met him briefly," said Gaius, "but it could work. The bigger problem will be getting him to accept the nomination. He doesn't care about politics."

Proculus groaned. "Gods. Even better." As if suddenly remembering the jug in his hand, he stared at the blood-red wine within. "The Rome we knew is dead, my friends. We need to adapt." He paused in thought, then brought the jug to his lips and drank.

This time it was Hostus's wife who navigated attention away from the general. "Priestess Amata," said Lucia, "I was saddened to hear of Lady Sellia's death. I know she was a dear friend of yours. She always struck me as a very kind woman."

"Perhaps too kind," said Gaius. "Rumor has it she was impregnated by one of her own slaves, and that's what pushed Naevius over the edge."

Amata felt Proculus's eyes on her, but avoided looking at him. Of every person in Rome, only the two of them knew what had truly befallen the couple, and why. She only hoped Proculus would retain his better discretion despite the drink.

"You shouldn't gossip," Valia said to her son. "No one knows if that slave business is true or not."

"What's wrong with a little gossip?" asked Proculus. "There is no food that goes better with wine." He laughed and spoke to Amata. "In fact, I'll bet that I know something you don't about my royal cousin Sextus and his lovely wife Penelope..."

Amata tensed. "Stop it," she said.

"Ah, so you do know."

"Don't, Proculus."

Everyone was rapt. Nonetheless, Proculus seemed to think twice about it and fell silent. Amata's relief was short lived, however, as Valia could not stop herself.

"What?" she asked her husband.

Proculus looked at her. In that moment, his head swimming in wine, he wanted nothing more than to please her. "Queen Penelope and our own King Romulus," he said wryly. "It lasted almost a year. I thought they'd wear out the road between Alba Longa and Rome."

"You are lying."

"I am not. Penelope is Mamilian's daughter, and you know how it was between him and Romulus. I think the only way Romulus could stick it to Mamilian was to stick it to his daughter."

The men laughed, but Valia threw them scolding looks and they settled down. "Does Sextus know?"

"No, he doesn't," asserted Amata, "and he can never know. There is no point. It would only hurt him, and he does not deserve that. Neither does Mamilian, for that matter. Regardless of how you all feel about him, he was Rome's ally when you most needed one and you should be grateful for that. He is old and frail. Learning of this will only open old wounds." She put her hands on her lap. "Please, out of respect for my friendships in Alba Longa and Tusculum, I ask that you keep this private."

"No one will hear it from me," said Gaius. His voice was sincere.

"Nor from me," said Hostus, and the others echoed him.

A procession of slaves approached carrying trays of suckling roast pigs, cooked to mouth-watering perfection, just as the music of the citharae grew louder to celebrate the main course. The culinary excitement dissolved the tenseness of the conversation as everyone dug into the succulent meat. The main conversation branched into a series of smaller discussions that, happily, strayed from the gossipy revelation and floated up to lighter matters. Gellius told a joke, and those around him laughed.

Despite the change in tone, however, Proculus kept his eyes on his wine jug. Even in his drunken state he could feel Amata's contemptuous glare land on him. It was so hot and focused that he wondered, with the proper prayer to Vesta, whether she just might make him burst into flames.

The Comitium boasted its share of public structures and monuments. Among them was the Curia where the senators met, as well as the decorated speaker's platform, various altars and shrines and, of course, the new larger-than-life statue of Quirinus. The area was evolving into the vital civic space that Rome's founder had always envisioned. But there was one monument that was more private, more somber. Although it was barely noticeable, everyone knew it was there.

Amata had heard the stories about that day, long ago, when Romulus had beheaded his brother Remus on the top of what they used to call the hill of Saturn, but what she had always

known as the Capitoline Hill. She had also heard that Romulus's
adoptive father, the shepherd Faustulus, had tried to stop it. In
his desperation to reconcile his sons, he had tried to ascend the
Capitoline but had been restrained by Proculus. When he continued to resist, Proculus had slain him, on orders of Rhea
Silvia...and it had happened on the very spot where Amata now
stood waiting in the dark.

Once, Amata had summoned the courage to ask Romulus
about it. *Do you hate Proculus for killing your father?* She had
asked. She hoped he would say yes. She wanted him to hate
Proculus as much as she did. But Romulus had been adamant.
My mother and Proculus were following the will of Mars, he had
said. *I can only have one father, and it is him.*

Yet as much as Romulus had accepted the necessity of
Faustulus's death, he had also mourned for him. He had buried
the shepherd's ashes deep in the earth near the spot where he had
fallen, and he had ordered a slab of black stone from the moun-
tains to be placed on top as a sort of bleak tombstone. Amata
looked down at the stone and saw the flames from her torch re-
flect in its smooth surface.

At the sound of approaching footsteps, she held out her torch
against the darkness. A moment later, Proculus's form stepped
out of the still blackness of the midnight Forum and into her little
point of light. He was not carrying a torch, but only a shovel and
an urn. His face was drawn, but his eyes were alert and clear.

"How righteous of you to sober up before we bury the king,"
she said. She knelt down and pushed the handle of her torch into
a spot of soft ground. Still on her knees, she reached up to take
the urn out of the crook of Proculus's arm. She opened the lid
and looked inside. It was full of gray ash and small pieces of bone.
An unwelcome vision flashed through her mind: Proculus digging through the mud for his friend's bones, then burning and
crushing what remained of him. "Thank you," she said.

"I did it for him," replied Proculus, "to send him to the gods
properly. I didn't do it for you."

Amata stared at him. It wasn't like Proculus to be so openly hostile to her. Usually he was more subtle. Considering the morbid duty he had been tasked with, perhaps she had been too insensitive. But then he knelt beside her and she smelled the wine on his breath. It promptly reminded her of the way he had divulged the king's affair.

"No one can ever know about this," she said. "You can't tell anyone, not even Valia."

"It was a misstep tonight," he replied. "A momentary lapse."

"You were drunk, Proculus. And when you're drunk, you talk. Must I worry, every time you have a cup in your hand, that you are going to spew out the truth? That the fierce King Romulus was hacked to pieces by his own smooth-skinned senators, then buried in an unmarked grave?"

Proculus scoffed. "You don't care about Romulus's legacy. You only care about your own."

"That is not true."

"It is the holy truth." He glared at her. "Because if Romulus was just a mere mortal, if his great Trojan ancestry meant nothing, if his Silvian name could not survive death, then neither can yours. And your name is all you have."

"If it's all I have," flared Amata, "it is because of you."

Proculus pressed his lips together and slammed the sharp tip of the shovel into the ground at the edge of the black stone, then used the handle as a fulcrum to lift one of the smaller paving stones that abutted it. He pushed it aside, then worked silently, shoveling and boring out a tunnel under the black gravestone. It took a while, but finally he sat back and looked at Amata.

"That should do."

Gripping both sides of the urn, Amata leaned forward and poured the king's remains into the void below the black stone. "Father Mars and Mother Vesta, we petition you in the name of King Romulus Silvius. We ask that you open the gates of the Elysian Plain to your favorite son. To you, we offer this image of your greatness and this spark of your eternal flame." She twisted to retrieve the terracotta statuette of Mars and the small lighted lamp she had brought with her, placing each as far down the tunneled-out hole as her arm could reach.

Proculus withdrew the dagger at his side. Holding his hand over the opening in the ground, he sliced his palm with the blade and squeezed his hand, dripping a stream of sacrificial blood into the king's resting place. "I offer to you, Hades, for the king's soul," he said.

Without waiting for Amata's permission, Proculus took up his shovel again, refilled the hole with dirt, and wedged the paving stone tightly against the edge of the black stone. He stood and held out his arm to her. She took his hand and he pulled her to her feet.

"Aule told me something once," said Amata. "He said that after Faustulus's ashes were buried here, Romulus told him to place a curse on the spot...to curse anyone who violated it."

"The gods have no right to curse us," replied Proculus, "not when Romulus's murderers still live and breathe." He wiped his bloody palm on his tunica. "How can we let them sit in the Senate and vote for the next king of Rome when they murdered the last one?" He looked down at the gash on his hand, and then looked up at Amata. "How can we let them walk freely around the streets of Rome, unpunished, enjoying their food and mistresses, thinking they got away with it? How am I supposed to face them here in the Comitium and not open their throats?"

"They will face justice at our hands," assured Amata, "just as Naevius did. The rumors about his wife and slave made his suicide believable, but it won't be as easy with the others. We have to wait for an opportunity. The gods will give us a way, I know it. Pray for patience."

"You pray for patience," said Proculus. "I will pray for vengeance."

He glanced at the ground and the king's secret grave, but in that moment any grief he might have felt for Romulus was overwhelmed by the hatred he felt for his murderers. He squeezed the handle of shovel as if to strangle it, then turned and walked away.

He could sense Amata behind him for a distance, but then lost
her as he veered off in the darkness toward the Campus Martius.
Valia had told him to stay away for the night. And anyway, it
would look strangely suspicious for him and Amata to return to
the Palatine together at such an hour.

By the light of her torch, Amata saw him march off toward the
field of Mars. She kept her trajectory and soon arrived at the Palatine Gate. Although she usually preferred to walk at night, she
was tired and wished she would have at least left a lectica at the
base of the Palatine to carry her up. Still, her thoughts were so
distracted that the distance closed quickly and she found herself
nearing the soft light of the Shrine of Vesta.

She knelt before the moving orange flames and retrieved the
urn that she carried under her indigo cloak: she had saved some
of Romulus's ashes within. Reaching her small hand into the urn,
she scooped up some of the remaining ash and sprinkled it into
the goddess's sacred fire, letting the gray remnants of the king
slip through her fingers.

After all your trials, cousin, she thought to herself, *after all
your sacrifices and everything you built... this is your funeral?*

And then regardless of what she had just told Proculus, she
too prayed for vengeance.

CHAPTER IX

Sabinum

Numa Pompilius found it hard to catch his breath in the mornings. It was not ill health that made it difficult, but rather the way his chest failed to fully expand until he had completed his morning sacrifice. Ever since he was a young man, he had suffered from the same recurring dream—although to him, it was not a dream at all, but rather a glimpse into the world beyond. The dream always started the same way—with Numa asleep, floating upwards in spirit while his physical body remained in bed. As he watched from above, his dark bedchamber would fill with golden flashes of lightning, the silence shattered by terrifying rolls of wall-shaking thunder.

Next, the gods would materialize from thin air. Great bearded Jupiter, with his robust frame and fearsome eyes, wielding a crackling thunderbolt. Majestic Juno, with her beautiful face and a cloak of peacock feathers draped over her shoulders. Armor-clad Minerva and snarling Mars, and Vesta, too, with flames pouring out of her hands, making the bedchamber so hot that the tapestries on the wall would catch fire. As the gods appeared, Numa would continue to float upward until his back pressed against the ceiling. He would hear voices outside his door: Neptune, Mercury, and Apollo, all discussing godly matters, and as he tried to tune his ear to listen, a frightening awareness would settle upon him—he could not breathe. The weight of the gods' presence would press against his chest, crushing his ribs, suffocating him. And then he would hear a final voice—Hades, his ungraspable words as creaky as the black staircase he ascended from the underworld, a staircase that seemed to be directly below Numa's bedchamber.

At this point in the dream, as he gasped for air, any lingering awe or curiosity that Numa felt at being in the presence of the gods would dissolve and be replaced by panic and the certainty that he was about to die. He could sense that his spirit was about to slip through the tiniest cracks in the ceiling and float up and away, diffusing like insubstantial clouds on a windy day, until there was nothing at all left of his existence.

Then, at last, the dream would begin its final act. The charred walls of his bedchamber would start to bleed with a rich, summer greenness. Trees and flowers would sprout and grow, and the sound of a babbling spring would fill his ears. He always wondered—was he in Elysium? As the consciousness of life began to fade away, he would hear laughter and look down to see a goddess—he didn't know this one's name—shrouded in mist. He could see her shining fingers through the fog as she sent a cloud of mist, cold and invigorating, upward to strike his face. In that selfsame moment, he could breathe again.

The goddess would then speak to him. "*Who are you?*" she would ask.

And then he would wake with a start.

It was no different this morning. The unknown goddess's voice was still ringing in his ears as he opened his eyes and gulped for breath. He sat up quickly, straightening his shoulders to expand his chest and lungs, but the weight of the gods would not fall away. He forced himself to his feet and shuffled across the floor, pushing open the door and stumbling outside toward a small pen of restless chickens. Beside the pen, a sacrificial tripod with a round bowl on top held the low but steady flames of a fire. Numa reached into the pen and gripped one of the birds by a leg, lifting it out with one hand as his other hand retrieved the small sacrificial knife perched on a fence post. He knelt on the ground.

"Healer Apollo, a morning offering for my breath," he croaked, and cut off the chicken's head. He hastily plucked a few handfuls of feathers off the headless body and set the bloody lump in the flames. His breath came easier and he inhaled deeply as the smell of burning flesh filled his nostrils. He put his hands over the tripod and waved the smoke upwards.

"Now that's a pious man," said a voice behind him. "Sacrificing before his morning piss."

Numa rose and extended an arm in greeting. "Gaius Julius," he said, his breaths still labored. "What brings you to Cures?"

Grinning, Gaius brushed a bloody chicken feather off his arm and regarded Numa. His hair was uncombed but cropped, and his chin showed a few days' growth. "I could ask you the same thing," he replied. "I was surprised to hear you'd left Athens."

"It's only a temporary absence. I'm disposing of what's left of my land and property in Sabinum. My herds, my slaves, everything. It's too hard to manage everything from Greece."

"I see."

Numa's eyes shifted and he looked over Gaius's shoulder. "Ah," he said. "I forgot about this."

Gaius took a step back as two burly slaves dressed in tunicas finer than their master's bowed their heads to Numa. They were restraining a third slave, although this one had an angry face and a swollen eye.

"Domine," said one of the finer slaves. "This is him."

The two men threw the defiant slave at Numa's feet. Numa cocked his head at him. "So you're the troublemaker who's been siphoning off my herds for the last year. What do you have to say for yourself?"

"My actions speak for themselves," the slave replied.

"Ha!" Numa picked a chicken feather off the back of his hand and dropped it to the ground. "Your actions say you are thief."

The kneeling slave remained obstinate. "A man's actions never lie," he said. He knew he was going to die. He would not grovel.

"Perhaps, but they rarely tell the whole story," said Numa. "Why are you a thief?"

The man looked at the ground and wiped some ooze off his swollen eye. Gaius suppressed an irritated sigh. He had important business to discuss with Numa. Why didn't he just kill the villain—nothing was worse than a slave who betrayed his master—and get on with it?

"I asked you a question," Numa said to the man at his feet. "Why are you a thief? You have been my slave for ten years. Have you ever gone hungry?"

"No, Domine."

"I am not a cruel master," said Numa, "and I am more generous than most. Only yesterday I freed twelve of my best slaves as thanks for the years they toiled on my fields. Why would you steal from me when you could someday receive the same reward?"

The slave thought about this. "I am impatient."

The answer made Numa throw his head back in laughter. When his amusement subsided, he looked questioningly at the man. "Do you know what the priests of Apollo at Delphi say?"

"Where is Delphi?" asked the thief.

Numa nodded, impressed. "See? You are more than a thief. You are a curious man. Delphi is in Greece, my friend. And the wise priests there teach that mercy is a virtue. So I will strike a bargain with you. I will spare your life, if you swear to work your next master's field in honesty." He tilted his head. "Because honesty is a virtue as well."

The thieving slave looked up at Numa and blinked his one good eye in disbelief. He had spent the night in shackles and in horror, coming to terms with the inevitability of his death and retreating into spiteful anger as it neared, but now the hope of seeing another sunrise filled him with new life. "As Veritas looks down on me, I swear it!"

Numa gave a nod to the two better-dressed slaves, and they led the thief away. Gaius regarded Numa: the messy hair, the unshaven face, the bloody chicken feathers stuck to his fingers. Was this to be the next king of Rome? A man who would rather philosophize with a thief than kill him? There was no way he could rule a place as unruly as Rome. Romulus had beheaded, stabbed, disemboweled, hanged, hacked, and lashed more criminals and con men than anyone could remember, and he still struggled to do it. Gaius frowned with an unpleasant realization. Maybe Hostus Hostilius wasn't such a bad choice after all.

"I've been away too long," said Numa. "My land suffers from a lack of guidance."

"It is the same way in Rome," replied Gaius, clinging to his purpose. "Since the king disappeared...ascended...the city has been without strong leadership. The void has left us dealing with our own share of thieves and opportunists. In fact, that is what brings me here. Senator Claudius—you've met him before, I believe—has nominated you as a candidate in our regal election. I am here on behalf of the Senate to see if you will accept the nomination."

Numa crossed his arms and stared off toward the green Sabine hills in the distance. He looked more analytical than taken aback, as if he were scrutinizing the hills for the reason such an unexpected matter would materialize in his quiet, almost solitary life.

"You don't look surprised by the nomination," Gaius noted.

"Only fools are surprised by what the gods lay before them," said Numa.

"True enough," agreed Gaius. He waited a beat and briefed, "You have significant support in the Senate. Most of the moderate Sabines and Etruscans, and the Romans—"

"The Romans support me?" Numa chuckled. "Does that include you?"

"Yes."

"Why?"

"My fellow Romans and I believe that it is time for change in Rome. There is much infighting in the city, both in the Senate and in the streets, between the various tribes and factions. We need someone from the outside who can unify us. There are also those who feel that Rome has become too warlike, and perhaps—"

"Rome is the tyrant of Latium," Numa said matter-of-factly. "It has been since the day it was born."

"Sabinum has birthed its share of tyrants," Gaius replied, "and would-be tyrants."

The insinuation was clear, and Numa nodded as if accepting the fairness of the rebuke. "I have spent my entire life living in shame because of my father's insurrection against Tatius. It is one of the reasons I have chosen Greece and not Sabinum as my home. Here in Cures, as in Rome, my name rings of insurgency." He looked at Gaius. "Not kingship."

"You have spent too much time in self-reflection, Numa. You can only see yourself from within. I would have thought a man who so regularly communed with the gods would have a broader perspective of his place in the world."

"I know myself, Gaius."

"And I know Senator Claudius. He is one of the wisest and most respected men in Rome. If he nominated you, it is because he sees a king. I don't understand your hesitation. Your name has been disgraced. That disgrace has defined you. Yet when the gods lay a path to salvation before you, you refuse to take it."

"Rome cannot be subdued by a man like me."

"Then don't subdue it," said Gaius. "Change it."

Marcius was a brooding sort, but then Numa knew that most religious types were. He himself fell into excessive introspection more often than was reasonable, so he could not fault his friend Marcius for doing the same. The difference between them, at least as far as Numa could tell, lay in their capacity for happiness. Numa could feel joy. He could feel pleasure, whether from the company of a woman or the warmth of wine in his belly, whether from the stormy cracks of Jupiter's thunderbolts in the black clouds above or the flapping wings of Apollo's crows as they flew across a blue sky. Marcius, however, rarely smiled. The only time he seemed to be close to happy was when he was relating some anecdote about how the people in the many lands to which he had traveled honored their gods. Whether it was the Egyptians or the Hittites, the Persians or the Phoenicians, or even more exotic and distant peoples, the talk of foreign gods filled him with an excitement that formed something smile-like on his face.

There was no smile when he spoke of the Romans, though.

Marcius sat forward in his chair, his elbows on his knees and a cup of wine between his hands. "I was last in Rome about five years ago," he said. "They are a fanatically pious people, but their ideas and rituals are a miscellany. They're sloppy, too. In the middle of a sacrifice, someone will cough or drop a knife, and they'll just keep going. They mean no disrespect by it. They just don't know any better. My father once witnessed a sacrifice to Janus, back when the Vestal Tarpeia was still alive. She suffered from an affliction, you will remember. She had an episode in the middle of the rites, and apparently her guard stepped right inside the sacred boundary to retrieve her. Then, instead of ending things and starting again the next day, another priestess stepped up to take her place and they continued on. My father said he saw her pick a dropped bowl of salt off the ground and use it to purify the sacrifice."

Numa's heart quickened for a beat or two. Deviations from flawless ritual always made him anxious. "Perhaps he was exaggerating to tell a good story. You know how it is."

"My father was not prone to dramatics," replied Marcius. "He saw it with his own eyes, and I saw the same kind of thing when I was there. I once went to a riverside sacrifice to Tiber where the whole of the king's prayer was drowned out by the sound of two quarreling ducks. Someone else might have found it comical, but I found it a sacrilege." He sat back in his chair and extended his legs. "But that's my point. They don't recognize religious mistakes, and they don't offer contrition when they happen. It's just ignorance. It's too bad, really. They were off to a good start when the priestess Rhea Silvia was there. She taught Romulus what she knew about how things were done in the temples at Lavinium and Alba Longa, sacrifices and offerings and such. I heard rumors that Tarpeia taught him a thing or two about the gods in Sabinum as well, but like I said, nothing is nearly as organized as it should be. The fault lies in that Etruscan priest who's been at the helm for ages. He's an augur at heart and unmatched when it comes to the auspices, but other rites and rituals have been patched together. If you ask my opinion, it's only the Romans' zeal for the gods that keeps them in their favor."

"And now they have a new god," said Numa. "Quirinus."

"That's what I mean," said Marcius. "They have their own way of doing things. Romulus declared himself a living god, and they went with it. It's like the kingdoms of Egypt where the pharaoh is an incarnate god. But to bring such ideas to Latium..." he nearly grinned, "that took some balls."

"Ha," Numa laughed aloud. It was not like the abstruse Marcius to speak coarsely. He usually thought himself above that kind of thing. "So you admire them, then?"

"I didn't say that," Marcius clarified. "Still, with the right king and the proper guidance..." he continued speculatively, letting his thoughts float free for a moment. "I tremble to think what Rome could accomplish if it actually honored the gods correctly, formulaically, instead of just fervently."

Numa pondered this. "The Greek way, perhaps."

Marcius shook his head. "The way the Romans honor the gods is idiosyncratic, haphazard even. Some of the Alban rituals go all the way back to old Troy, others are from Cures or Veii, others seem to be taken from nameless peasant villages. Some seem to have no basis whatsoever, and yet the people are fiercely devoted to them. Simply overlaying the rituals of another place would not work. You would have to build something new and coherent from the foundation that is already there."

"You speak as though I've already agreed to go," said Numa.

"The Romans are a lost people, my friend." Marcius reached down to set his wine cup on the floor and then shook a finger at Numa. "They need their shepherd king."

"Perhaps," Numa indulged, "but you know it is not that simple for me. Living in Athens has afforded me a comfortable anonymity. My father, and his mistakes...I don't know if I want to wear the cloak of that."

"It is not about what we want," said Marcius "It's about what the gods ask of us."

"So you think I should go?"

"Yes, even if only to see what that den of wolves has been up to."

"You know what I am going to ask next," said Numa.

"I do indeed," replied Marcius, "and yes, I will go with you."

CHAPTER X

Alba Longa

It was good to be back in Alba Longa among the comforts of home. Real home, not her house on the Palatine. Her Roman house was comfortable in a sort of earthy way, but it did not compare to the sprawling Silvian palace that generations of kings and queens had called home, and that Amata now lived in with a respectable staff of slaves and servants. The divide between Rome and Alba Longa was just as wide when it came to the Roman Aedes Vestae and the Alban Temple of Vesta, and Amata felt equally relieved to leave the folksy hut-like Aedes behind and return to her duties as the chief Vestal in the ornate Alban temple. She was pleased to find the temple and the order as she had left it: efficient, pious, and organized.

In fact, all of Alba Longa had remained so. The pestilence that was hitting Rome's crops and vineyards had not extended to the fields that fed its more urbane and well-established mother city, and the powerful yet peaceful Alba Longa continued to be ruled by the competent King Sextus Julius. The result was a happy people and a carefree summer.

Well, mostly carefree. There was only one thing nagging at

Amata, and she had spent the entire morning debating with herself about how to handle it. *Straight on,* she had finally decided, *and honestly.* There really was no other option. That is why she had no sooner arrived at the home of Sextus and Penelope than she had sought out the Alban queen and pulled her aside to speak privately behind a statue of Venus in the lush royal courtyard.

"Amata," said Penelope, "can't this wait? Our guests are still arriving."

"That's why it can't wait," replied Amata. She eyed the steady stream of well-dressed and well-connected guests filing into the courtyard for the royal couple's annual summer garden party. It was a large and prestigious event, with people coming from all over Latium—including a number of aristocrats, priests and wealthy merchants from Rome—to attend. Amata knew them, and also knew they moved in the same circles as some of her friends on the Palatine. And although Queen Penelope didn't know it, that had left her vulnerable.

"Then get to it," urged Penelope. "Sextus will be cross with me soon."

You don't know the half of it, thought Amata. "It is about Proculus," she said. She put her fingers to her lips, as if that would hide the words. "He knows about you and Romulus."

Penelope blinked through the fog of Amata's words. As the fog cleared, she felt her heartbeat quicken, the dangerous implications of the revelation now beginning to circle her like bodiless predators. This could destroy her life in so many ways. Cobwebbed, unwanted memories came to the foreground of her mind.

"My gods," she said, her voice thin. "How did he learn of it?"

"I have no idea," said Amata. "Maybe Romulus told him, or maybe he just figured it out. Not much gets by the man. But what does it matter how he found out? He knows."

"Who else knows?"

This is the part Amata had really been dreading. "Just about everyone who lives on the Palatine," she said. "Proculus was drunk at supper and he blurted it out. I'm sorry, Penelope. There was nothing I could do. I pleaded with everyone to keep it a secret, but"—she shook her head in frustration as the guests continued to arrive—"word might have spread to some of the Romans here."

Penelope turned her back to the gathering on the other side of the large courtyard. "If Sextus finds out...gods help me, Amata, if my father finds out..."

Amata glanced at the guests. Even as Penelope struggled to absorb the news and restrain her worst fears, Sextus was gripping the elderly Mamilian's arm in welcome and directing him to a high-backed cushioned chair reserved for the queen's notoriously intractable father.

"It may come to nothing," said Amata. "I begged them not to say anything. They may have already forgotten and moved on to fresher gossip. Don't assume the worst. Isn't that what you told me?"

The queen frowned. "Yes, and look how that turned out."

"Sorry. Bad example." She touched Penelope's shoulder. "But good advice. Come, let's have some wine."

Penelope hesitated. "Just give me a moment. Sextus can tell when something is bothering me." She took a few steps to a gurgling fountain with a dolphin in the center and leaned on the edge of the basin, careful not to get her dress wet. "It was so long ago, Romulus and I. And so foolish." She let out a sardonic chuckle. "Did you know that my father had once suggested to Rhea Silvia that Romulus and I marry? My sister Phaidra was to marry Remus."

"I am glad Phaidra was spared that insult," said Amata. "Remus was a butcher."

"Many would say the same of Romulus."

Amata could not argue with that. "Did you love him?"

The queen smiled sadly. "Perhaps for a little while. Had things worked out differently, had we married as my father had wanted, I think we would have been happy. Although considering how Romulus and my father were with each other, it probably turned out for the best."

"For me, too," said Amata, sitting on the edge of the basin next to Penelope. She elbowed her friend good naturedly, trying to lighten the mood. "Shortly before my father was killed, I over-heard him talking to Albus Julius. They were going to wed me to Proculus."

"No!"

"It is true."

"Thank soft-hearted Juno for saving you from that torment," said Penelope. "Imagine living with the constant stench of Procu-lus's wine breath on your face. I don't know how Valia does it."

"She loves him, and despite his boundless faults, he loves her, too."

Penelope's eyes searched for and found her husband amid the gathering. "I love Sextus very much," she said with emotion. "Even when I was with Romulus, I never stopped loving him. I just got caught up in it all. You know how Romulus was. He was a force of nature. But after the deaths of his children, and then Hersilia, he seemed so broken. My sympathy for him turned into comfort, and then something else."

"How did it end?" asked Amata.

"Painfully," replied Penelope, "but I suppose that is always how it ends." She stood, and Amata stood with her. "Let's go say hello to my father before he berates me in front of my own subjects."

The two women left the fountain and the statue of Venus, cas-ually making their way across the courtyard toward where Mamilian sat, and exchanging pleasantries with the royal couple's guests along the way. Amata noted the way Penelope scrutinized the face of everyone she spoke with, looking for a revealing smile or a certain glint of the eye that might betray who knew her secret.

Reaching Mamilian, they took chairs opposite him just as slaves arrived with wine and cheese. Mamilian accepted a cup and stared at Amata for several long moments. She endured it. With the exception of Rhea Silvia, the leader of Tusculum had never cared for those who bore the name of the Silvii. It was his prejudice, one born long before her, back when he and Prince

Egestus were young men. Yet their rivalry was as irrelevant to Amata as the old man himself, and she was unmoved by his arrogant demeanor. If it weren't for her friendship with Penelope, she would ignore him altogether.

"It is good to see you, Master Mamilian," she lied.

He grinned. "The living and immortal Quirinus," he said.

"Pardon me, sir?"

The grin shifted into a cynical snigger. "I heard about Proculus's speech." He waved a hand mockingly in the air. "The divine ascension." He took a sip of his wine before again shooting a barbed look at Amata. "Only in fucking Rome."

Amata felt a hand on her shoulder, and looked up to see Sextus smiling diplomatically down at her. "Priestess, may I have a word?"

"Of course, Your Highness," said Amata, using the honorific she always used when speaking to Sextus in public. She rose and followed him into the Julian palace and into a sitting room decorated with frescos of ocean scenes. "That Mamilian—" she began, but stopped when she saw the serious look on Sextus's face. Her stomach sank. Had he already heard about Penelope and Romulus? Had he taken her aside to ask her what she knew about it?

"I have a request to make of you, Amata," he said. "It is a religious matter, but a sensitive one."

Amata subtly exhaled a sigh of relief. "Go on, Sextus."

"Many years ago, something sacred was taken from our city, something that belonged here. Romulus took it."

"The Palladium," said Amata.

"The founder brought it to Alba Longa himself, and with all respect to Romulus, he should never have taken it to Rome. Now that he is gone, we have an opportunity to set things right. Whoever is elected to be the next king of Rome, I would like you to speak to him, to petition him to release it, so you can bring it back to where it belongs."

Amata paused before answering. Sextus's altruism was not quite as absolute as he was pretending. If he managed to have the

Palladium returned to Alba Longa, the accomplishment would become part of his own royal legacy. Still, he was right—the ancient Trojan relic belonged in Alba Longa.

"I will do my best," she said, "but whether or not I am successful will depend on the man who is elected king. If it is a Sabine or an Etruscan, he may allow it. But if a Roman is elected, it is unlikely."

"I have heard the favored man is Numa Pompilius," replied Sextus. "That is good and bad."

"How so?"

"Well, he's a pious man, and an intelligent one, so he may respect the provenance of Alba Longa and agree to return the Palladium. But politically, I'm not sure he's the best fit for Rome. He's a Sabine, but he's spent his life in Greece. That makes him an outsider, a man with no identity who grew up with no loyalty to any city. Some might see this as a good thing—a lack of bias—but I don't think so. A man who has never felt loyalty for his native city cannot suddenly feel it for a foreign one. If a man is to be king, he must already have the capacity for loyalty. You cannot simply hand it to someone with a crown and expect them to wear it."

Amata rubbed her temples. Romulus's death, Penelope's secret, the politics of the Palladium and the upcoming election...it was all too much. "Sextus," she said, "you're giving me a headache."

"I've had a headache for nearly forty years," replied the Alban king. "You'll learn to live with it."

It was Amata's first time passing through the iron gates of the necropolis in Alba Longa, and it was nothing like she had imagined. She has always envisioned it to be a deserted and colorless graveyard of neglected tombs, of forgotten lives and a dead past. Instead, she had been met with rows of decorated, meticulously maintained and fastidiously manicured trees that housed loudly chirping birds and even louder chattering squirrels that darted here and there, scampering down the paved stone pathway with her like small, self-appointed, high-strung escorts. She was happy for the company. Watching them playfully clamber up and over the colorful statues of birds and animals that lined the path helped assuage the sadness that accompanied her purpose.

As she walked, she clutched Romulus's smooth, unadorned urn to her chest. She and Proculus had poured most of his remains under the black stone in the Comitium, and she had sprinkled some of his ashes on the shrine to Vesta on the Palatine. But she had kept enough of him to bring home to Alba Longa, where he could reside forever in the city of the dead alongside the great Silvian kings who had come before him.

For better or worse, that included her father, Nemeois. He had been the king of Alba Longa for nearly twenty years, until that fateful day when Rhea Silvia and her son, the rightful king, had deposed him. Afterward, Nemeois had been brought here, to the necropolis, and sealed inside his tomb. Alive. Amata had never summoned the courage to visit it. Not until today.

Reaching the royal section of the necropolis, she noted the larger-than-life statues of Aeneas and Ascanius at its entrance and kept walking until she spotted a shrine to Vesta. It was here that Rhea Silvia had performed—endured—years of solitary service as a priestess. A bowl of milk sat on the edge of the shrine, and Amata stopped just long enough to drizzle a few drops into the low but steady flames.

She kept walking along the rows of royal tombs until one of the life-sized statues that stood before a hut-shaped sepulcher made her gasp aloud. She had not seen the face of her father since she was a child, but here it was, staring at her. She could almost see the hard mouth crack into an adoring smile, as if amused by some witticism she had delivered or some prank she had played on him. He had been a good father. By all accounts, he had also been a good king. She felt sympathy for him, but anger, too. It was his ambition that had enclosed him in his tomb before his time. It was his ambition that had led to the deaths of her mother and brother, and to her grief-stricken childhood and perpetual service to the goddess.

At least that is what she had been told by his killers and what her tutor Nikandros had been instructed—likely upon pain of death—to teach her. But Nikandros had also taught her how to think for herself, and in later years, Amata had tried to understand her father's reasons for orchestrating the usurpation of King Numitor and murdering the crown prince Egestus. Was it really just ambition? Or was her father correct—justified, even—in seizing the throne from an incompetent king and an incestuous prince? Though not part of the royal line, her father was nonetheless a Silvian and had always honored his great ancestry. Perhaps he had not been driven by ambition, but rather by a desire to restore the dignity of the Silvii.

Wrapping one arm around Romulus's urn and holding it close to her body, Amata extended her other arm and touched the thick wooden door of her father's sealed tomb with her fingertips. Behind this door lay his bones. Unlike the kings around him, he had not been interred with dignity. She wondered: had he resisted as the soldiers pushed him into the blackness of his tomb? Had he begged for mercy? And after the heavy door of his crypt had been closed and he had been left in total darkness, cut off from the living world outside, had he wept? Raged? How long had he lived in the dark, without food or water, until he felt the waters of the Styx pour into the tomb to carry him to the underworld? His fate had been nightmarish, and Amata had spent countless nights crying herself to sleep, unable to get the horrific images of him locked inside his tomb—clawing at the door, gasping for breath, the flesh rotting off his bones—out of her mind.

Interred alive. Could there be any worse way to die?

She pulled her gaze away from the tomb's door and glanced at the trees and flowers around her, compelling herself to remember the happy times. Their family—Amata, Amatus, and their mother and father—laughing over supper, singing funny songs by the fire, or playing hide and seek in the garden. Even as a child, she had been able to tell that her parents didn't love each other. They loved their children, though, and that had been enough to keep them together.

A cloud covered the sun, making her skin prickle with coolness and sapping the warmth from the memory so Amata moved on, continuing past the royal sepulchers and statues of dead kings until she arrived at her destination: the temple-shaped tomb of Prince Egestus Silvius. This tomb, she knew she had to enter.

Still holding the urn, she pulled on the heavy door. It opened easily despite its age and weight. Steeling herself, Amata stepped inside where the air was even cooler, but the sight of the colorful frescos that adorned the walls and the large sculpted sarcophagus in the middle of the chamber distracted her from her discomfort. Beside the stone coffer, as if guarding it, there stood a somewhat terrifying statue of Mars. The god's face—black eyes, bearded chin, severe expression—was unnervingly similar to Romulus's.

She moved further into the chamber, noticing the urn that sat on top of the prince's sarcophagus. It was no surprise to see the urn of Rhea Silvia here, entombed with her brother. Amata looked thoughtfully at it for a moment, finding a certain poignancy in the painted orange and red flames that decorated its surface. She knelt before the statue of Mars, placing Romulus's urn at its feet. It was fitting that what remained of his body would rest here, in the very spot where it came into the world.

"I have fulfilled my duty as your kinswoman," Amata whispered. She stood and walked back toward the door, casting a glance over her shoulder at the urn on the floor. "Until we meet again, cousin."

She stepped out of the tomb and closed the door behind her. Turning, she stopped and put her hand to her chest in startled surprise to find Mamilian sitting on a stone bench not more than a few paces away. Amata met his eyes and found them clear with the certain knowledge of the task she had just completed.

"Who did it?" he asked.

She tried not to react. "What do you mean?"

"Who killed him?"

Amata gave him a withering look. "Go home, Master Mamilian," she said, and walked past him.

He sprang to his feet. Seizing her from behind, he spun her body around to face him, clutching both of her arms and immobilizing her. His imposing height, the edge of violence in his voice, and the force of his piercing stare—it all gave Amata a fleeting glance of what a terrifying man he must have been in his younger days. It was no wonder that Romulus had always maneuvered so carefully around him.

"Who killed Romulus?" he demanded. The aggression in his voice dissolved into anguish. "Who killed Rhea's son? I need to know."

Even through the pain of his grip, Amata felt a rise of sympathy for the old man. Suddenly, she wanted to tell him. But she could not.

"He is at rest," she said. "They both are."

Mamilian let her go. She held his gaze for a moment, then walked away, leaving him and the city of the dead behind.

CHAPTER XI

Rome

The Roman Forum looked the same to Marcius as it did the last time he was in the city. The only difference was the smell. It was awful. The reason was immediately clear. The large above-ground sewage system that snaked through the area—it was nothing more than an open channel packed on both sides with stone—was filled to, or rather over, its brim.

Grim-faced city slaves walked along the length of the rancid channel's stone borders, toiling with shovels and pickaxes to break through the sludge that blocked the sewer's flow from the Forum to where it emptied into the Tiber River. The unluckiest of the slaves stood knee-high in the fly-covered brown muck itself, using tools, sticks and their own bare hands to remove the stomach-turning blockages. All around, more griping workers shoveled and swept the sewage that had spilled over onto the streets, piling the sloppy, stinking mess into carts, which were then emptied into the Tiber.

Numa lifted the neckline of his tunica to cover his nose and mouth. "It is inhuman," he muttered to Marcius as they walked along the Forum streets. "Hygeia has forsaken the place."

Marcius opened his mouth to say something in response, but felt the foul stench settle on his tongue and closed it. He groaned.

They kept walking until their path was blocked by a small, unfolding drama. Just ahead, a slave with a shovel at his feet was growling some obscenity at a young man. The younger man unhooked the lash at his side and unfurled it with a snap. The slave cried out in pain as the fabric on the back of his dirty tunica split open, and streams of flesh blood mixed with the unsightly brown stains already there. The slave caught his breath, picked up the shovel, and hopped back into the blocked sewer.

The young man continued to stand in the middle of the street, blocking Numa and Marcius's path and huffing in anger. When he noticed the two finely dressed men behind him, though, he immediately stepped aside.

"I am sorry, sirs," he said.

"Not all," replied Numa. "You do important work."

The young man looked testily at Numa—things were bad enough, he didn't need this one's attitude—but, gleaning no mockery in the man's face, his own expression relaxed. "Sure," he said wryly.

"What is your name, boy?" asked Numa.

"Theo, sir."

"And how did you come to be doing such work, Theo?"

"I was given a bad job to do, and I made the mistake of doing a good job of it. Now it's the only work I can get. I used to work the Circus, but now they've given the track to that idiot Bannus, and I get the sewers, which used to be his job. So Bannus gets rewarded with glory work for doing a shitty job"—he scowled at the filth on his tunica—"and I get stuck with doing his shitty job."

"There's a riddle in there somewhere," said Numa, glancing at Marcius.

"More like a cautionary tale," replied Theo. "Why do the right thing? They'll only find a way to punish you for it. I smell so bad these days my goat won't share a room with me."

"Perhaps you should aim for higher company," said Marcius.

The young man looked off in the direction of the nearby Aedes Vestae. "It isn't fair," he muttered to himself.

"And yet it could be worse," said Numa. "After all, the lash is in your hand"—he pointed to the whipped slave in the sewer—"and the wounds are on his back." He leaned in closer to Theo. "Injustice is a gift from the gods, boy. It helps build our character."

"Does it?" asked Theo. He fastened the lash to his belt, picked a filth-covered stick off the ground, and held it out to Numa. "Then why don't we change positions for a while. I will do your business, while you clear the sewer and become a better man."

"But you don't even know my business. It may be worse than yours."

"I will be the judge of that," said Theo. "What is your business?"

"I am trying to decide whether I want to be the king of Rome."

Theo sighed, turned his back to the two men, and trudged back to the sewer. Maybe this dainty pair had time to dawdle about and mock people, but he certainly didn't.

More charmed by the hardworking man's slight than offended by it, Numa led Marcius to the perimeter of the Aedes Vestae where two soldiers stood guard on either side of the door.

"Is Priestess Amata Silvia in there?" asked Numa.

"Who wants to know?" asked the guard.

Marcius snorted, and the guard raised an unimpressed eyebrow at him.

Just then, the door opened from the inside and an attractive but frazzled young woman stepped outside, handing a bucket of foul-smelling water to one of the guards. He set it on the ground and motioned to Numa and Marcius. "These two are looking for Priestess Amata. They haven't said why."

Petronia regarded the strangers. "Why are you looking for her?"

Marcius snorted again, a pretentious snort, and let his eyes wander despondently over the modest Aedes before settling on Petronia's soiled hands. The sewage on the street had clearly made its way into the sacred space. "Perhaps we want to discuss the abysmal state of the goddess's sanctuary and ask her why she hasn't done anything about it."

Petronia had just selected a few choice words for the moping snob when she thought twice and bit her tongue. His sandals were cleaner than most. He could be someone important. She smiled tightly to his companion. He seemed a little friendlier.

"I am the sacerdos Petronia," she said. "And you are?"

"Numa Pompilius."

Numa Pompilius. She had heard that name recently...but where? She struggled to place it. "Priestess Amata has returned to her home in Alba Longa, sir," she said. "I can have a message sent to her, or may I be of service?"

"Do you know where we can find the augur Aule?"

"Why?" This time, Petronia met Marcius's derisive chuckle with a stern look. These were her colleagues, and she had every right to ask.

"Young lady," said Numa, "Senator Claudius has proposed my name be entered in the regal election. But I am a stranger to Rome, and I wanted to see your temples for myself before I accept. I put nothing above the proper worship of the gods, not even kingship."

Now Petronia could place the name. She had overheard the generals Gellius and Appius discussing him in the market. Though from what she had taken from their conversation, they were reluctant supporters only and had doubts about his ability to bridle the city. She had to admit, Numa didn't exactly blend into the background of Rome in its current—how did the mopey one say it?—oh yes, abysmal state.

"Sacerdos Aule will be at the Auguraculum," she said. "I will take you." After a quick word with the sacerdotes Lollia and Elissa who were in the Aedes with her, Petronia led the two men through the streets of the Forum, sidestepping the worst of the sewage and a fistfight between an Etruscan carpenter and a Sabine merchant, until they arrived at the base of the citadel. They climbed the steps and reached the top where a contingent of red-cloaked soldiers looked past Petronia to assess her two unfamiliar companions.

"This is Numa Pompilius," she announced. "He is here on senatorial matters with his companion." She did not bother to acquaint herself or the guards with the companion's name. Perhaps that would put him in his place. "They wish to speak with Sacerdos Aule. I can take them."

"I'll accompany you," said Statius, shouldering his way through the guards. After surviving his foot-roasting interrogation in the wake of Romulus's death, the head of the king's personal bodyguard had been promoted to acting commander of the citadel. He was grateful for the confidence that General Proculus had shown in him by granting him the second prestigious posting—one he would hold until the new king was declared—and he now ate, slept and lived on the hilltop. He also insisted on escorting anyone he did not personally know if they had business anywhere on the Capitoline.

"Is a military escort really necessary?" asked Numa.

"If you are elected king, sir," said Statius, revealing he too had heard the name before, "you will have one at all times. Might as well get used to it."

Numa studied the situation atop the Capitoline: it was crawling with a small army of soldiers, and it seemed impossible to go more than a hundred paces without being stopped, questioned, and searched. Even the toga-clad priests and magistrates who moved in and out of temples and other buildings were subject to it.

With Statius's permission, and before heading to the Auguraculum, Petronia walked Numa and Marcius along the Capitoline. She showed them the various shrines, as well as the Tarpeian Rock, the high cliff from which traitors to Rome were thrown to their death. She showed them Romulus's greatest architectural achievement, the Temple of Jupiter, built on the site of a sacred flint stone found by Romulus himself. As they walked toward the Asylum, where Rome's founder had first welcomed strong and weak to his city, she described the place where his royal basket had been found on the banks of the river. She talked about the building of the Campus Martius, the Circus, the Comitium, the Forum, and the appearance of the *ignis mirabilis*—the miracle fire of Vesta—that had been ignited with a spear of lightning thrown by Mars to mark the spot where Romulus was to build his great city.

The tour of the hilltop and the abridged history lesson incorporated everything Aule had instructed her to say to visitors to Rome. Since beginning her tenure in the Aedes, Petronia had given the same tour to a number of dignitaries and priests from other cities. Yet unlike other visitors who asked questions, Numa and his companion remained silent throughout.

It was only as they reached the north summit of the Capitoline, where were even more soldiers were stationed, that Numa spoke. He turned to Statius. "It is always this heavily guarded?"

"It is the citadel, sir," said Statius, "and the Temple of Juno"— he motioned to the rectangular temple—"is the site of our gold and silver reserves."

"Then from what I hear," said Marcius, "it isn't heavily guarded enough."

It was humorless comment, but Numa laughed.

Statius eyed them: they were an odd pair. The younger man seemed as grave and serious as death, but Numa was the opposite. He was almost too quick to laugh. Statius had heard that Numa was a man of the gods, but just the same, he seemed somehow irreverent. He certainly could not be any less like Romulus had been, but then regal matters were well above Statius's pay grade. He chose diplomacy and ignored the gibe about the missing gold. Anyway, the ongoing theft of the precious metal from the city's forge was common knowledge. It was also the biggest mystery in all of Latium—how were gold nuggets managing to disappear from the treasury on an almost daily basis, despite the meticulous vetting of its workers and the unblinking eyes of a hundred provoked guards, pissed off by how bad it was making them look?

They continued past the Temple of Juno, at last arriving at the boundary stones of the rectangular, open-sky sanctuary of the Auguraculum. Aule was sitting at rest on a wooden chair in the middle of the space, looking out over the distant hills and the blue sky above. Statius held back a bit, while Petronia knelt at one of the boundary stones. When her two companions remained standing, she shot them a sideways glance. Numa may have been on the verge of kingship, but he was still below the gods. Numa looked down at her and smiled, as if amused by her indignation, and knelt beside her. But to her shock, the mopey one not only remained standing, but passed through the boundary. It was everything Petronia could do to not reach forward and grab him by his ankles.

"Stop," she whispered.

He didn't listen, but walked brazenly up to the augur's chair, put his hands on his hips, and looked out at the same section of sky that Aule was looking at. The augur didn't seem to notice the younger man's presence, but then Marcius pointed in the distance and spoke.

"That house there, on that hill, it blocks the line of sight. It must come down."

Startled, Aule jumped to his feet. The lituus that had been resting on his lap fell to the ground. "Gods above!" he said. "Where are the bloody guards?" He turned, and his angry gaze met the stunned eyes of Statius. The soldier gave him an exasperated look.

"May I cross the boundary, Sacerdos?" Statius asked.

"You damn well better!" shouted the augur.

Statius marched past the carved stone boundary markers and gripped Marcius by the arm.

"That house must go!" Marcius said angrily to Aule.

Aule faced him. "That area is not within the templum."

"It is still significant," said Marcius, "and you know it. So why has it not been torn down? Perhaps it is your house. Or the house of a friend, or your mistress."

"Enough!"

They all looked to see Petronia standing at the boundary stone, her arms straight at her sides, her fists clenched. She looked down at Numa.

"He has no right to speak to Sacerdos Aule like that! How dare you come into our city and disrespect us! If you are so offended by our ways, you will find the nearest city gate over there," she said, raising her arm and pointing.

Numa stood. He looked uncertain—like he wasn't sure if he should laugh or take this more seriously—but the young woman's protectiveness of the old priest was sincere in its nobility, so he erred on the side of tact and offered an apologetic bow to Aule.

"Forgive us, sir," he said. "My friend is passionate about the gods. Sometimes too passionate."

"Many are passionate about the gods," replied Aule, "and yet still politic around men."

Hauling Marcius back outside the boundary of the Auguraculum, Statius gave the pretentious young man an extra shove for good measure. Marcius stumbled but found his feet. He rubbed his arm: the skin where Statius had grabbed him was red and burning, and welts were already forming. The soldier spoke to both men.

"Do you have other business in Rome?"

"No," said Numa. "Our horses are stabled by the north gate. We will be on our way."

"Allow me to provide a military escort," said Statius. "If you don't object, of course." Without waiting for a response, he waved over two soldiers who had been watching the incident from a prudent distance. "Take these fine men to their horses."

Happy to oblige, the soldiers approached. One of them put his hand on the hilt of the dagger at his side, while the other took a more gracious role.

"This way," he said to the visitors. "We'll have you out of Rome before you know it."

✻   ✻   ✻

Numa Pompilius could not stop chuckling.

"You and I have stood before the sacred fire in Delphi and asked questions of Apollo's Oracle," he said to Marcius. "We have descended into the bowels of the earth to experience the mysteries of Eleusis. We have stood too close to the Ploutonion at Hierapolis, and we have communed with Amun at the great Temple of Ramses at Ipsambul"—he wiped tears of laughter from his eyes—"but we are kicked off a horrid hilltop in Rome like misbehaving children at a dinner party!" He looked at his friend who rode beside him. Seeing the ill humor in his face, he tried unsuccessfully to stifle a snicker. "Do not take it personally, Marcius."

"I take very little personally, Numa. You know that. But what about you? Do you want to be king of a city that threw you out on your ear?"

Numa pretended to hear something. "I think Athens is calling my name."

Marcius nodded, and Numa inhaled the fresh, crisp air. Rather than immediately returning to Cures, they had decided to first ride southeast of Rome to visit a villa recently purchased by one of Marcius's friends. The journey had taken them over land unknown to either of them. It was beautiful.

"These fields are as green as the eyes of Demeter," Numa observed.

"My friend has boasted of them since he bought his villa. He says this land and the springs on it are home to water nymphs the locals call the Camenae. He says there is a grove where—" he stopped when he noticed Numa was no longer riding alongside him. Pivoting on his horse, he looked back to see that Numa had dismounted and was standing, transfixed, next to a softly babbling spring that he himself had not even noticed when passing. Marcius slid off his horse and approached his friend's side.

"I have been here before," said Numa, staring into the cool mist of the green spring. His expression was uncharacteristically severe.

"When?"

"Every night, when I fall asleep."

Without further explanation, Numa pulled his eyes away from the verdant spring. He returned to his horse and mounted it, turning the animal around—back toward Rome.

"Where are you going?" Marcius called out. But Numa did not answer. He just nudged his horse into a gallop and rode away, as though imbued with newfound purpose.

Marcius scrambled to mount his own horse. Unsure as to why, he followed his friend back to the city that had just cast them out.

CHAPTER XII

Proculus shifted in his seat in the Curia, his eyes on Numa Pompilius. The man was exactly how Gaius had described him. Erudite. Eccentric in the way a man tended to be when he had spent too much time in temples and not enough time on the battlefield. He sat with the confidence of the educated smug, yet now and then he tugged at the fabric of his toga, betraying a level of discomfort that amused Proculus, and no doubt the rest of Rome's old guard. It was probably the first time the man had worn a toga, at least one in the unique Roman style.

As he and the rest of the senatorial assembly waited for Senator Oppius to count the votes yet again, Proculus curled the fingers of his right hand into a fist. He had forced himself to avoid wine this morning, and whenever he went without at breakfast, it was always his right hand that fell into tremors first. The left would soon follow, but with luck, the vote would be over by then and he could go home and drink himself into stability. His gaze shifted from Numa to those he did not merely dislike, but rather hated with a fury he had never before felt for anyone, not even Rome's worst enemies: Senators Calvisius, Carteius, Antonius, and the droopy-eyed Pele. Proculus did not dare let his stare linger on them for too long. He could not let them see the rancor in his eyes. They had to think, for now, that they had gotten away with it.

Yet he could not imagine what they were feeling at this moment, sitting in the same chamber in which they had torn apart the king, and waiting for the new king to be declared. Did they feel relief? Confusion? Satisfaction? Their faces were expressionless. Despite the way that Rome had moved on, they knew better than to draw attention to themselves.

Enjoy the reprieve, thought Proculus. He tightened both hands into fists and remembered Amata's words. "They will face justice at our hands." But when? How?

He swore to himself that once the election was over, and once enough time had passed to quell suspicion, he would commit himself to leveling the bloodiest, most painful forms of vengeance he could conjure up against Romulus's assassins. Every horror he had learned in war, every torment he had mastered as an interrogator, he would bring to bear against them.

Acrisius, seated next to him, leaned in. "Looks like the old man's done," he said, as Senator Oppius turned away from the voting urn and moved toward the lighted altar in the center of the chamber. "Not a moment too soon. I have to piss like a stallion."

The elderly Oppius poured a libation of oil into the altar fire, picked up the crown of oak leaves that sat on the pedestal next to it, and turned to the assembly of senators—one hundred men in total, all seated shoulder to shoulder in the Curia, anxiously awaiting the results of the final count. The regal candidates waited as well: Senators Hostilius, Sertorius, Occius, and Rasinius, and the newcomer Pompilius, all trying to appear above it all while praying that the numbers favored them.

"Under the all-seeing eyes of Jupiter," said Oppius, "under the protection of Mars and Vesta, and with the permission of our beloved Father Quirinus who watches over his city from his heavenly throne, it is the will and legal declaration of this assembly that Numa Pompilius be crowned king of Rome."

Despite the significance of the declaration, it was anticlimactic. So too was the reaction. The truth was, no one really wanted a new king in the first place. Romulus may not have been loved by all, but he was effective—if brutally so—and predictable. He was even fair, in his own way. But most of all, he was reassuring. With Romulus in charge, no one imagined that the slaves would get lazy, or that the guards at the city gates would start accepting bribes from criminals, or that the treasury would keep leaking gold. No one worried that the armies of the Volsci or factions of the chronically untrustworthy Etrusci might once again begin to provoke the city by sending their scouts ever deeper into Roman territory.

Assessing the mood, Numa stood and moved to Oppius's side. Yet instead of lowering his head to accept the crown in the senator's hand, he took the *simpulum* off the altar and drizzled oil into the sacred flames.

"I am made a king by the votes of men," he said, "but Rome is a city of the gods, and I cannot accept the crown until Jupiter himself casts his divine vote. For while I am humbled by the faith you have placed in me, I place my faith solely in the divine." He looked at Oppius. "Make no declaration to the people until the auspices have been taken and the gods have had their say."

Murmurs moved through the assembly. Some were skeptical, cynical even, but most were surprised. Impressed. Such deference to the gods and modesty among men—it was a good start.

Hostus Hostilius was one of the cynical. As a hundred men rose to follow Numa through the columned portico of the Curia, all filing out of the Comitium, Hostus walked alongside Proculus and spoke complainingly.

"This will be trickery," he muttered. "The man would put Odysseus to shame."

"He cannot control the flight of the birds," said Proculus, "nor can he corrupt Aule. It is showmanship, and risky showmanship at that. Let's see if it snaps back to sting him."

As Numa and the procession of senators in his wake exited the Comitium, they were greeted by an austere aggregation of

Rome's magistrates, notable citizens, and priests and priestesses, including Amata, who had arrived the day before from Alba Longa. Like all of them, she had waited since dawn to see the new king emerge from the Curia with a crown on his head, a purple cloak over his shoulders, and Rome's regal insignia—a staff, with a golden she-wolf on top—in his hand. Instead, the stranger Numa Pompilius emerged first, as plain as when he had entered, with Senator Oppius carrying the regal accoutrements behind him. Were it not for the excited whispers of the senators that spread like flames in wind throughout the crowd—"Numa won, but he seeks the gods' approval!"—one might have assumed no winner had been chosen at all.

With Numa in the lead, the expectant congregation of Rome's elite continued to the base of the Capitoline Hill and ascended, passing the Temple of Juno and the bewildered guards, and finally reaching the stark openness of the Auguraculum. Aule was standing next to a boundary stone, his augur's staff in hand. Although his expression was impervious to most, those who knew him best could see the annoyance in it. Numa had not notified him of this potential spectacle, and had it not been for the Olympian speed of a subordinate priest running ahead with the news, Aule would have been caught off-guard before all of Rome.

With a large crowd gathered behind him, Numa knelt before Rome's chief priest. "Sacerdos Aule, on behalf of the Senate and the people of Rome, I ask that auspices be taken to determine the right and success of my kingship."

The unsmiling augur bid the king-elect rise, and together they entered the templum where the divination would proceed, Aule using his lituus to designate the sacred area of the sky to be observed as he called out the rites. Avoiding Numa's eyes, he reached up and drew a fold of the man's toga over his head, covering it in reverence to the gods. Finally, he laid his hand on Numa's veiled head and again looked to the skies, this time praying to Jupiter for a sign. Was it the god's desire that Numa should be king or not?

A hushed silence fell on the gathering atop the Capitoline. The silence flowed down the slope of the hill, covering the multitudes who had packed the Forum. They stared eagerly up at the Auguraculum, and then even higher into the sky, searching for a sign or an omen—a flock of birds coming from this direction or that, an odd-shaped cloud, even a flash of faraway lightning or sudden loud sound emanating from the east or west, the south or north.

Amata watched from the boundary. She could feel her own suspense grow and mingle with the suspense of those around her, those below her, perhaps even the gods above. She turned her head in all directions—where had all the birds gone? Her feeling of suspense began to fade, replaced by a feeling of unease. This silence, this empty sky, was unnatural. Unless Numa's agents had secretly caught and caged every crow, sparrow, eagle, pigeon and starling in Rome, the gods were indeed deliberating Numa's worth. Everyone could feel it. Even Aule's expression turned from annoyance to apprehension at the sense of foreboding that hung heavy in the air, filling the space where the birds should have been.

And then—there it was. A moving spot in the sky, approaching on the right. The birds neared the hilltop lazily and soared effortlessly overheard, not one of them breaking the solemnity of the scene with a call that might corrupt the augur's interpretation. When they passed, Aule bid Numa rise.

"The signs are clear," he said loudly, "and the omens favorable. With the blessing of Jove, Numa Pompilius shall be king!"

At that, a mighty cheer went up—it wasn't the mightiest that Rome had ever given, but again, it was a good start. The dramatic taking of the auspices had done what the senatorial vote had not—it had roused some excitement for the new king of Rome. As the cheer died down, the aged senator Oppius, Romulus's first senator, pushed thoughts of the old king aside and placed the crown of oak leaves on the new king's head. He set the purple cloak over Numa's shoulders, and placed the royal staff in his right hand.

As King Numa Pompilius faced his subjects, Proculus stood within the crowd on the Capitoline and studied him. Whatever discomfort Numa's toga had initially caused him, it was gone. He looked as though he'd been wearing one his whole life. The general turned away. He wound his way through the gathering and down the Capitoline, heading to the market and praying that the wine vendors were open.

"Tell the king that Numa Pompilius was crowned in Rome this morning," Amata said to Sextus's messenger, who had arrived the day before from Alba Longa. "Tell him also that Numa at first refused the royal insignia, only accepting it after the auspices were taken and the signs proved favorable. Tell him"—she smiled—"that he and the queen missed a dramatic scene."

The messenger bowed and exited Amata's Palatine home. The Vestal knew that the Senate would have dispatched messengers throughout Latium, Sabinum, Etruria, Samnium and other regions to spread the news the moment that Numa was elected king, but courtesy and their friendship dictated that she personally send one to Sextus as well. She could picture him and Penelope sitting by the fire as they received the messenger, hearing the undertone of harmless gossip in her message about Numa's religious theater—who knew if his demonstration at the Auguraculum was sincere or strategic—and then falling into more gossip about whatever stories they had heard about the new king of Rome. The thought of that made her smile widen.

She finished dressing with the help of two slaves, choosing a white dress but topping it with a *palla* of lively orange rather than the mourning indigo she had worn lately. One of the slaves fastened a necklace around her neck: three loops of carnelian beads with a gold medallion that boasted a fine engraving of sunrays. The other slave moved to the door to answer a knock.

The door opened, and Valia sauntered inside. "Look at you,"

she said. "The color's returned to your cheeks and your wardrobe."

Amata glanced at Valia's vivid blue dress and the vibrant emerald-studded jewelry draped around her neck and arms. "Look who's talking. I at first thought a peacock had strutted into my home."

Valia shouldered the slave aside and arranged the loops of the necklace around Amata's neck. "It will be easier now," she said. "The city can move on. We can, too."

"Not everyone shares your confidence in Numa," said Amata.

"*King* Numa."

"All right, King Numa. I know Sextus has his reservations. Acrisius, Gellius, your husband and half the Romans in the Senate...they didn't cast their votes out of confidence in the man. Quite the opposite."

"Well, no one survives in Rome by being altruistic, do they?" asked Valia.

"*Ita vero*," replied Amata.

The sound of a distant cheer found its way into Amata's hut. Even from their location on the Palatine, the two women could hear excited shouts from the Circus float upward. Games were well underway in the arena—chariot races, boxing, sword fighting and more—to celebrate not just the crowning of Rome's new king, but the auspicious timing of it. Happily, the coronation coincided with the *vinalia*, the city's largest wine festival of the year.

Yet what was a happy coincidence to most of Rome was an unhappy curse to Valia.

"Proculus will be drunk as Silenus by now," she muttered. "He'll need to be carried home on the back of a donkey."

"He might surprise you."

"I've been married to him too long to be surprised by him."

They left Amata's home together, taking the street down the slope of the Palatine to the Circus, with three well-armed soldiers following closely behind. The guards chaperoned the pair to the canopied viewing box along a long stretch of track, the one that was reserved for Rome's elite. Spotting Gaius, they took the two empty seats next to him.

Gaius turned to Valia. "You came at the wrong time, Mother."

Valia exhaled, exasperated. The two women had arrived in the middle of an archery competition featuring Rome's generals, including Acrisius, Gellius, Paeon, Appius, Hostus, and of course, Proculus. Proculus was clearly intoxicated. To bursts of amused laugher in the wooden stands, he fumbled to string his bow, and then dropped it onto the ground, toppling onto his hands and knees in a shaky effort to retrieve it. Acrisius tried to mitigate the embarrassing spectacle by helping him, but Proculus pushed him aside and tried again. This time, he landed on his face. The crowd laughed louder.

"Do something," Valia whispered to her son.

A shadow appeared in Amata's line of sight, and she looked up to see a man standing at her left shoulder. She recognized his face—he was a minor magistrate—but did not know his name.

"Priestess Amata," he said. "King Numa has summoned you to the Curia. I am to accompany you."

The interruption and the surprise order was enough to distract Valia from the embarrassment her husband was currently causing her on the track. She nudged Amata. "Go. But come right back and tell me what he wanted."

Amata followed the magistrate to an area behind the viewing box where a lectica awaited her. She slipped inside and felt the porters lift the vehicle. After several minutes of easy travel but confusing speculation—why in the world would the king want to see her so soon after his crowning?—the lectica arrived at the Comitium. She stepped out and walked past the lighted altar just outside the Curia's entrance, pausing respectfully at the portico. While it was permissible for a woman or priestess to enter the Comitium this far, entering the Curia itself was forbidden.

Inside the temple-like assembly space, the purple-cloaked Numa stood in discussion with a crowd of eight or ten senators and a younger man with a staid face whom Amata assumed was his personal priest of sorts. Petronia had told her about him: his name was Marcius, and the young sacerdos had gone red-faced with anger when speaking of him.

Numa himself showed little trace of regal deportment. While Romulus had crafted an aura of preeminence, Numa seemed more accessible. He looked the senators in the eye as they spoke, laughing at their tired anecdotes while absently adjusting the gold chain around his neck. But then again, he hadn't even been king for a full day yet. That easy bearing could change when confronted with the ceaseless bickering and raucous outbursts the Roman senators were famous for. The kings' physical appearances also revealed their differences: Numa's light-brown hair and eyes were a less menacing shade than Romulus's black hair and black eyes. Numa's face was lined from his travels and his introspection, however, and even though he was a little younger than Amata, he looked older.

The magistrate approached the king and gestured to Amata. Numa bade her enter.

"Priestess Amata," he greeted. "Come sit with me."

The senators around him seemed to twitch with indecision. Should they inform the new king that, according to Roman convention, women were not permitted to enter the Curia? Or should they let it slide this once and inform him at a more discreet time? They were still twitching when Numa walked away from them and sat on a chair, leaving another invitingly open for Amata.

She passed through the portico and bowed to him. "King Numa," she said as she sat.

A droll grin appeared briefly on his face, as though it was the first time he had heard the regal title before his name.

"Amata," he said, mulling her name. "It means beloved one, does it not? It is fitting, since you are so highly regarded in Latium."

"I don't know about that, sir," she lied.

"Would you like some wine?"

"Thank you, but no, Your Highness."

"I am told this wine festival hearkens back to your own ancestry."

"It does, sir. It is an old Latium festival they say was started by Aeneas, to celebrate his victory over the Etruscan king Mezentius. The best wines of the harvest were offered to Jupiter, Mars and Vesta." She paused, thinking that might be enough of an explanation. Surely the king had more important matters to attend to right now. The group of senators he had been speaking with were standing impatiently on the other side of the Curia, waiting for his return. Numa didn't seem to care, but instead nodded as if interested in nothing else but the story, so she continued. "Romulus was often too busy for festivals, but he always participated in the vinalia. As I'm sure you know, he too had a long-standing conflict with an Etruscan king, Velsos, and was grateful to the gods when he was finally able to defeat him."

"And yet the Etruscans are still a force to be reckoned with," said Numa. "It is not easy to conquer a people through violence. It is like cutting down a tree. Sprigs will always rise up."

"I suppose that is true, sir." Amata wasn't sure—was the comment mere philosophy, or was it a slight against Romulus's rule?

"Your cousin accomplished more than any mortal could be expected to in a lifetime," said Numa, sensing her uncertainty. "I find it fitting that the gods sought to reward him with immortality."

"Indeed, Your Highness."

Numa wagged a finger at her, his expression taking on an aspect of curious rumination. "You know, Priestess, you and I actually have a lot in common."

"Oh?"

"Both of our fathers were usurpers." He stopped wagging his finger. "And both were killed on Romulus's orders."

Amata bristled. She held his gaze, her eyes becoming more examining. Numa was not her king. King Sextus of Alba Longa was her king. If she wanted to, she could stand up and excuse herself, and head straight back to Alba Longa without stopping. Numa would not detain her—the political fallout from the Latin Confederation would be swift and harsh. And anyway, who would he give the order to? Rome's old guard would never stand for it. The man would lose control before he'd even fully established it.

Yet as the initial impact of his bold words faded away, and as she considered him, she soon realized his words bore no threat, no insult. Rather, they were reflective in a benign, almost sympathetic way.

"I suppose that is also true, sir."

He smiled, pleased that she understood. "I trust you don't mind my speaking bluntly," he said, his voice adopting a more businesslike tone.

"I prefer it, sir."

"Half of Rome's temples have fallen into ruin," he began, "and the other half are managed by priests whose prayers are as haphazard as the flight of a one-winged bird. It is embarrassing. One of my first priorities will therefore be to double the number of temples and shrines in the city in the first year of my rule, and to renovate the existing temples. I also plan to implement a *collegium* of priests, and to reform the prayers and rites of the priesthoods." He dipped his head toward Marcius. "My priest Marcius has heard rumblings that you have often lamented the state of the Aedes Vestae and how the order is managed in Rome."

"Yes, I have."

"Marcius also says the temple and the Vestal order in Alba Longa are second to none. As such, I am hoping that you would be willing to help mold the Roman order into what it should be."

"I am happy to hear of your plans," said Amata. "Very happy, in fact. I will of course provide as much guidance as I can."

"I don't want guidance," replied the king. "I want you to stay in Rome." When she hesitated and began to fidget in her chair, he added, "That is, unless you are thinking of retiring."

Amata stopped fidgeting. She stared at him, baffled. "What?"

Numa shrugged casually. "Well, it's my understanding that Romulus wasn't just your cousin. He also held legal power over you."

"Yes," replied Amata. "He was the last male in the Silvian line."

Numa let a moment pass. "But Romulus is gone," he said. "Now what?"

Amata shook her head. "I don't understand what you mean, sir. Romulus made arrangements for my care."

"How so?"

She frowned in thought. What had Proculus said? Oh yes. "I believe he arranged for my emancipation. I imagine it makes no difference though, as I—"

"Ah," said Numa. "So you are now a free woman."

Amata pursed her lips. She had not thought about it that way.

"It must be strange to suddenly be free. To have no overseer. For the first time in your adult life, you have a choice. You can choose to live life as a private woman. You never have to step inside one of Vesta's temples ever again if you don't want to. You can enjoy your home, your friends, you can even take a lover or marry if you wish. There is no one to stop you." He leaned forward, as if to emphasize his point. "You can leave the old order at Alba Longa—it can't offer many challenges to you at this point—and create a new order in Rome, and a new life for yourself in the process."

"I am content with the life I have, sir."

"One should not say so too quickly," he replied, "the gods may hear and fix us to the spot." He grinned and stood, and began to pace nonchalantly about the room. "It is the same in Latium as it is in Sabinum, I believe—girls serve in the temple for six months before marrying." He stopped pacing and faced her. "It could not have been easy for you to watch so many women come and go, all leaving to begin their new lives as wives and mothers while you remained a sacerdos."

Amata laced her fingers together. It was as everyone had said—Numa Pompilius was a hard man to decipher. His words were piercing and he knew where to strike, but his tone was innocuous. What was his intention? To provoke? Or was this just the way he got to know people?

"You make it sound as though I have languished in the temple, starving for food and human contact. I can assure you that is not the case, Your Highness. I have led a privileged life."

"Privileged, yes. But not independent. Not free, not truly."

"It is all relative," replied Amata. "Is a starving free man happier than a spoiled slave?"

The moment the word *slave* escaped her lips, Amata regretted it. She should have known he would pounce, and he did.

"So you see yourself as a slave, then?"

"I do not."

"I see myself as a slave," he replied earnestly. "A slave to my name, to the gods, to the Fates, and now a slave to Rome."

Amata put her hands on her lap in a way that indicated she would prefer the conversation draw to a close. "Sir, it pleases me to know that Rome is in good hands. I will offer my best guidance to your sacerdotes, but I much prefer to do so from my own home in Alba Longa."

He opened his arms magnanimously. "Then you are free to do so. Thank you for coming to see me, Priestess. I look forward to your input with respect to the Aedes. With your help, the Roman order of sacerdotes may one day be as revered as the Alban order."

That is unlikely, thought Amata. She stood and bowed again.

"I am sure it will be," she said.

Like most of Rome, Petronia had spent the morning waiting for the results of the regal election. She had stared up at the Auguraculum and watched with bated breath as Aule took the auspices on behalf of the king-elect, silently praying the whole time that Jupiter's messengers would fly in the wrong direction, in the unfavorable direction, and that Numa would have no choice but to refuse the crown in front of everyone. It hadn't happened that way. Then again, maybe Numa wouldn't be as bad as she thought. She did tend to think the worst. It was one of many bad habits that she had tried, unsuccessfully, to change over the years. Plus, it wasn't actually Numa that she disliked. It was his priest, Marcius.

Within moments of King Numa accepting the royal insignia on top of the Capitoline, city slaves and workers had spilled into the Forum to begin decorating and setting up for the wine festival, and the mood transitioned from political to celebratory, the wine flowing before Numa had even made it off the hilltop. While most people grabbed food and drink and headed to the Circus for the games, Petronia had gone straight to the Aedes Vestae where she was on afternoon watch, and had immediately begun to scrub the floor. Overflow from the nearby sewer was still somehow leaking through the walls.

She had been in the middle of her labor when Priestess Amata had come by to do a surprise inspection. Yet it was Amata who had been surprised: she had walked in to find three sacerdotes idly gossiping by the altar while Petronia alone was on her hands and knees, cleaning the goddess's floor. The priestess had abruptly turned around and walked out of the Aedes without uttering a word.

After finishing an otherwise uneventful watch over the sacred fire, Petronia returned to her nearby hut where Malla helped remove her tunica—it stank of smoke tinged with sewer—and washed her with cool spring water, the slave complaining the whole time about her mistress's unholy state. Finally, she helped Petronia change into a fresh white tunica with a lightweight cream-colored palla. Rejuvenated by the clean water and clothes, Petronia slipped her gold bracelet with the garnet stone onto her arm, bid Malla goodbye, and ventured out of her hut and into the festive Forum, weaving through the revelers until she spotted Lollia standing at the base of the gilded statue of Quirinus.

"What took you so long?" asked Lollia.

"I spent the afternoon scrubbing shit off the floor and then Malla had to scrub it off me."

Lollia wrinkled her nose. "That's nasty, Petronia. Anyway, you smell sweet as a rose now. Let's get something to eat."

"Let's get wine first. From what I hear, whatever hasn't already been offered to the gods will be gone before sunset, and it's already dusk."

"I've heard the same thing," said Lollia. "The pestilence hit the wine crops hard. It won't be much of a wine festival without wine."

Inadvertently eavesdropping on the pair's conversation, a gruff man in a good tunica tilted his head up toward the Capitoline. "You're right about that, young missies. The king's priest—what a strange bugger he is—has been offering libations to Jupiter since midday. If he doesn't lay off soon, there won't be any left for us mortals."

The man lumbered off, and Petronia cranked her head over the crowd, looking up toward the Temple of Jupiter on the Capitoline. "Come on," she said to Lollia.

She grabbed her friend by the wrist, nearly dragging her through the celebrants, many of whom were wearing wreaths of grape leaves and dancing to the sound of lively pipes and drums. Yet a closer look revealed an unpleasant reality—less than half of those around them had wine cups in hand. Those that didn't weren't celebrating as much as searching for their share.

As the two women navigated the crowd, finally achieving a clear line of sight to the Altar of Jupiter on the Capitoline above, Petronia huffed in anger. It was exactly as the gruff man had said. It was Marcius who was overseeing the ritualistic offerings to the gods, and not Rome's chief priest, Aule.

"That is wrong," said Lollia.

"Wrong in a thousand ways," replied Petronia. "I have to go. I'll find you later."

Ignoring Lollia's exclamations of protest, Petronia lifted the bottom of her tunica and doubled back to the street that led up the Capitoline, flirting her way past the guards as always, and proceeding to the far slope of the hilltop where Aule's home was located. She rapped on the closed door. After a moment of shuffling, the door opened and she found herself staring into the glazed eyes of Aule. Clearly, he had apportioned some of Rome's dwindling wine stores for himself.

"Why is that pretender offering to the gods when you should be doing it?" Petronia asked him.

"He is no pretender," slurred Aule. "He is the new chief priest of Rome."

Petronia's mouth dropped open. "He is not!"

"He is, my dear." The augur pounded his chest with a fist to suppress a wine belch, then regarded the sacerdos as kindly as he could in his compromised condition. "You are a sweet girl, Petronia. Make your peace with Marcius. Things will be easier for you that way."

"I don't care what is easier. I care what is fair!"

Aule chuckled. "Only the gods of the underworld cast judgment."

"What does that even mean?"

"It means life isn't fair." The old priest looked at Petronia, looked at his wine cup, and then closed the door of his home.

Already irritated, a burst of carefree laughter in the near distance grated Petronia's nerves. She followed the revelry back the way she had come, until she came upon a group of priests, generals, and their wives, all standing by a large brazier as General Acrisius's wife, Lady Rufina, waved her arms in the air in the telling of some amusing anecdote. Priestess Amata was among them. From what Petronia could glean as she neared the group, Lady Rufina was acting out some kind of drunken embarrassment suffered by General Proculus at the Circus. The sacerdos stood at arm's length and waited until Amata noticed her.

"What is it, Petronia?" inquired the priestess.

"It is Sacerdos Aule"—Petronia turned and pointed back in the direction of the priest's home—"I have just seen him. He's drinking himself into a stupor, and I don't blame him. King Numa has just stripped him of his priesthood!"

Amata tactfully excused herself from her company and ushered Petronia aside to speak more privately. "He has not been stripped of his priesthood," she said, "but things have changed."

"You knew about this?"

"Who do you think brought him the wine?" Amata sighed. "Aule will not be Rome's chief priest any longer, but Numa is making him the head priest of a new college of augurs. He will be in charge of reforming the auspices. It is an important task and augury has always been Aule's true passion."

"It is a sham posting," said Petronia. "Marcius will do whatever he wants with the auspices, no matter what Sacerdos Aule advises. You must do something."

Normally, Petronia's impudence would have awarded her a curt dismissal by the older priestess. Yet her loyalty to Aule was noble. Endearing. Amata had to admire it.

"Numa is the king of Rome now," she said. "It is not my place to challenge him, nor is it yours. Regardless of what changes he makes, I believe that he truly reveres the gods. The rest is between him and them."

A swell of angry voices coming from the area of Jupiter's temple where Marcius was still offering to the father of the gods nearly drowned out the last of Amata's words. A rage-filled shout rose above the others—"Jupiter's drunk enough, you prick! Leave some for the rest of us!" There was the sound of things breaking, of being knocked over. In an instant, two burly soldiers were at Amata's side.

"Trouble's brewing," said one of them. "General Acrisius has ordered the wives and priestesses to return home immediately. We will escort you, Priestess."

As the guards ushered Amata away, Petronia heard her hastily order a soldier to stay with the young sacerdos, but the order was lost in the shouts and scuffles of the quickly mounting chaos, and the soldier did not hear it.

Petronia could sense the change of mood as viscerally as a change in temperature. The promise of wine, food, and a good time had kept tempers in check all day, but now that night was falling and it was clear none of those things would come in abundance, Rome was losing its collective composure. Petronia was surprised it had remained composed for this long. Between the pestilence, the growing violence on the streets, the increased security, the ongoing interrogations due to the disappearing gold, the stench of the open sewers, and finally the sight of precious wine soaking into the earth on the Capitoline...if Marcius and Numa had any real understanding of Rome's nature, they would not have so blithely provoked its already testy citizens.

Yet Petronia understood Rome well enough to make a run for it. As she scrambled down the Capitoline, she felt the black clouds of the burgeoning riot swirl and pick up strength all around her. In the few moments it took her to arrive in the Forum below, the storm had swept in fully and she struggled to stay on her feet as shouting, angry bodies crashed into her from all sides. By the time she had fought her way to the Shrine of Vulcan, it was chaos.

Roman soldiers moved in pairs, pummelling the closest of the rioters with their shields and openly stabbing the most persistent of the troublemakers with the blood-wet blades of their daggers. Petronia fell painfully onto her knees as a man roughly shouldered past her. She managed to stand only to be knocked down again, this time by four or five men carrying buckets of water and running toward a trio of rowdy youths who had set a vendor's wooden stall on fire. One of the men dumped his bucket on the flames and then turned toward the boys, slamming the empty wooden bucket into their heads. Two of the youths fled, but the third collapsed and lay unmoving on the ground.

Petronia crossed her arms in front of her chest to instinctively shield her body, pushing her way through the throngs of people until a hand wrapped around her long hair and yanked her head back hard. She stumbled and lost her footing, this time landing on her back. A toothless, leather-faced man straddled her from above and laughed, reaching around to shove his hand up her dress.

She screamed.

As she stared up in horror at her attacker, the bottom of a soldier's shield met the side of the man's face, violently jerking his head sideways and causing thick blood to spew from his nose and mouth. Dazed, he teetered above her and began to slowly fall forward, but she twisted and freed herself in time to avoid being crushed by him.

Clambering to her feet yet again, Petronia jostled for space in the moving crowd. Her objective was to reach the street that led to the gate, but the thrust of rioters tossed her body this way and that, as if it were a piece of helpless driftwood on a raging sea. Once, she made the mistake of extending her arm to try and push her way through the mob, but it got stuck in the swarm and she was lucky to pull it back with the bones still straight.

And then, as if the fearful situation couldn't get any more terrifying, she saw a sight that stopped the blood in her veins—Theo, just several paces ahead, being beaten by two men in slave tunicas. At least she thought it was Theo. She only caught a fleeting glance before the sea of people swept her away, ever closer to the speaker's platform in the Comitium.

"Theo! Theo!" she cried out.

She heard a loud voice—not Theo's. It was a voice she knew, though. It was King Numa's voice. She turned her head to follow it, and saw him standing on the decorated tribune, a crown of oak leaves on his head and the purple cloak of royalty on his shoulders. The captain of the celeres, Statius, stood beside him, his long sword drawn and ready to slay anyone who got too close to the new king.

"Friends!" Numa called out, "Romans! Your king speaks, and by the gods, you will listen!"

They didn't listen.

Numa marched to one side of the speaker's platform where there stood a large sacrificial tripod and a bronze firebowl that burned with Vesta's fire. Gripping the handles of the firebowl, he lifted it from the tripod and carried it to the front of the tribune. Once there, he swung the bowl forward, sending ash and flame flying into the crowd before and below him. The firebowl now empty, he dropped it upside down and stepped on top of the overturned basin so that he stood even higher above the mob.

"Romans, I have now done as you!" Numa hollered, stomping on the sacred firebowl. "I have vandalized my city! I have offended the gods with my insolence!"

The antics caught the attention of a few in the crowd. They elbowed those next to them and pointed up to Numa in wonder. Before long, whatever the king was up to on the tribune seemed far more interesting than the riot—that was proceeding as predictably as riots usually did—and most people stopped shouting, pushing, and fighting in favor of watching the drama unfold on Rome's main stage. As they gawked up at him, Numa ripped the crown of oak leaves from his head and flung it in the crowd. He shrugged off his regal purple cloak and did the same with it.

"Romans!" he held up his arms, waiting for silence to speak again. When it came, he inhaled a deep breath through his nose. "Who are you?" The question was out of place. The question made no sense. And yet something about it struck the men and women at Numa's feet, and they raised their eyes to their strange new king. "Who are you?" he asked again, this time tinging the question with weighty awe, with profound wonder, as if no matter in the world could be more important or more fascinating to him.

"We are only men," he heard a voice from the crowd call out.

"If you are only men, then the gods are only gods," Numa replied. "But who would dare tell Jupiter that he is *only* a god? Is Jupiter not more than that? Is he not a being filled with passion, with purpose, with love and fury? Can Jupiter be defined by the word *god*? I tell you, truly, that you are not *only* men. You are more than that, just as I am more than a king. I am one of you. I am a Roman! And I make this vow to you—I will take no wine, I will eat no fine bread, until each and every one of you can do the same!"

A surging sense of appreciation radiated from the crowd. People began to whisper and murmur to each other, repeating Numa's words and passing them along to the person next to them, behind them, sending the king's words soaring through the streets of Rome like birds on the breeze.

"*Ave*, King Numa!" someone shouted, and that voice was joined by others. The crowd began to grow restless again, although the violence that had so recently filled the Forum was gone, replaced by renewed piety and a newfound admiration for King Numa. Bodies moved forward, all wanting to touch the king's feet.

At that, Statius stepped closer to Numa and signaled for other members of the king's bodyguard to mobilize. A heartbeat later, some thirty celeres had surrounded the tribune, the tips of their daggers pointed threateningly in the faces of the awestruck subjects at the front of the crowd.

"Get back, you bastards!" shouted Statius, and jabbed his sword at a young man who dared to reach up and touch the king's sandal.

"Stop!" cried Numa. He faced Statius before looking back toward the crowd. "My fellow Romans," he said, then pointed at Statius, "this man believes that you will do me harm. But I know your hearts. I know you are men of honor, men of the gods, and I am not afraid of you. I do not need to be protected from you. Therefore, here and now, I dissolve the royal bodyguard known as the celeres! I will walk among my people not just as their king, but as their friend!"

"Your Highness!" Statius shook his head, stunned. He shouted to be heard above the clamorous cheer. "I advise against this, sir!"

Numa did not reply. Instead, he turned and walked off the speaker's platform, moving through his amazed subjects as casually and carefree as a farmer strolling through his fields. Not one person grabbed him. Not one person threw anything at him or called him a disparaging name. The people merely bowed and parted, letting him pass freely and peacefully.

But Petronia didn't care about the king's passage. There was only person she wanted to reach, and that was Theo. She had spent the entire duration of the king's speech trying to locate the spot where she had last seen him, if indeed it was him, being beaten by slaves. At last, she found the spot—but it was too late. The beaten man was nowhere to be seen. All that remained were puddles of blood on the ground.

Moving in the opposite direction as the king and his follower-subjects, Petronia pushed her way through the capricious gathering until the crowd thinned enough that she could break into a run, not stopping until she reached the city gate. Although she usually passed without delay, the riot had put the guards on high alert and they were scrutinizing passers-through more than usual, eager to catch any instigators who thought they could slip out of the city.

One of the guards, a young man alternately posted at the gate and on the citadel, spotted her. "Lady Petronia. Come here."

She held her breath and moved toward him. "It is pandemonium in the Forum," she said.

He stepped close and leaned in toward her. "I hear the king threw his crown into the crowd. Did you see it?"

"Oh, yes. It was all very dramatic. He tossed it into the mob, and then—you will find this particularly shocking—he dismissed the celeres!"

"No!"

"It is true. He says that he trusts his subjects to not harm him."

The guard laughed. "He *is* new to Rome!" The laugh subsided. "Heading to the Viminal?"

"Yes."

It was not unusual for Petronia to go to the Viminal. A friend from childhood had married a man with a large home there, and the sacerdos was known to visit often. The only drawback to the pretext was the fact that this particular friend was abysmal company—the endless complaints of an unhappy wife, the shrieks of her vexatious, sticky-fingered children...it was unbearable, but at least she was simple-minded enough to never suspect that Petronia had another reason for making the trek.

The guard motioned to another soldier, indicating that Petronia could pass. "Would you like an escort?" he asked her.

"No, the road is busy," she replied. "I think it's safer outside the city than inside right now."

"You're probably right."

Petronia exited the gate, finally allowing herself to breathe freely and stepping up her pace as she prayed. *Please Juno Regina, let him be at home...let him be safe.* Walking quickly, but not quickly enough to draw attention to herself, she reached the settlement on the Viminal and took the footpath that led to Theo's humble little hut, oblivious to the thistles that tugged at the bottom of her dress and the wasps that darted threateningly in the air around her.

She reached the open field and the post where his goat was usually tethered. The animal was there, but free of its rope. It perked its ears when it saw her, but remained beside the bunch of tasty tall grasses it was munching, as if guarding its sweet find. Petronia ran past it, into Theo's hut.

He was there, kneeling before his modest household shrine. Petronia caught him in mid-prayer—"Mother Vesta, protect your sacerdos." He sprang to his feet when she entered and ran to her, wrapping his arms around her and pushing his face into the nape of her neck. "I could see the smoke from here...I could hear it from here..."

"It is fine," she soothed, panting. "I am fine."

"Were you hurt?"

Petronia shook her head, trying to lose the feeling of her attacker's foul hand sliding up her dress, touching her privately. Violating her. "Not at all."

"I should have stayed in the city," he said. "I left after my shift, but I should have stayed. I should have known something like this would happen."

Petronia forced herself to smile. "It was not as bad as you think. It was kind of exciting, actually. King Numa was on the tribune and said—"

"I don't care what King Numa said on the tribune! Petronia, why are we staying here? Why are we letting Rome tether us, like dumb animals to a post, milking us for whatever it can take? I have a job I hate and I own a single goat. You have no dowry and a slave on loan from some distant relative you've never met. There is no future for us in Rome. Not in Cures, either." He pulled her close and kissed her on the lips. "Marry me. We can take what little we have and build a life for ourselves somewhere else. We can have children. I can learn a trade and start my own business. You know I can do it!"

Petronia stepped closer and laid her head against his chest. "Theo, you could master the work of Atlas if you wanted to. I have never known a more capable man."

"Do you not love me?"

She glanced around his tiny hut, seeing the worn bed linens, the chipped cups, the overturned crate that served as the household shrine, and the manure-stained sandals just inside the door. Theo was capable, but he would never be a rich man. Perhaps she could overlook that if she loved him, but she didn't love him. She knew she never would.

Theo rested his chin on the top of her head. "Do you not love me?" he asked again, and although he could feel her arms squeeze him tighter, no answer came.

CHAPTER XIII

To someone who lived on the Palatine Hill, the worst thing about a Roman riot wasn't the violence, theft, or destruction. The walled and well-guarded hilltop meant they were, quite literally, above all of that nonsense. Rather, the worst thing about a Roman riot was the gods-forsaken, ear-splitting, unending *noise*. The screams. The crashes and bangs. The drunken shouting. The profanity-laced curses. Sadly, the walls were not nearly high enough to keep the noise down.

So while Amata had escaped the riot unscathed, she had nonetheless spent a sleepless night tossing and turning, covering her ears with her pillow and finally depleting her own stores of wine, all in an effort to fall asleep for a few luxurious moments. It had worked, sort of, but the patchy nature of her sleep and the wine had left her welcoming the dawn feeling worse than if had she not slept at all.

From what she had heard from the soldier who delivered her morning firewood, the riot had resulted in the usual kinds of damages. The temples and altars on the militarized Capitoline were unharmed, but the Forum was a mess. Rioters had smashed many vendors' stalls to kindling, littered the streets with any-thing they could find and break, stolen offering vessels from the shrines, and deliberately clogged the already overworked sewer with everything from city banners to their own sandals. Amata didn't even want to think about what kind of condition the Aedes Vestae would be in when she arrived.

She had not yet finished dressing when she heard a knock at the door. She ignored it. The person knocked again, this time more insistently, so she quickly tied a belt around her tunica and marched irritably across the floor of her home, opening the door to find one of Sextus's messengers standing in the threshold.

"Yes?" she snapped. "What is so important you must knock twice?"

"Priestess Amata," bowed the messenger, "King Sextus requests an update with regard to your stay in Rome. He asks whether you have made any progress with respect to the holy item the two of you previously discussed."

The Palladium, thought Amata. It seemed that Sextus was more eager than he had let on to have the Trojan relic returned to Alba Longa.

"King Sextus also reminds you that your duties at the temple in Alba Longa require your attention, and requests that you return home as soon as possible"—the messenger raised his eyebrows for emphasis—"with the aforementioned holy item, of course."

Amata chewed her lip. "Tell him..." She frowned. This was irritating. Her head throbbed, her stomach felt scarily untrustworthy, the morning sun stabbed at her eyes, and she should have already left for the Aedes where she was expected to meet Numa to discuss his plans for the structure and surrounding area. Yet here was Sextus, demanding she answer to him as well? There was only one explanation for his brusque message: he had found out about Penelope and Romulus, and wanted to know whether Amata had known about it. "Tell him you delivered the message," she said, and closed the door in the surprised man's face.

She moved to the hearthfire in the center of her round home and poured hot water from a pot into a cup stuffed with mint leaves, blowing on the hot beverage to cool it and then taking a sip, hoping the peppermint would settle her stomach. It helped a bit, and she soon felt brave enough to venture out and risk the journey down the Palatine Hill to the Forum.

By the time she arrived at the Aedes Vestae, whatever progress she had made in settling her stomach was lost. The work of vandals had clogged the nearby sewer, and a film of foulness on the street forced her to lift the bottom of her dress as she walked along. She looked ahead and saw a young man standing in the open sewer. He reached in, gagged, and withdrew a dead dog, tossing it to the side. Amata put her hand on her stomach and entered the Aedes.

Petronia was there, once again on her hands and knees, this time scrubbing the bottom of the altar. The other sacerdos on watch was a young woman by the name of Helen. Perhaps assuming her beautiful namesake put her above ugly labor, she was leaning against the curved wall, running her fingers through her long, curly hair. When Amata entered, she pushed herself away from the wall and put a piece of oak on the sacred fire. Amata stared at her. Things had become so lax in the Aedes that the sacerdos almost seemed to be goading the older Vestal to chastise her.

"Helen, you may go," said Amata.

"My watch is not over, Priestess."

"Yes, it is," said Amata. "All your watches are over."

"Priestess!" The young woman looked disbelievingly at Amata, but seeing no softening in her expression, slunk poutingly out of the Aedes.

Petronia rose and wiped off her hands with a wet cloth. "I'd be lying if I said that I didn't enjoy that," she said. When the priestess smirked, she continued. "The slop from the sewer keeps seeping in along the bottom of the wall, right here." Petronia tapped a portion of the wall with her sandaled toe. "I've asked for it to be repaired, but with the election, I think it just got overlooked. Anyway, Lollia will be here soon and she will help me clean."

Amata looked around the inside of the Aedes. Other than the occasional spot repair along the wall or ceiling, it hadn't changed in years. The goddess's eternal fire burned in a wide bronze bowl atop its round stone altar, while the Palladium still sat in its unadorned niche. The niches that used to contain traditional *sarcinae sanctae* were empty, the practice having been abandoned long ago. A few dry spindles and hearth branches from the *arbor felix* were tucked into a basket on the floor and a pile of sanctified wood was stacked beside it. Her gaze moved back to the ancient statue of Athena, a helmet on her head and a shield and spear in her grip. Amata still felt a nagging irritation at Sextus's demands, but he was right. The artifact did belong in Alba Longa. Romulus should never have taken it away.

"You will have all the help you need soon enough," said Amata. "King Numa has asked me to recommend some improvements to the order." She looked up, absently watching a wisp of smoke escape out the opening in the ceiling. "I hope he tears this whole thing down and builds a new temple altogether. This place is a disgrace to the goddess."

Amata's frankness surprised Petronia. She wasn't sure why, but the high priestess seemed more distracted than usual. More informal...more like an actual person and not just an important title.

"If you ask him to do it, he probably will," said Petronia. "Sacerdos Aule says the king thinks highly of you."

"How is Aule? I should visit him today."

"I brought him some broth this morning and told him a bad joke. That usually cheers him up when he's growly."

"Did it work?"

"Not really. But at least he's stopped drinking. That, or he's run out of wine, it's one or the other."

Another smirk from Amata. "Aule will be all right."

"He's worried that Marcius will erase his life's work in Rome."

Amata reached for an iron stoker and shifted a lazy piece of wood. Lively new flames appeared and reached upward, licking the nourishing oak that sat in their midst. "This change has many people re-examining their lives."

"Those are pregnant words, Priestess."

The sacred fire burned steadily, but Amata kept poking at it, stirring the ash. "I suppose you're right," she said. "Numa asked me to stay in Rome permanently to create a new order of Roman Vestals. He wants it to be on par with the Alban order."

"Will you stay?"

"No. But I will admit, his words have me thinking."

"His words have all of Rome thinking. He is our new philosopher king," Petronia said sprightly, opening her arms in a theatrical gesture, "standing on the speaker's platform, asking a mob of rioters to look inward."

"From what I hear, it worked."

"Like a charm. I saw it with my own eyes."

Amata laughed, and put down the stoker. The ash began to settle. "Petronia, I have another admission. I am afraid I may have misjudged you. I saw you enter the Aedes late one morning, and I assumed you were not taking your duties seriously. I was wrong. You are doing a fine job. I haven't seen another sacerdos who works as hard as you, or who is willing to clean the Aedes of this filth we're dealing with."

"Thank you for saying so, Priestess. I am not perfect, but I am trying to be better. I must tell you, though, that Lollia and Claudia have also scrubbed the Aedes nonstop. So has Aemelia. Sacerdos Gegania has just started her tenure, but I can already tell she is a hard worker, too."

"Thank you for letting me know," said Amata. Petronia's willingness to praise her sister sacerdotes, rather than simply aggrandizing herself, was a rare and admirable attribute. "General Gellius has a son by the name of Paullus," Amata said. "Have you met him?"

"I have not."

"He is a good man and a fine soldier. He's young, but he'll be admitted to the Senate soon. He is away from Rome on campaign, but I will arrange for a meeting when he returns."

"Thank you, Priestess," said Petronia. She tried not to smile too widely, but it was no use. "I look forward to that."

"Good. In the meantime, I'll speak to the other sacerdotes—the lazy ones. They can join Helen on the road out of Rome, or they can start performing their duties with more devotion." She opened the door to leave, immediately assaulted by the stench of the sewer. "That reminds me. I'm having special incense brought in from the Vestal order in Bovillae. With any luck, it will arrive today. We'll burn it continuously in the sacred fire to help mask the odour of the sewer."

Amata stepped out of the Aedes just as Lollia arrived. The sacerdos bowed politely and slipped inside to join Petronia, while Amata stood on the street staring absently into the distance. A voice jolted her out of her thoughts.

"Good morning, Priestess Amata."

"Your Highness," Amata lowered her head, trying to hide her surprise at the king's appearance. He wore a simple tunica—it looked like he had slept in it—and was barefoot. And unless she was mistaken, he had just emerged from a sacerdos hut located adjacent to the Aedes. She racked her brain—was there a sacerdos living in it? Had the king actually...

Numa laughed. "Oh, Priestess," he said. "It is not what it looks like." He gestured to the hut behind him. "This is my home now."

She put a hand over her mouth to stifle a laugh, but it didn't help. Her amusement turned to confusion. "Wait...you're going to live here? In the Forum, beside the Aedes?"

"This is where Vesta came to earth," Numa said seriously. "I am honored to live in such a blessed place. In fact, I am going to expand my home to include an office for my priests. They will meet here, in the holiest area of Rome."

"I have always thought of it that way myself, sir." Amata looked around. "This whole area of the Forum should be sacred to the goddess. The rest of the huts that have been housing the sacerdotes should be leveled. The sacerdotes should live in one house, a convent. That is how it is done not just in Alba Longa, but in Lavinium and Bovillae as well. It is the proper way."

"Agreed," said Numa. "I will issue the work order today. You can approve the plans."

"And the grove of Vesta," continued Amata, "it should be expanded. The Capillata tree should be fenced in, too. I caught a young boy climbing it a few days ago and had to pull him down by the leg."

"Anything else?"

"There is a spring right over there, closer to the Palatine. They say it is sacred to the nymph Juturna, and it has healing properties. I once burned my hand badly in the sacred fire and soaked it in there, and the wound healed overnight. Now I always have the sacerdotes wash there if they are scalded. The spring should be developed, and there should be an altar there to Juturna to give thanks."

"And?"

She exhaled, and let her gaze settle on the hut-like Aedes itself. "Your Highness, look at it. I could walk a donkey through some of the cracks in the walls. The wind and rain enter at will, and so does the sewage. It is crumbling before our eyes. And it isn't just the structural problems either. It is the most unattractive building in the city. The new latrine on the citadel evokes greater feelings of reverence. The goddess's blessed fire deserves a more beautiful home."

"So what should I do?"

"Tear it down. Build something more suited to the purpose. Trust me, it is no small task to keep the sacred fire going day and night. The building needs to be bigger and the roof needs to be higher. There needs to be better air exchange and drainage. There should be more storage as well, hidden away, for sacrificial implements and offerings, for wood and even for ash. In Alba Longa, there is a depository under the floor for the ashes so they don't have to be carted away every day, but can be stored and disposed of in Lake Albanus with the proper rites. It could be the same here, with the ashes put into the Tiber. And the altar itself is too small—the sacred fire should be bigger. It will be easier to sustain, and much easier to divine the goddess's will, if the flames are more substantial."

"I did not think Vestal sacerdotes practiced divination," said Numa.

"Most do not," replied Amata. "Sacerdotes are taught to observe the flames for obvious signs, but that's usually the extent of it. There are only a few older priestesses in Alba Longa and Lavinium who practice true fire divination. They follow the ancient Trojan practices. I have been instructed in those techniques, but I have also learned much from Aule and the Etruscan customs. I have found the combined method to be very accurate."

"Is it wise to bond different practices together in that way?"

"Trojan Vesta is one thing, but Roman Vesta is another. I think it is the nature of the city itself. Romulus accepted people from everywhere. He accepted their customs, too, especially those of Etruria. The gods have been patient of variation."

"Perhaps that is how it should be," said Numa. "I have seen that most rituals, even those that seem pure, have elements of others. The Trojans and Etruscans took of the Greeks, and the Greeks took of the Egyptians."

"My tutor used to tell me the same thing," said Amata. "Although he is Greek, so he would not admit they took from anyone."

Numa smiled. "The divination method you have crafted...will you teach it to me and Marcius? It should be formalized for my college of priests."

Amata hesitated. Was this the time to ask that the Palladium be returned to Alba Longa? No. Numa would see it as mere bartering—which of course it would be—and would be offended.

"I must return to my duties in Alba Longa, Your Highness, but I would be happy to teach you before I go."

"Excellent." Numa scraped a bare foot on the cobblestone. "Building a proper temple to Vesta will be my priority," he said. "I will complete it before I begin work on any other temple. The sacerdotes' house will also be prioritized." He looked around in satisfaction, imagining how the sacred area would soon be changed. "After all my travels," he said, "it will be here where I finally, truly, live among the gods."

Theo had been holding his breath for most of the day, and it wasn't only because of the sewage. Mostly, it was because the man he had openly mocked in the Forum only days earlier was now the king of Rome. Even worse, the king had decided to live in a hut that was within a stone's throw of where Theo was still toiling to clear the sewer. And if that weren't stressful enough, there was also the constant parade of important people that now filed past his formerly anonymous work station, all of them on their way to meet with the king. Priestess Amata had been the first, followed by a number of senators. Most recently, General Proculus and his son Gaius had arrived. Even from a distance, Theo could hear the general's stern words for the king as they stood outside his home.

"Dismissing the celeres? In the middle of a bloody riot?"

"I didn't dismiss them, General. I disbanded them."

Proculus scoffed derisively, and Gaius stepped between his father and the king.

"Your Highness," he said, "we are only thinking of your safety."

"I am safe enough. I have been going about my business all day and not a single sword is sticking out of my back."

"You may make light of your own safety," said Proculus, "but what about the safety of your people? How can they feel secure, knowing that at any moment some pissed-off merchant or sewer slave can just walk up to their king and open his neck? Then where will they be? I'll tell you. Back hiding in their homes with the doors barricaded, praying the Senate gets it shit together and elects a new king so the streets can be safe again."

"If someone is determined to kill me, they will find a way through a thousand bodyguards," said Numa. "I put my faith in the gods. You should do the same, Proculus. You will find life much more tolerable."

"I'll be sure to do just that," replied the general.

Numa ignored the caustic tone. "Anyway, I have other uses for those men. You can take half of them for the army. Choose the men you like. I will use the rest according to their talents. I need to staff the new workers' guilds I'm creating—blacksmiths, bakers, leatherworkers, potters, and so on. The city is too tribal, General. Etruscans monopolize the building projects, and the Sabines squander the vendors market. Each guild will therefore include men of all tribes. They will find brotherhood that way, and pride in the work they do together."

Gaius was impressed. "And they will see themselves only as Romans."

"That's right," replied Numa. "The idea came to me the first time I visited Rome, and I've been thinking about it ever since. I believe the guilds will make the streets safer than a fleet of soldiers bashing in heads every time an Etruscan and a Sabine throw insults at each other." He looked at Proculus, and saw the general's grizzled face working it over.

"Could work," Proculus admitted. A waft of sewer stench struck his nose, and he pinched his nostrils. "You there!" he called out to Theo.

Theo, who was just about to unfurl his lash on a chronically lazy slave, stood up straight, swallowed his trepidation, and faced the three important men approaching him. He bowed to the king. "Your Highness," he said, and then faced Proculus. "Yes, General?"

"I'm not seeing much progress here, boy. Maybe I should put the lash in the slave's hand and see if that make a difference."

"No, sir...I'm sorry, sir..."

Numa slapped Proculus on the back. "The boy is doing his best," he said.

The general grumbled something, and headed off in the direction of the Capitoline. Gaius flashed Numa an apologetic smile, hoping it would compensate for his father's cantankerous nature. "Excuse us, sir."

When the father and son were gone, Numa looked at Theo. The younger man's face was a mosaic of expressions: embarrassment, uncertainty, fear.

"Your Highness," he stammered, "about the other day. I had no idea. I am sorry."

The king laughed. "For now, the lash is still in your hand." He turned and strolled back to his hut, still laughing.

Theo kept working. He kept working even as the blue sky took on the colors of predusk and his slave workers grew so tired and useless he had to send them away and order fresh ones. He kept working as Petronia walked past him, leaving her watch in the Aedes to fetch supper in the market, and then returning to walk past him again. He tried to catch her eye, but she deliberately refused to look at him.

She is nervous with the king living so close by, Theo told himself. *That is all.*

He kept working, and he was making progress, too, even as cold drops of rain began to fall on his bare arms. Wading along in the open channel, he could feel the sludge begin to flow past his legs more steadily. The slaves he had positioned along the length of the sewer line were doing their job. A rumble of thunder overhead celebrated his success, and the man who toiled just ahead of him turned around to nod encouragingly.

He waved to the slave, but immediately braced himself as a virtual tidal wave of fast-moving sewage struck him from behind, flowing past him with such speed and force that it nearly knocked him off his feet. The sudden release of a large blockage from upstream, plus the extra volume added by the rain, had created a hazard.

"Watch out!" he called to the slave ahead of him in the channel. "It's opened up!"

But it was too late. The slave's arms went up as his legs went out from under him. Caught in the sewer's current, he vanished from Theo's view. Theo scrambled over the stone border of the channel and landed on the ground, running as fast as he could along the sewer line, trying to outrun the flow of waste and rainwater to reach the man who had been swept away. On any other day, it would have been an easy enough task for such a young man. But this late in the day, exhausted and slipping on the muddy ground, Theo struggled to reach half the speed he was normally capable of.

"Help me! He's fallen in the sewer!" Theo shouted, but the thunder and crashing rain drowned out his voice.

He ran on, feeling his legs tremble with fatigue as he followed the channel along, every now and then gripping the stone border and leaning over it to look inside—but no, the slave was nowhere to be seen. Desperate, Theo looked around for help, but the rain had sent everyone indoors. He ran by a large military tent and saw a group of soldiers huddled around a brazier inside, but they pretended not to see him. Whatever trinket the fool had dropped in the sewer was his problem. They weren't about to get soaked to the bone in filth to help him.

The sound of the rain hitting the ground changed as the terminus of the sewage channel came into view: just ahead, the great Tiber River flowed wide and steady, welcoming the rainfall. In another moment, it would also welcome half of Rome's sewage and a particularly unlucky slave. With no other choice—after all, the cost of the dead worker would be deducted from his salary— Theo dove into the river just as the channel belched the sewage and the slave into the water.

Theo grabbed the back of the man's tunica and pulled him close, but it was too late. The man's skull was caved in on one side. Whether he had struck it on the stone border of the channel when he first fell, or whether he had hit a rock when ejected out of the sewer, it was impossible to tell. Impossible and irrelevant. He was dead, and Theo would be poorer for it.

"Miserable gods!" he shouted.

He was rewarded for his sacrilege by a mouthful of foul sewage. Spitting it out in disgust, he pushed the corpse away. But then something even fouler flew out of the sewer line to strike him—a huge, solid mass of what felt like congealed animal fat. The massive plug of lard and suet—no doubt the result of Forum vendors dumping too much animal fat in the sewage system— lolled heavily in the current for a moment before lodging itself against the shore. It was the obstruction that had been blocking the line for days.

As Theo stared, revolted, at the dislodged obstruction, the light still fading and the rain still falling, he thought he saw something in it, something mixed in with the clumps of hair and bone shards. He coughed and waded closer to it, eyes narrowed in scrutiny.

The slimy surface of the fatty mass was studded with a number of small, shiny nugget-like objects. He reached out and plucked one out of the large lipid ball to inspect it closer. His heart skipped a beat. *Gold.*

Gold, stolen from Rome's treasury.

"They're using the sewer," he said breathily, hearing the disbelief, the excitement, in his own voice. "By the gods, they're using the sewer!"

CHAPTER XIV

It had been some three months since Amata had been in Rome, but as her carriage passed through its gates, her thoughts were still in Alba Longa. They were still stuck on the way Sextus had all but interrogated her on what she knew about the affair between his wife and Romulus. Amata was sympathetic—the look of betrayal and fury on his face was unforgettable—but what could she tell him? She could hardly reveal that she knew about it, so she had denied knowledge and done her best to reassure him of Penelope's love for him. Of her remorse.

Yet the whole time, Amata had struggled to contain her own resentment. Why was it her duty to console the king and mitigate the queen's sin? Yes, they were her friends, but she was a priestess of Vesta, not Venus. Matters of marital love and suffering were beyond her religious purview.

Her carriage stopped inside the gates and she heard soldiers talking. A moment later, the door of her carriage opened and Proculus offered her an obligatory smile of welcome. She didn't return it. It was his drunken revelation that had made her life in Alba Longa so stressful in the first place. Now, it was almost a relief to be back in Rome, away from the royal drama between Sextus and Penelope. King Numa's message that both the new Temple of Vesta and the sacerdotes' house in Rome were complete, and his invitation for her to come and see them, had given her the perfect excuse to leave.

And yet the excuse wasn't an empty one. Petronia's regular messages updating her on the progress of the temple and surrounding area had piqued Amata's interest. She stepped out of her carriage but declined a lectica. She had been sitting long enough and it would feel good to walk. Proculus looked around for a free guard to accompany her to the Forum, but finding none, had no choice but to do it himself.

"I'm sure you have better things to do with your time than chaperone me," said Amata. "I am quite capable of finding my way."

He fell into step beside her. "How was your trip, Priestess?" he asked lifelessly.

"Fine."

They walked in silence until they came across the familiar figure of Hostus Hostilius, kneeling in prayer before a street-side shrine to Ceres. He poured a libation of wine into the flames on the altar and stood to greet Amata.

"Come to see the temple, have you, Priestess?"

"I have, Hostus."

"You will be impressed. Let's hope the gods are, too. We need something to keep them in Rome."

Amata understood what he meant. The pestilence that had struck Rome's crops showed no signs of abating, and both the stores of grain and the herds were dwindling. And the less the Romans had to eat, the less they had to sacrifice to the gods.

Proculus spat on the ground. "The crops wilt because we have a wilting king."

"I've heard the city is peaceful, though," said Amata. "Is that true?"

"No one has the energy to fight," replied Proculus. "They're too weak from hunger."

Hostus chuckled. "The general would rather swallow fire than give any credit to Numa," he said, "but things are calmer than they've been in a while. The workers' guilds were a good idea. They're keeping people busy and keeping order at the same time. But more importantly"—he grinned at Amata—"Numa's managed to import a sea of wine from Campania."

"That's the real secret to our king's success," said Proculus. "Everyone's too drunk to realize how vulnerable our city is under his rule, or lack thereof. Just yesterday, I told him that we had to figure out how the gold was disappearing from the treasury. I asked him for permission to expand my interrogations. And do you know what the fool said to me? He said, 'Perhaps whoever is stealing the gold needs it more than we do.'"

Amata turned her head and looked into the distance, trying to hide her smile. In his short time as king, Numa had clearly learned how to give as good as he got when it came to his prickly top general.

They walked on. Soon, the pleasant smell of incense—Amata recognized it as the incense she had requested from Bovillae—filled her nostrils, and the priestess saw it all at once. The area sacred to Vesta had been transformed. The grove of Vesta teemed with colorful flowers and a new cobblestone footpath wound through it. The indiscriminately placed individual huts that had formerly housed the sacerdotes were gone, replaced by a single house—a large rectangular complex that looked to be as comfortable as it was functional.

The Capillata tree was no longer overgrown and neglected, but pruned and bordered by an encompassing shoulder-height fence. Colorful painted panels beautified the fence's solid surface, panels that depicted the symbols and scenes of Rome and its history. Amata recognized Aeneas fleeing Troy with his son, the Palladium and the sacred fire. Next to that scene was a veiled woman holding two infants on her lap—Rhea Silvia and her royal twins. Beside that panel, a snarling she-wolf stood on the banks of the Tiber. Finally, there was Mars, throwing a fiery spear to earth, and Romulus following its trajectory.

And then there was the new temple itself. It had retained its round structure in tribute to the hut-homes of the region, but it was much larger, its encircling wall now pure white and bolstered by an outer ring of six wooden columns in the Etruscan style, their shafts painted a vivid purple and their capitals encased in sculpted terracotta. The frieze that banded the top of the exterior wall boasted stuccoed and painted images of sacrificial ox heads, rosettes, and swooping garlands. Crowning the temple, and standing near the oculus in the domed roof, was a statue of Vesta holding a scepter and reaching down to stroke the head of a protective serpent at her feet.

In no way was the temple as ornate as the one in Alba Longa. Yet it was beautiful. Perfect. Beautifully and perfectly *Roman*. It did precisely what a Temple of Vesta should do—it inspired feelings of piety for the goddess. However, the temple and its surrounding structures went further. They inspired feelings of pride for Rome itself, for Rome's founding, and Amata realized something important about Numa. Despite his eccentric nature and his often irreverent ways, he had deep respect for the extraordinary history and unique culture of the city he now ruled.

She opened the temple's door, noting the pretty rosette carvings now upon it, and stepped inside to find the sacerdotes Lollia and Claudia on watch. They stood beside a new and larger round stone altar: it was positioned off center within the circular sanctum and was prettily adorned with garlands of fresh green laurel. The fire-bowl that held the sacred fire on top of the altar was also larger, and smoke from the thick flames rose effectively to the ceiling to slip out the oculus. The sounds of the snapping flames resounded within the embrace of the crimson encircling wall. It was a lovely way to hear the voice of the goddess, and for the first time, Amata felt the space was reverent enough to hold the spirit not just of the Roman hearthfire, but of the ancient *Iliaci ignes Vestae*—the Trojan fires of Vesta—of Romulus's, and her own, ancestors.

"Priestess Amata," said Lollia. "Do you like it? Oh, it is too bad—Petronia was so excited. She wanted to be the first to show you."

"It is wonderful," replied Amata. "What is behind that curtain?"

Lollia pulled aside a heavy deep-purple curtain to reveal a window of fine latticework.

"Fresh air!" she said, and all three women laughed. "You will like this, too." She crossed the floor of the sanctum, poking her finger into an unseen crevice in the wall and then pulling open a hidden door. The Palladium stood in a chamber inside. "The king believes ancient relics should be kept from view. He said that makes people honor them more." She closed the secret door and pointed to the floor. "The ashes are hidden as well. There is a depository under the floor for them."

Amata smiled. Numa had implemented all of her suggestions and more. "It is all wonderful," she said. And it was. Yet one thing nagged at her—the care that the Roman king had shown for the Palladium was a bad sign. He would be resistant to parting with it. Perhaps she should have asked for its return earlier after all. No doubt, she would face even more tedious questioning from Sextus when she returned home.

Unless she didn't return to Alba Longa. Unless she decided to retire to some cozy coastal village near Lavinium. One where the sun always shone and the open water soothed the spirit, one where the people were carefree and the gods were benevolent.

So you are now a free woman...You never have to step inside one of Vesta's temples ever again if you don't want to. You can enjoy your home, your friends, you can even take a lover or marry if you wish. There is no one to stop you.

She had heard Numa's words in her head a lot lately.

Amata faced the sacerdotes. "I know that both of you have extended your tenure to the goddess because of all of this," she said, looking around the sanctum. "Thank you."

"Petronia has done most of the work," said Lollia.

"That's funny," said Amata, "she says the same about the two of you."

"She had the overnight watch and is resting in her room," said

Claudia. "Would you like to speak with her? I can show you our house."

"Let her sleep," said Amata. "I will call on her later this afternoon, after I've had a rest myself." She smiled. "I have news that will interest her."

Malla rubbed her hands together and grinned madly at her mistress. "Domina, just think. Soon, we'll be living the good life on the Palatine!"

Petronia laughed at her slave. "Malla, I haven't even met the man yet. What if he doesn't like me?"

"He will like you," assured Malla. "Any man with eyes would like you. Take my word for it, the betrothal will be official by this time tomorrow night. As for the wedding date"—she glanced at her mistress's backside and winked lewdly—"he won't want to wait long."

"I hope you are right. Priestess Amata is confident in the match."

"Of course she is. She's known General Gellius and his son forever. Those uppity types always take care of their own. Just promise me one thing..."

"What is that?"

"If my master recalls me to Cures, you won't send me back. I have grown fond of you, despite all your faults." She paused as Petronia laughed, then continued with affection. "How I long to see a pudgy little Petronia splashing in the bath."

"If Paullus does marry me, I will make him buy you," said Petronia. "And if the price is too high, I will just tell my uncle that you died from some bad pork and we threw your body in the Tiber. He won't come looking. You're not a good enough slave for that."

"That is true." Malla sat on the edge of Petronia's bed. "Tell me again what the priestess said. Don't leave anything out."

Petronia beamed and sat next to Malla. "I gave her a tour of the sacerdotes' house—I'm very good at giving tours, you know, everyone says so—and she was very impressed by the kitchen and the bathing quarters. She thought the private rooms of each sacerdos could have been a bit bigger, but I told her we were pleased enough. I thought she would leave after that, but she asked the kitchen slaves to bring us some supper, and she and I dined in the garden. We talked about the new temple and she thanked me for all my hard work. It was then that she told me General Gellius's son, Paullus, was back in Rome and wanted to meet me. She said that Paullus's mother—that's Lady Safinia, you've seen her around the marketplace—is hosting a dinner party tomorrow night at her home on the Palatine, and has invited me."

"And?"

"And the priestess said she expects an engagement to come out of it. She said Lady Safinia wouldn't bother to invite me unless she'd already made up her mind about the match."

Malla rubbed her hands together again. "I am so happy for you, my dear."

Petronia stood. "Lollia says I can borrow her good jewels and whatever palla and sandals I want. Go to her room and take what you think is best. I am going to pray in the grove."

"Yes, Domina."

The two women went their separate ways, Malla heading to Lollia's private quarters and Petronia walking along the carpeted floor of the sacerdotes' communal domicile. The smell of bread baking in the kitchen made her stomach growl, but she continued to a side door of the complex, opened it, and stepped into the secured area of Vesta's grove. It was dark, but the light of the full moon and the torches lit the serene space well enough to see by. A carved wooden altar held a sleepy fire, so she knelt before it and placed two pieces of kindling on top before pouring a libation of wine into the waking flames. She dipped the simpulum back into the wine jug beside the altar and this time drank the ladleful of wine herself. Thanks to Numa's resourcefulness, there was enough for the goddess and those who served her.

"*Vesta Sancta*," she prayed. Hesitating, she looked over her shoulder, just to make sure she was alone. "Forgive me the faults I have made in your service, and know that I have always tended your eternal fire with a loving heart and a pure spirit. Goddess, bless my union with Paullus, younger son of General Gellius of Rome. I vow to honor you in my household hearth as I have honored you at the altar in your temple."

"So that's it," said a young male voice. "You've finally found him. Your rich man."

Petronia gasped and leapt to her feet. "Theo! How did you get in here?"

He was standing awkwardly in the dark, holding a shovel. "I have access to the grove day and night," he said, trying not to sound as embarrassed, as crushed, as he felt. "For sanitation purposes."

"It is clean enough here."

"How else can I speak to you? You haven't come to my home in months, and you won't even make eye contact with me in the street."

Petronia tried to speak kindly. "It is over between us, Theo. I told you from the beginning that I did not love you and that I would never marry you. Why can't you be content with what we had?"

"When you thought I was killed in the riot...you cared then."

She sighed, letting her shoulders drop as she stepped closer to him. "Yes, I cared. I still care. But that is different than love."

"You don't love Paullus. You don't even know him." He dropped the shovel and looked down as his fingers searched for something in the small leather pouch at his hip. He held up a ring—roughly made, but made of solid gold. "I am not as poor as you think."

She moved to take the ring from his fingers, but stopped herself. That would give him the wrong idea. "Where did you get that?"

"I have been doing well for myself." He smiled excitedly, his face still full of that naïve hope Petronia had expected would fade, but never had. "Between my salary and what I make from my goat—the tooth paste, remember?—I have much finer things. You would be comfortable."

She narrowed her eyes as she inspected the ring in the dim light. "Did you find it somewhere?"

"I bought it," he said. He took her hand and tried to slide the ring on a finger, but she pulled away.

"I will not marry you, Theo," she said. "Not now, not ever. I will always care about you, but I will never love you." She backed away from him. "Now go."

"I wonder what a fine man like Paullus would think if he knew..." his voice trailed off.

She stopped and stared at him. "I don't deserve that."

He looked away, ashamed of the empty threat. What a child he must seem to her. No wonder she refused to marry him. He had only spoken out of pain, a pain of his own making. She had never lied to him, never misled him. He picked his shovel off the ground and left the sacred grove, taking the pain with him and hoping that, despite her words, she was left with a little of her own.

CHAPTER XV

No one would call General Gellius a handsome man. He had the physique of a lifelong soldier and the confident carriage that came from being a prestigious member of Rome's old guard, but the positive attributes stopped before they reached his face. Maybe it was nature, or maybe it was just *his* nature. Like many of the older men in Rome, the ones who had seen battle after battle, and who had only reluctantly accepted the new king of the city they had fought for in their youth, he was a chronically serious man whose face simply wasn't that adept at showing happiness.

Yet as Priestess Amata led Petronia through the crowded garden of the general's Palatine home to meet his son, the young woman felt a flush of pleasure as Amata discreetly pointed Paullus out to her. He had clearly taken his looks from his attractive mother, Lady Safinia. In fact, it was Petronia's own good looks that had apparently convinced the noblewoman to favor Petronia as a match for her son. According to the gossips in Rome, she wanted to ensure her grandchildren had every advantage.

With Petronia at her side, Amata neared the food table where Paullus and Safinia were chatting idly, wine cups in one hand and fingers hovering over a large bowl of fat olives. When Safinia saw them approach, she elbowed her son and both of them put down their cups. Paullus immediately stepped toward Petronia. She felt her stomach flip as he reached out to take her hands in his. If she had feared an aloof reception on the part of the young nobleman, she quickly realized Paullus had no such ego.

He looked at Petronia, but spoke to Amata. "Priestess," he said. "Have you plucked this one from the gods?"

Petronia laughed, and Paullus's lips burst into a warm smile.

Safinia grinned in satisfaction and turned to Amata, nodding. As far as she was concerned, that settled it.

"My mother is as subtle as a Jupiter in a tempest," Paullus said to Petronia. "Shall we walk together? We will not be alone, of course. We will have the eyes of everyone here following us."

Petronia didn't fight the look of elation that she knew was forming on her face. She bowed respectfully to Safinia, then accepted Paullus's arm. They walked off into the garden together, meandering aimlessly and falling into easy conversation.

"She is a beauty," said Safinia, as she watched the young couple from afar.

"She has no dowry," replied Amata, "but she is loyal beyond measure. Anyway, you are rich enough."

"She is perfect," said Safinia. "Thank you, my friend. Just look at Paullus shuffling along with Cupid's arrow sticking out of his back. He is already taken with her. I would like them to marry next month, on the ides. Would that cause an inconvenience at the temple?"

"Not at all. That is more than enough time for her to train the next senior sacerdos."

"Good." Safinia's expression soured as she looked over Amata's shoulder. "Oh gods, look at Proculus."

The two women turned to see Proculus standing behind a bench, gripping the back of it for support as he bent at the waist and vomited on a small terracotta rabbit statue nestled in a flowerbed. A slave rushed over with a bucket to clean it up, while Gaius whispered something in his father's ear and Valia stood behind both of them, glaring at the back of her husband's head. Proculus straightened and locked eyes with Amata.

"I want to talk to you," he said, and pointed at her.

Amata moved to a more private spot in the garden and waited impatiently for Proculus to stumble over. "What is it?" she asked. "You're embarrassing your family, and Safinia will kill you if you ruin this party for Paullus."

"Look at that bastard!" Proculus said in a strident whisper. "Do you fucking believe that?"

She followed his stare across the garden. In an instant, her anger at Proculus was overwhelmed by an even greater rage. Senator Calvisius was there, eating and drinking merrily with a group of other senators, including Hostus and the elderly Oppius. Calvisius laughed at something so hard that he spilled wine on his toga, then scowled at a passing wine slave as if it was her fault.

"I'm telling you, woman," said Proculus. "I can't wait much longer."

"I know."

"We've waited too long already."

"No, we haven't. But we do need to think of something soon. I don't like seeing him, or any of them, any more than you do." The wine slave approached carrying a tray of cups. Amata took one and drained it. Maybe Proculus was on to something. Maybe drink was the only way to make peace with some kinds of hatred. "I have a few more things I need to finish for Numa and his priest. For the new temple. After that, we'll figure what to do, once and for all." She squinted, probing his expression. "Agreed?"

"If you say so."

"Are we agreed?"

"Yes, damn it. Stop your nagging. I get enough of that from my wife."

"Don't tell me what to do, Proculus. I'm not the one making a fool of myself at a friend's garden party, not that anyone is surprised, especially your poor wife. Just promise me one thing. After you finish emptying your stomach on Safinia's garden decorations, you'll keep your mouth shut. I don't need you blurting out anymore secrets."

He wiped his mouth with the back of his hand and staggered off, though looking slightly more stable than he had a few moments earlier. That was something. Amata turned and walked in the opposite direction. As she watched her friends socializing in the garden, she happened to notice the priest Marcius standing by himself, inspecting the leaves of a laurel bush. She could not say he was a likeable man, but nonetheless she felt obligated to be polite.

"Marcius," she said, "does the laurel meet your approval?"

His reaction at seeing her was as flat as his monotone voice. "I am working on a prayer to be spoken whenever the sacerdotes burn laurel in the sacred fire. I was just thinking about it now."

"I see."

"I was going to ask for your input," he said, his tone almost dipping into apology, "but I thought I would finish it first. I hope you are not offended."

"I am not. I would be very happy to hear it when you are ready." She waited for him to say something else, but when she realized he wasn't going to, she continued. "The temple is beautiful, Marcius. Truly, it is. You and the king should be proud of your work. I am sure the goddess is pleased."

To her surprise, he almost smiled. "I have the utmost respect for the Vestales Albanae. Your words are therefore meaningful to me."

She nodded her head. Marcius was unusual. He was brooding and had little social tact. But he was sincere, had an astute understanding of how to honor the gods, and was obviously determined to make Rome's temples and religious protocols as sophisticated as anywhere in the world. The potential of that made her speak without thinking. "I wish Romulus was here to see what you are doing." The wine from Campania was stronger than she was accustomed to and was making her emotional. She changed the subject. "I thought the king might attend tonight."

"He has too much to do, but he forced me to come. He says I need to learn how to enjoy parties."

"Are you enjoying this party?"

He looked around. "Not at all."

Amata watched Proculus trip over a stone. "Well, if it makes you feel any better, neither am I." Sighing, she took two cups of wine off a table, passed one to the priest, and they both drank.

"Did you see the spring of Juturna today?" asked Marcius.

"No. Have they finished work on it?"

"Yes, just this afternoon." Marcius took the wine cup from her hand. "An excellent excuse to leave." In a move that Amata surmised was as wild as the priest ever got at parties, he emptied the remaining wine from their cups into the soil of the laurel bush and left the cups on the ground. "Shall we go?"

Amata gave it a moment's thought. "Why not."

The Vestal bid goodnight to her friends and waved at Petronia—the girl couldn't smile wider if she tried—and walked with Marcius into the night air, sauntering along the Palatine and down its slope, and passing through the gate into the Forum. The Forum was well lit by torches and as they reached the small temple to Jupiter that Romulus had built shortly after the crisis of Tarpeia and the invasion of the Sabine army, Marcius stopped to say a prayer to the father of the gods. In Romulus's day, the temple had only been a rough hut with an altar in front, and it had suffered neglect in the years since. But Numa had restored it as well. It had never looked better.

"I can't believe how changed this area of the Forum is in such a short time," she said as they strolled through the area sacred to Vesta. Nearing the king's residence—formerly a nondescript sacerdos hut, now expanded and called the Regia—Amata saw a figure move past a latticed window. A moment later, King Numa stepped onto the street outside. He was chewing something meaty and swallowed, then coughed, before greeting them.

"Good evening," he said. He looked at Marcius, as if impressed that his usually asocial priest had at least been pleasant enough to make one friend. "How was the party?"

"Is this one of those times I'm supposed to answer honestly or diplomatically?" asked Marcius.

"Honestly," said Numa.

"Tedious. At least until the priestess took pity on me and came over to talk. I was about to show her the improvements at the spring."

Numa wiped his hand on his tunica. "I will take her, Marcius. You have practiced enough diplomacy for one night."

The priest bowed his head to Amata. "It was my pleasure. Good night, Priestess."

As Marcius left, the king led Amata to the nearby spring where she was treated to yet another change. The natural rocky embankment of the little spring where she had soaked her scalded skin had been transformed and expanded. The babbling water was now surrounded by a smooth stone border that was perfect for sitting comfortably on. A stone altar to Juturna rose from the middle of the clear water. On the side of the spring closest to the Temple of Vesta, there stood a statue that made Amata's mouth drop open in surprise.

The statue was of a Vestal sacerdos—one who looked strikingly similar to her—leaning over, as if about to dip her hand in the healing water, just as Amata had told Numa she had once done. A serpent was coiled innocuously around one of her ankles as a symbol of regeneration, of shedding one's old skin and the power of renewal.

The wine from Campania again brought her emotions to the surface and she felt moisture in her eyes. "It is beautiful, Your Highness." She sat on the spring's stone border and looked into the water. By the light of the torches, it somehow looked even clearer than it did during the day.

Numa sat beside her. "I have finished organizing the religious collegium," he said. "The high priest of the college will be called the *Pontifex Maximus*. It is a term that reflects his role as the bridge between men and the gods."

"So Marcius is Rome's first Pontifex Maximus."

"He is. He will be responsible for appointing the *flamen* priests who will serve each god. The most important of these will be the three major flamens for Jupiter, Mars, and Quirinus."

She looked seriously at him. *Not Vesta?*

He smiled indulgently. "And Vesta," he said. "The high priestess of Vesta will hold a place of particular prestige and influence in the college. She will be called the *Vestalis Maxima*." He looked into the water as he spoke. "I have prayed to the goddess that you would be Rome's first. It is auspicious that a Silvian priestess would be the first to hold the position."

"I don't know, Your Highness." Her eyes fell on the serpent wrapped around the foot of the Vestal statue. Like the creature, she too felt like she was shedding one skin and growing another. She just wasn't sure what she wanted it to be. She spoke honestly—Numa's philosophical nature had that effect on people—and dipped the toes of her sandals into the water. "The day of your crowning, when we spoke in the Curia...I've been thinking a lot about what you said. I am a free woman now. That is true. But it's strange. The more I think about that freedom, the more aware I am of the ties that bind me to my responsibilities."

"And you are beginning to resent those ties."

"No, not resent. Not exactly."

"I have always wanted to ask you," said Numa, "was there ever another option open to you?"

"What do you mean?"

"Romulus knew that you and he were the last of the Silvii. I am surprised that he did not release you from your temple duties so that you could marry and continue the Silvian line."

Amata shook her head. "Romulus would never have let me marry. He would have seen my children as a threat to him and a bastardization of our royal bloodline. He was so proud of his pure Silvian blood. Once, we were walking along the Tiber when a drunken merchant from Alba Longa tried to insult him by shouting, 'There he is, the crown prince of incest!' That's what some of the older people in Alba Longa still call him. But instead of punishing the man, Romulus gave him a purse of silver and a good horse, and told him he was welcome in Rome anytime." Her head was swimming from the wine, and she laughed somewhat indecorously at the memory. Numa joined her. "Not many people know this," she said less frivolously, "but shortly after his children were murdered and his wife left him, he went to a kinswoman of ours named Amulia. She was Rhea Silvia's cousin. She was older than him, but still in her childbearing years. He tried to have a child with her, but it came to nothing. Proculus once hinted of a stillborn, but I'm not sure and I never asked. Romulus paid her great honors when she died."

Numa turned his head to face her. "He must have asked the same of you."

Amata dipped her feet further into the cool water. "He did. When I was twenty years old."

Numa could see her mind stretching back, remembering. "Did you couple with him?"

Amata withdrew her feet from the water. "Never."

"Did you consider it?"

She met his eyes. "Briefly, yes. He said I could be the queen of Rome if I wanted to. But I just couldn't accept the physical part. Not with Romulus. We were cousins, but he was more like a brother to me. And the way people would look at us..."

"Royal incest was in his blood," said Numa. "So to speak. It would have been easier for him than for you. Do you miss him?"

She leaned her head back and looked up into the starry night sky. "Yes, but perhaps not as much as I should. That doesn't mean I didn't love him."

"I understand." He hesitated. "What really happened to him?"

She blinked up at the star-strewn heavens. "I suppose the same thing that happens to all of us." She turned back to him. "Thank you for what you have done for Vesta in Rome. The temple, the sacerdotes' house, the spring, all of it. For years, I asked Romulus to improve things, but he ignored me. It feels good to be listened to."

"I should be thanking you, Amata. You've made it look like I know what I'm doing." He scratched his head worriedly. "I wish it were that way in all respects. The pestilence, the disappearing gold..." he raked his fingers harder through his short hair as his thoughts darkened. "Proculus and Rome's old guard, as you call them...they drool with the anticipation of my failure."

"That is not true. Not exactly. They want you to succeed for the sake of the city, but only on their terms. It is why they elected you."

"Ah," he said, understanding. "You and I are very alike, you know."

"Because both of our fathers were usurpers," she said, echoing his earlier words, "and both were killed on Romulus's orders."

"No, it is more than that." His voice took on an esoteric timbre. "Look at our lives. Our paths were scythed not just by Roman politics, but by the Fates. We have both been called to serve the gods. But at times, the task terrifies me. I am finding my way as I go along. Marcius is indispensable to me. As you have seen for yourself, he has no confidence in anything but how to properly serve the gods, and that confidence is absolute. It is not the same with me. I hear the calling as clearly as I hear the babbling water of this spring, but I'm not always sure how to answer. That is why I want you to stay in Rome."

"You overestimate my confidence," replied Amata. She glanced again at the snake coiled around the foot of the statue. *You overestimate my piety too*, she thought. *I don't even know if I want to serve the gods anymore.* She stood. "The wine you brought in from Campania..." she smiled. "I think I will find myself an empty bed in the sacerdotes' house for the night."

Numa rose. To Amata's shock, she suddenly felt his lips pressed against hers. The pleasurable warmth of the sensation spread throughout her body as his arms wrapped around her, pulling her close and kissing her more deeply. She didn't resist. She didn't resist, even as he took her by the hand and led her along the quiet, torchlit street, away from the house of the Vestal sacerdotes and toward the house of the king.

CHAPTER XVI

The nausea was the first thing she became aware of. She awoke to the feeling of it, not overpowering, not enough to make her vomit, but enough to make her groan unhappily. Her temples were throbbing. She felt moisture and discomfort between her legs.

It was not yet light in the king's home, but by the flame of an oil lamp she could see the rise and fall of his bare chest as he slept beside her in the bed. One of his legs was draped over hers. It was heavy, and she pulled herself free and sat up. The wool blanket that had been covering her slipped off and she felt suddenly, horribly, exposed. Covering her breasts with an arm, she slipped out of the bed and searched in the dim light for her dress until she found it on the floor. She fumbled with the fabric, finally managing to arrange it properly on her body.

Numa sat up.

"Amata."

She clasped her hands to her mouth and slumped onto the edge of the bed. Numa put his hand on her back, but she shook away his touch and began to weep, harder and harder, until her body convulsed in anguish and she collapsed onto the mattress, rolling onto her back and covering her tear-stained face with her hands.

"What have I done?" she cried. "*What have I done?*"

Numa touched her head. "There is nothing to be ashamed of."

She pushed his hand away. The nausea was worse now, though not from the previous night's wine, but rather from the shocks of sickening, oppressive regret that struck from the inside, making her limbs tremble and her stomach cramp. She got up and instinctively looked for something she could retch into if it came to that, but seeing nothing, shuffled miserably to the snapping embers of the hearthfire and stared into it, mesmerized by the sight of the red coals and the painful reality of her own sacrilege.

"Nothing to be ashamed of," she muttered, mocking Numa's words. "I have defiled myself."

"Amata," said Numa. "Hardly." Cautiously, he got out of bed and walked, naked, toward her. She looked at him, but the revulsion in her face compelled him to reach back and pull the covers off the mattress, wrapping the wool blanket around his waist. "You are as honorable as ever. It was my fault." He came closer and saw that her teeth were softly chattering as if from cold or fear. "It was my fault," he repeated. "No one has to know."

"The gods know."

He touched her arm, and when she didn't pull away, he moved his hand up to stroke her long hair. "Does that matter? Last night, I had the sense that you wanted to—"

"Wanted to what?"

"To leave the order."

"How could you know that," she asked, "when I did not know it myself?" She stepped away and began to pace the carpeted floor of his hut. Whatever ambivalence she had felt the previous night, whatever doubts she had had about continuing to serve the goddess, had disappeared. She had total clarity now. And she hated herself for her weakness. She fell into tears again. "I have been a virgin priestess of Vesta for over thirty years." Her eyes moved to the bed—the messy sheets, the king's tunica on the floor—and she swallowed, her throat tight and dry. "Who am I now?"

"You are the same person, if you want to be."

"You know that is not true, Numa."

"No," he admitted. "It is not true. But you can atone with the goddess, and she will forgive the lapse. If that is what you want..."

"Lapse? I am changed forever! Vesta is a virgin goddess. Her sacerdotes must be as pure as she. You are a man of the gods. Do you think she will allow a polluted high priestess to lead her priesthood? Do you think she will let vulgar hands place kindling in her holiest fire?"

"I have been in a thousand temples," said Numa, "and I've seen that many priests and priestesses, but I have never a seen a priestess as devoted or as diligent as you. Vesta knows who you are, even if you do not. She knows you are mortal. She will be forgiving."

"I don't want her forgiveness. I want her respect."

"Maybe it isn't Vesta's respect you're afraid of losing," said Numa. His voice was harder now. More inquisitorial, almost impertinent. "Maybe you just don't want everyone knowing you're no different than the rest of us."

"No, you saw to that."

"I did not tie you to the bed, Amata."

"You could have had any woman in Rome. You should not have tempted one in divine service."

"Tempted," Numa scoffed. "Temptation involves some measure of resistance, and I saw none from you."

Amata leaned her back against the wall. Slowly, she slid down to sit on the floor, subdued and weakened, with her head in her hands. Numa knew he should not have been so cruel. Their impulsive coupling had no consequences for him. It was much different for her.

She let out a long, shaky breath. "Give me a moment to collect myself, and I will leave."

"You don't need to leave," he replied. He sat on the floor beside her. "Amata, I am sorry. I should not have spoken so harshly." He gave her an abashed smile. "It's just that your reaction to our love-making...well, it's not what a man wants to see from a woman."

"I am sorry that I hurt your ego," she said bitterly, "but in case you didn't notice, my life is falling apart."

"It is not. I will never speak of this, not to anyone. You can return to Alba Longa if you wish, whether to the temple or not. Or you can stay here in Rome as my Vestalis Maxima, or simply as a private noblewoman. You have choice."

"Then I *choose* to be a virgin again. I *choose* to serve the goddess with a pure spirit and an unprofaned body." She wiped away her tears, and although she spoke jeeringly, he could see the devastation in her eyes. "Can you make that happen?"

Numa brushed the hair off her face. They sat together on the floor, watching the morning sun come through the window, Numa wishing—for her sake—that he could make the heavens move backward.

CHAPTER XVII

Theo crouched in the trees on the banks of the Tiber, staring through the darkness at the sewer's terminus, the point where it dumped its foul contents into the river. He thought about leaving and going home. After all, it was risky to confront whoever was using the city's sewer to steal gold from its treasury. The thief—or maybe there was more than one of them—might kill him on the spot.

But he knew he had to take that risk. He needed more gold. He had already spent the twelve nuggets he had pulled out of the fatty mass. It was amazing how fast he went through it, really. He had treated himself to the best food and wine in the market, bought several new tunicas and pairs of sandals, and splurged on a few nights with the pricier prostitutes in the city. Before he knew it, it was gone. That included the wedding ring he had made for Petronia, but which she had rejected in favor of a betrothal to Paullus Gellius. Still, that didn't matter anymore. Petronia wasn't the only one making a new start in life. He was, too.

He smiled when he thought of her. Cyra. She was a city laundress, and a slave one at that, but Theo had fallen for her at first sight. Yes, it had been that way with Petronia too, but this time was different. Cyra was sweet. Innocent. Theo had met her the day after Petronia had rejected him in Vesta's grove. She had delivered a basket of clean tunicas to his workstation, and her blue eyes and demure smile had captivated him. That same day, Theo had asked General Acrisius for permission to take her, and the general had granted it. Cyra was less experienced than Petronia had been, and definitely less experienced than the pricy prostitutes he had hired, but that didn't matter. Theo had enjoyed her all the same.

And now, he could think of only one thing: getting more gold to purchase her from the city, free her, marry her, and buy a house somewhere far, far from Rome where they could live in peace.

Feeling his legs cramp from crouching in the same position for too long, he gripped a nearby branch for balance and fell onto his bottom, stretching his legs in front of him and sighing with the relief of it.

"More comfortable now, friend?"

Theo gasped and looked up. Two men—one around his age, the other middle-aged—glared down at him. Both were holding daggers. It was the younger one who had spoken, and Theo looked squarely at him.

"What's it to you?" he asked.

"Why are you out here?" inquired the older man. He was heavyset, with a balding head of patchy hair and an accusatory, though not necessarily aggressive, voice. "Who are you?"

Theo stood. "I work for the city," he said. "I'm in charge of the sewer." He leveled his gaze at the older man. "And I'll ask the questions. What are the two of you doing out here?" When the two men exchanged uncertain glances, Theo adopted the most authoritative stance he could—legs apart, chin held high. "Or should I call General Proculus and have you interrogated?"

"For what?" asked the younger man. "Being awake at night?"

"For sneaking around the sewer in the dark like you're up to no good."

The older man laughed. "We could say the same of you."

"Fine," said Theo. "Let's let the general have the final word."

He took three militaristic strides forward, but stopped as the younger man grabbed his arm. He pivoted to face both men.

"What do you want?" asked the older man.

"I want to know how you're doing it," Theo replied. "And I want in on it."

The two men looked at each other, communicating with their eyes. The younger one spoke. "We're not saying we've done anything, but if we had, how do we know we can trust you? What's to stop you from reporting us?"

"I know you're stealing the gold," said Theo, "and I know you're using the sewer to do it. If I wanted to report you, I would've done it already. You'd have half the army crouching in wait for you, not just me. So the way I see it, you have two choices. You can kill me. Then you can spend the whole day tomorrow pissing yourselves as the city turns the sewer upside down, thinking that I've fallen in like that weak-legged grunt I'm sure you heard about a while back. If they do, you can be damn sure they'll find gold in the line somewhere. Your second choice is to divide your loot three ways instead of two." He raised his eyebrows. "Like I said, I'm basically in charge of the sewer. King Numa's even hinted he's going to make me the head of the sewer workers' guild. I will control when, where, and how the whole line is swept and inspected."

The older man, the one with the patchy hair, frowned. "Fuck off."

Theo laughed in his face. "You must've been beside yourselves..." he shook his head and let his voice trail off, deliberately goading the pair.

"What are you talking about?" asked the older man.

"When the sewer was blocked," Theo replied, smiling widely, "when you couldn't retrieve the gold you'd stolen because of the blockage. You've must've been terrified of being found out."

"Fuck off, you little—"

The younger man put his hand on the older man's shoulder, subduing him. "Shut up for once, Glaucio." He looked at Theo, assessing him. If they had to be found out by someone, this was probably their best option. It might even work to their benefit. The sewer worker was correct—the blockage had led to some stressful, sleepless nights. In fact, they had been so shaken by the close call they had reduced the amount of gold they were stealing. It now made the job of scouring the brown water at the sewer's terminus for a nugget or two hardly worth it. They needed someone on the inside. He glanced at his more senior companion. "This could work," he said, then turned to Theo. "My name is Larce. This is Glaucio. What's your name?"

"I'm Theo. How are you doing it?"

The older man grumbled, but resigned himself to the complicity. "We work in the treasury," he said. "I'm a metalworker. My job is to portion the gold, silver, and bronze into the right sizes and weights. If I get little pieces, I melt them together to make a bigger piece. If I get a big piece, I melt it down into smaller nuggets." He gestured to his friend. "Larce works in the latrine. The metalworkers shit in buckets, and he empties the buckets in the sewer." He shrugged. "And that's it."

Theo frowned. "Impossible. The guards check the buckets."

Both thieves burst into laughter.

"It can't be that easy," said Theo.

"Easy?" exclaimed Glaucio. "I eat only prunes and solid gold. That is not as easy as you think. A bottomless cup holds wine longer than my guts do these days."

"There's no way you could have passed that much gold."

"There are three of us," said Glaucio. "Me and my two brothers. We are all metalworkers, and believe me, all our guts are goldmines." When Theo grimaced at the thought, Glaucio chuckled. "We had it good for a while. After the king died, the guards were pretty slack so we started stuffing gold pieces into our loincloths before we went to the latrines. But then this Statius prick came along and ordered that all treasury men had to work

Petronia, you are like a sister to me. I care about you. Paullus is a good man and you deserve to be happy. Don't sabotage yourself."

Petronia kissed Lollia on the cheek. "You are right," she said seriously. "I am done with him. I am done hurting him. I will sacrifice to Juno, and she will grant me a long marriage to Paullus and a fine home on the Palatine." She smiled, feeling her spirits lift. "She must, Lollia. I am allergic to fish."

CHAPTER XVIII

The Pontifex Maximus Marcius sneezed loudly. He wasn't used to the thick air of the horse stables. He scraped the bottom of his sandal on a pile of straw to dislodge a chunk of manure, waved away a fly, and furrowed his brow in worry. "Whose mare was it that birthed the creature?" he asked.

"It belongs to a man named Geganius," answered Proculus. "He's originally from Alba Longa, but he's lived in Rome for years."

"What do you know about him?"

"He comes from an old family. They're descended from Gyas, a priest who fled Troy with Aeneas. He's married. Two daughters. The elder is a sacerdos in the Temple of Vesta. He's been trying to gain a senatorial seat, but hasn't been admitted yet. He doesn't meet the land requirements. He's not been any trouble though."

"Whose horse is the sire?"

Here, Proculus hesitated. "It was a stallion from Romulus's stable."

"Romulus bequeathed his horses to you, did he not?"

"Yes."

"So the sire is yours?"

Proculus stared at the newborn foal—the *two-headed* new-born foal. It had been a long time since Rome had received such a disturbing omen. He hated to be associated with it. "Yes, the damn thing is mine," he said. "So what?"

"It is no coincidence that both mare and sire have notable ownership," replied Marcius, in that unperturbed way that perturbed almost everyone he spoke with. "Men of the Silvii, Julii and Geganii...all relate back to Troy. This can only be a sign from the gods. From Mars in particular."

"Troy did not fare well with strange horses," added Acrisius. He had been listening from a step behind, but now joined them.

The three men leaned on the top of the stall door and stared at the black two-headed foal lying on its side on the straw-covered floor of the enclosure. The animal was still alive, though frail and fading. Its skulls were fused above the neck, and of the four eyes, only two blinked. The foal's mother had been moved to an adjacent stall, and she was thumping about inside, snorting and neighing anxiously.

"The mare and sire should be taken to the Altar of Mars and sacrificed there," said Marcius. "The foal should be taken outside of the city to be sacrificed. I will perform the rites myself."

"Should Numa see it first?" asked Proculus.

"No," said Marcius, "under no circumstances should the king be near it. We must make sure it is crated up well, and we must take the path farthest from the Regia."

Proculus felt a tug at his tunica, and turned to look down at the face of a wide-eyed six-year-old girl. "Grandfather, can I see it?"

"Veneneia," he said. "Where is your father?"

"I'm right here," said Gaius, entering the stable. "I just can't keep up to her anymore." He strode to his daughter and picked her up. "The word is out," he said to the men. "Half of Rome is on its way here to see it."

They all looked at Marcius, but the priest only shrugged indifferently. "They can see it if they want to. It was born to be seen. But it must be sacrificed before it dies."

The men moved aside as a crush of young girls arrived as a pack to peer over the stall door at the deformed animal. Tullia and Canuleia were among them, the former being the daughter of Hostus Hostilius and the latter being the granddaughter of the distinguished Senator Canuleius. They fell into silence at the sight.

"It is hurt," said Tullia.

"Yes," agreed Veneneia, from her father's arms. "What do you always say, Father? Put it out of its mystery."

"Put it out of its *misery*," corrected Gaius. "Although both might be correct in this case."

Canuleia, at ten years old, studied the animal with less sympathy and more shrewdness. "Sacerdos Aule should disembowel it," she said. "He should study the entrails."

Marcius nodded. "Agreed."

The pack of girls was soon shouldered aside by the sons of Rome's generals and senators who stormed in herd-like, many of their parents trailing behind like outpaced shepherds. The boys were less contemplative at the sight of the two-headed beast and jostled with each other for position, pointing and shouting with excitement. Their antics quickly annoyed the girls who skipped out of the stable in search of lighter amusement.

Proculus followed them out of the stable to find Valia standing at the threshold, as if afraid to step out of the sunlight and into the shade of the omen's presence. He couldn't blame her.

"Should I look at it?" she asked him.

"I wouldn't."

"Then I won't." Valia picked a piece of straw off her husband's cloak. "What do you think it means?"

He avoided her eyes. He knew exactly what it meant. At dawn, he had been informed that Senator Pele had died of natural causes. Of old age. He had died in his sleep while lying naked next to his mistress. But he should have died screaming in agony. He should have died while staring at his own teeth and testicles in Proculus's blood-soaked hands as the general exacted excruciating vengeance for the king's murder. Proculus knew the omen was meant for him. It was a sign from Romulus, a sign of anger, of discontent, at his inaction.

"Proculus," said Valia. "Did you hear me? I asked what you think it means."

"That's a question for the priests," Proculus replied, "including Amata."

"She's still unwell."

But Proculus wasn't listening. He was lost in his own thoughts. He wandered off with them and without another word to his wife.

Amata regretted sending her slave away. Now she had to answer the call at the door herself. She groaned, kicked off the bedcovers, and crossed the floor of her home to open the door. The wise but wrinkled face of an old man smiled at her from the other side.

"Nikandros!" She took the elderly tutor by the forearms and pulled him gently into her home. "What are you doing here? Is everything all right? Has something happened to the king or—"

"Everything is fine in Alba Longa," he replied, taking quick stock of her. Her hair, which was normally neat and pulled back from her face, was uncombed. Even though it was in the middle of the day, she was still wearing an overnight tunica. She hadn't even bothered to put a shawl around herself before opening the door. Her eyes looked listless, and now that her tutor had unexpectedly arrived from Alba Longa, confused. "Can an old teacher not visit his favorite student?"

"You hate to travel, and you cannot stand Rome."

"Yes, and I have recently been reminded why. The road is cratered and the city reeks."

She smirked, gesturing for him to take a chair in front of the hearthfire. He did, and she stoked the flames, knowing he was easily chilled. Moving to a table along the wall, she put some dates in a bowl and poured some water in a cup, handing him both. He drank thirstily and she poured him a second cup.

"Why are you here?" she asked.

He settled into his chair and looked around. Amata's hut-home was larger than the one the Palatine guards had pointed out as once belonging to Romulus, but it was still modest by Alban standards. Circular with a central hearth, its various rooms were curtained off by heavy drapes. Fine colorful tapestries—almost too fine for the home itself—decorated the walls. It was the same way with the furnishings. The chair he sat on was gilded, and he recognized it as once having stood in the private dining room of Amata's parents, King Nemeois and Queen Cloelia, in the Silvian palace. But that was a lifetime ago.

"So this is where you lay your head when in Rome," he said. "It seems strange after all these years that I have never had occasion to visit your private house."

"Why have you come?" she asked again.

"Lady Valia sent me a message. She said you have been ill for days, although..."

"Yes?"

"She suspects there is more to it. She says that you and Proculus have been even harsher with each other recently. Now that King Romulus is not here to maintain the civility between you, I wonder—"

"You don't need to wonder, Nikandros. Everything is fine—or at least unchanged—between Proculus and me. I am upset with him for revealing Penelope's secret, though. It was none of his business."

"Perhaps not, but is your judgment not misplaced? Penelope's indiscretion was the larger betrayal. She broke her vows."

"And yet had Proculus kept his mouth shut about it, Sextus would never have been hurt."

"No," agreed Nikandros. "Only disrespected."

Amata said nothing, the spirit of argument suddenly gone. Nikandros ate the last date in the bowl and held out the vessel to her. She got up and refilled it, then sat back down next to him as he picked through the fruit for the best ones.

"Would you like something more substantial?" she asked. "I can call for a slave."

"No, I only pick at my food these days. That is how the stomach ages."

"I haven't had much of an appetite myself these last few days," she said, and then as if realizing what she had said, forced a tone of perkiness into her voice. "We will take supper by the Tiber," she said. "Fresh air always makes a person hungry."

"What is going on with you, my dear?"

Amata plucked a date from his bowl and inspected it. There were so many ways to answer that question. She chose an easy one. "Yesterday, a deformed foal was born in the stable. It had two heads. The Pontifex Maximus believes it was an omen."

"Is it still alive?"

"No, it was sacrificed to Mars. The mare and sire, too. But the sire was one of Romulus's best stallions. He left it to Proculus. The mare belonged to Geganius."

"Ah," said Nikandros, "all Alban families and all with Trojan blood. No doubt, the Pontifex Maximus believes that is portentous. Another horse of doom."

"Something like that." Amata tossed the uneaten date into the fire and pulled a blanket over her legs. "Do you remember you once took me to see a two-headed calf that had been born in Tusculum? I was no more than ten years old at the time."

"I remember."

"After we saw it, you said, 'Tell me, Amata. What was it? Was it one calf with two heads or was it two calves with one body? If you can answer that, you will understand how the gods think.'"

Nikandros laughed. "How clever of me."

"What do you think the omen means?"

"Two-headed creatures usually signify a crossroads of some kind. Rome could be at one." His gaze became more inquisitive. "The king is the head of Rome. How is Numa? Does he seem uncertain or conflicted about something?"

Amata smoothed the blanket on her lap. Another question

with many answers. "No, he is a steady man. And a more capable king than expected." Before he could ask anything else about Numa, Amata looked at him curiously. "Nikandros, have you ever been at a crossroads? Personally, I mean."

He seemed to consider whether to answer that. "After your parents and brother were slain, I was brought before Romulus. I thought he might kill me—several of your father's advisers were killed, along with a number of high-ranking palace staff—but instead he gave me two choices. I could leave Alba Longa and return to Greece. Or, I could remain in the city as your tutor on the condition that he approved your instruction. He would only permit me to present your uncle and father as usurpers who acted without justification. I was forbidden from discussing their reasons for doing what they did. For me, it presented a dilemma. I feared for your well-being and wanted to stay, yet I did not want to compromise my values by only teaching Romulus's propaganda."

"But you chose to say with me."

"You were a terrified child, and I was terrified for you. The day the soldiers took you from your home to the convent on Mount Albanus was one of the worst days of both our lives. I feared it was a ruse...that Romulus would let you live for a while to appear merciful, but slowly poison your food or find some other way to dispose of you. So yes, I stayed to do what I could. I did my best to keep your thoughts distracted from your loss. And there were many times I wished I could have told you more about your father's actions. When Prince Egestus committed his incest, Nemeois faced his own crossroads. He could continue to support him despite what he saw as a sacrilege, or he could usurp him and maintain the dignity of the Silvii."

She wiped away a tear. "Thank you for staying with me, Nikandros."

"Do you believe I did the right thing even though I betrayed my values?"

"Yes."

He mulled her answer, then set his empty bowl on the floor.

"A crossroads can also represent something more ethereal. It can relate to the space between the world of men and the world of the gods. Some kind of religious matter or crisis..."

"You neglect the most obvious meaning of a deformed horse," said Amata. "Mars has sent it as a sign of his anger. Rome may be on the brink of losing his favor."

"Rome honors the god of war more than any city I have ever known. Why would Mars be angry with it?"

She fidgeted with the edge of the blanket. Again, so many answers.

Mars is not angry with Rome. He is angry with me for defiling myself before the gods, and for indulging in pleasure and thoughts of freedom instead of avenging his son.

"Did you hear that Senator Pele died?" she asked.

"I did not know Senator Pele, but the name sounds familiar."

"He was one of the senators who last saw Romulus alive."

Amata could see Nikandros struggling to put it all together. "Then whatever he knows, he will take it below with him," he said. He put a hand over his mouth and yawned. "Oh, forgive me, my dear. You know I cannot sleep on the road."

Amata rose from her chair. "Come."

Nikandros stood and followed her to a drape that hung from the ceiling. She pulled it back and directed him to lie on her bed, pulling the blankets over his body.

"Sleep," she said. "When you are rested, we will take a walk along the Tiber."

She looked down at him as he drifted off. How she longed to tell him everything. Who knew—perhaps he suspected. Regardless, since she had been a child, he had always found the words to comfort her. Here he was, now an old man and herself no child, and he was still doing so. But she could never tell him. Even Nikandros, as sage and learned as he was, could never fully fathom the breadth of her betrayal. She returned to her chair by the fire, wrapped the blanket around her bare shoulders, and stared into the purifying flames, wishing she could somehow use them to purify herself.

CHAPTER XIX

Gellius felt the sting of a mosquito bite on the back of his neck and slapped it. He wiped the bloodied insect off his palm onto his tunica and looked at the senior sacerdos Petronia, the young woman who would soon be his daughter-in-law. She was kneeling on the ground, scooping another large jug of water out of the spring. She stood, sealed the jug, and handed it to him. He took it smilingly, and together they began to walk back toward the path where he had left his horse-drawn carriage.

"It was kind of you to escort me out here," she said, "but you didn't have to."

"Tell Paullus that," Gellius replied. "I might be a general, but he's giving the orders."

Petronia laughed. "This spring isn't too far. I would have been fine." She returned his smile. "But I think it's sweet that he's worried."

"He would have taken you himself, but you are still a sacerdos. It might have raised some eyebrows."

"I am a sacerdos for six more days," said Petronia, "and I hope Paullus won't mind, but I might refuse to put any wood on our hearthfire for some time." Gellius chuckled and she continued, though less flippantly. "To be honest, sir, temple duty has been very hard work lately. I am looking forward to starting a new life with your son and your family."

"I can imagine the Pontifex Maximus is a demanding man."

"You have no idea. He has made so many changes to the city's religious rites and the priestly protocols. Yesterday, I had to perform a public sacrifice with him—we consecrated the new shrine to Vulcan at the foot of the Capitoline—and my hands were shaking the whole time. I was so afraid of making a mistake." She put her hands in front of her, mimicking the rituals she had performed. "I had to purify the bull calf just so and pour the oil just so"—she turned to look at him severely—"he told me beforehand that if I made any mistakes we'd have to start over the next day, and the next day after that if that's what it took. The prayers are all different, too. It took me forever to memorize them. Anyway, I don't like Sacerdos Marcius very much—that's our little secret, all right?—but I must admit he is thorough and very organized. He has strange ideas though. During the sacrifice, he threw ten live frogs from the Tiber into the fire. That's new, isn't it?"

"I haven't seen it before," said Gellius, "but that doesn't mean it's new."

Petronia glanced sideways at him. "Oh, you soldiers are such a practical lot."

The general slapped another mosquito. "I meant to ask. Has Priestess Amata been to the temple lately? My wife is worried about her."

"No, not for a while. She must be feeling better, though, since she had a visitor from Alba Longa yesterday. I saw them walking along the Tiber. I think he left Rome this morning. Wait, my sandal has come loose."

Petronia sat on a boulder and began to fuss with the strap of her sandal as Gellius held the jug and surveyed their lush green surroundings.

"Why does Numa insist on water from this spring anyway?" he asked the sacerdos. "What's wrong with a closer one?"

"He says there are nymphs in this spring. The most powerful is named Egeria, and she can—" she stopped in mid-sentence. Gellius had dropped the jug of water and was sprinting toward a muddy patch of earth. "General, what is it?" she asked. She fumbled to secure her sandal and ran over to join him.

He was already on his hands and knees, gripping the edge of something half-buried in the muck. A military shield. His expression was rigid, his face suddenly bloodless.

"Impossible..." he muttered. He pulled the shield free and wiped the mud off its surface. "It's not possible..."

Petronia felt her pulse quicken. If the general was this upset, it had to be something terrible. Yet his fear made no sense: the shield had some unique markings, but it was clearly Roman. "Sir, what is wrong?"

He stood quickly. "Hurry," he said. "We need to get back to Rome. I must speak with the king immediately."

＊　＊　＊

Gripping the shield with a blanched hand, Gellius passed through the gates of Rome on horseback. He dismounted and helped Petronia out of the carriage.

"Sir, will you tell me what the matter is?" she asked.

"Not right now," he said. He squeezed the shoulder of the soldier closest to him. "Send your fastest men to find generals Proculus and Acrisius...find Appius and Paeon, too." He thought. "And the Pontifex Maximus. Have them all meet me at the Regia immediately."

"Yes, General."

"I don't care what they're doing or who they're doing it with," Gellius added. "Tell them to come *now*. It's urgent."

The soldier turned to swiftly deploy his men. Leaving the horse and carriage at the gate, Gellius ripped the reins of another horse out of a soldier's hand. He ordered the man to hold the muddy shield while he mounted and pulled Petronia up to sit behind him.

The soldier passed the shield up to him. Gellius kicked the horse into motion and galloped toward the Regia, leaving the gate sentries to wonder what in the world was happening.

Quickly arriving at the king's residence, Gellius slid off the horse before it had come to a complete stop. He helped Petronia down.

"Go to the temple. Say whatever prayer to Vesta is most powerful. Make an offering into the holy fire. Do whatever it is that the senior sacerdos is supposed to do."

"I will, sir," she replied, and dashed off to the nearby sanctum.

Clutching the shield, Gellius marched to the king's door. As per Numa's orders, there were no guards outside, so the general knocked insistently. The door opened to reveal the face of a young scribe. He was holding a sheet of papyrus and a pointed reed, and Gellius remembered: unlike Romulus, unlike most Romans, Numa was literate.

"The king is occupied," said the scribe.

"It's urgent. Get him."

The scribe set his jaw indignantly, but Numa rose from a desk behind him. "I hope this is important, General," he said. "I am writing the pontifical laws. Focus is essential."

"Your Highness," said Gellius, barely bowing. "Send the scribe away."

Numa signaled for the scribe to leave and stepped forward, inviting Gellius into the royal house. It was Gellius's first time in the Regia and it was much like he would have expected from the eccentric king. A two-part structure, the first part of the expanded building served as the formal office of the religious college of pontiffs, which was headed by Marcius, and boasted a number of fine terracotta statuettes of the gods, wall paintings, and a shrine to Mars. Rows of sacrificial implements hung from the walls. The rear portion of the structure, cordoned off only by a heavy curtain, served as the king's private residence.

As Numa's eyes landed on the mud-caked shield in Gellius's grip, the sound of approaching voices floated in through the open door of the Regia. Their forms soon followed, and within moments the generals and pontiff were gathered together.

Seeing the armament in Gellius's hand, Proculus stared apprehensively at the shield. "Where did you get that?"

"I found it by a spring to the southeast," he looked at the king, "the one the Vestal sacerdotes are now drawing water from."

Numa moved to stand before Gellius and inspected the shield. "A Roman item," said the king, "no doubt dropped or abandoned by some forgetful soldier. Why would this be of concern?"

Proculus took the shield out of Gellius's hand and set it upright on the floor. He squatted in front of it, running his fingers along the edge. "There is no doubt," he said gravely. "This is Romulus's shield. His alone had this emblem—a wolf's head encircled by a wreath of oak leaves. The metalworkers were forbidden from making another. And this dent right here...it is where my sword landed while we were training. I remember because I knocked it out of his hand and he rewarded me with a gash on the shoulder." He turned the shield around and pointed to a piece of plating upon which a rough etching of a thunderbolt had been scratched into the metal. "Romulus used the tip of his dagger to do this. We were eating in his tent. He carved it while chewing a salted eel, and said, 'The work of Vulcan.' We laughed."

Numa clapped his hands together. "Then why so grim?" he asked. "Gellius, you have stumbled upon a precious relic of the founder. We will build a shrine for it."

Gellius turned to him. "You don't understand, Your Highness. This shield"—he looked fearfully at it—"I destroyed it with my own hands over thirty ago."

The pontiff Marcius squatted beside Proculus. He poured a cup of water over the shield's surface, revealing the brilliant gold hidden by the mire. Indeed, it could only have belonged to a king. "Did you actually destroy it yourself?" the priest asked Gellius, "or did you merely order it destroyed?"

"Like I said, I destroyed it with my own hands," said Gellius, holding his hands in front of him for emphasis. "I hammered it halfway to Hades, and then I melted it down. I did exactly what Romulus ordered me to do."

"Why did he want it destroyed?" asked Numa.

Proculus rose. With his lips pursed in trepidation, he stepped back from the shield. "This was the shield that Romulus threw down from the Capitoline Hill, onto the traitor Tarpeia below."

Numa let out a faltering breath. Feeling the muscles in his legs lose strength, he moved quickly to the closest chair and slumped into it.

Acrisius swallowed hard. "Two signs, and so close together," he said. "First the omen in the stables and now this."

"The foal was no omen," Numa said, his voice low. "It was just an oddity of nature."

"How can you be sure, sir?" asked Acrisius.

"When I was in Egypt, I caught a fish with two tails, but the great Nile did not stop flowing because of it." Numa stared ruminatively at the shield, turning the meaning of it over his mind. "But this...this is different. This is a message from one king to another." His lips moved as if he were speaking to himself. "You can all leave," he said, not taking his eyes off the she-wolf in the shield's center. "But go fetch Priestess Amata and have her come here without delay."

It was a bright afternoon, but as soon as Amata cracked open the door of the Regia, she found herself staring into near darkness. The king had ordered the two small windows in the office of the pontiffs to be boarded up, and heavy goatskins had been thrown over the roof to block out any sunlight that might filter in through the thatching. There was no fire in the hearth, but a few oil lamps were burning. A sacrificial fire also burned on the shrine to Mars.

Amata slipped inside and closed the door behind her. She took a cautious step, then another, toward the shrine, before which

Numa was kneeling in prayer. She felt moisture on her sandals and looked down, squinting, to see that the floor was streaked with blood. Several dead chickens lay around the base of the shrine's altar. Their innards sizzled in the fire on top.

Amata had been irked when Proculus had arrived at her door, banging on the wood boards and demanding that she go at once to the Regia to meet with the king. She had answered his impropriety by slamming the door in his face, but he had—incredibly—opened it and barged inside without her permission. The look of shock on his face had been enough to assuage her anger though, and she had listened to his incredible message: *Mars has re-formed Romulus's shield from the flames and thrown it to earth!*

After hearing that, she had dressed quickly and hastened down the Palatine to answer the king's summons.

"Your Highness," she whispered as she tiptoed toward him.

He turned to her, his face full of emotion. "Amata," he said. "What does it mean?"

She moved to the shield. By the light of the sacrificial fire, the wolf's head seemed to move, as if watching the king and the priestess, deciding whether to attack.

"Nikandros," she said softly, "he spoke of the space between the world of men and the world of the gods." She touched the shield. "That must be where it came from. But as for what it means—"

"It means I have been a fool," Numa interrupted. "The stolen gold, the diseased crops...they are signs of my weakness. This shield is a sign from Mars, and from Romulus, too, that I must be stronger."

"You have already accomplished great things in Rome, Numa."

"And now I must protect those things," he said. He reached up to take her hands, and pulled her down onto the floor to kneel before the shrine with him. He turned her head to gaze at the imagery on the shield. "Look, a wolf for me. It growls, and tells me that a king must inspire fear, that he must not hesitate to attack." He touched the shield's emblem. "And for you, a wreath of oak, the symbol of the Silvii. Do you see? I defend the walls of Rome, while you protect its sacred hearth."

Amata reached up to take a simpulum off the altar. She dipped it into a bowl of oil and poured the libation into the flames. "I am corrupted, Numa. I can no longer serve the virgin goddess."

"You are wrong," he said. "That space between the world of men and the world of the gods...I know where it is. Anything is possible there." He smiled at her confusion. "The spring where Gellius found the shield, there is a divine presence there. A purifying presence. I have gone into the waters. They are cold when you drink from them and when you approach, but when you step in, it is like walking into flames. The waters burn the skin like fire. They purify like fire, too. I can take you there, Amata, and we can burn away our sin. You can be as pure as the goddess again, and I can put the guilt of it behind me."

Amata sat back on her heels, captivated.

Emboldened by her enthrallment, Numa continued reverentially. "I used to dream of the place. I would be asleep and nearly suffocating when I would feel cool mist on my face. I would hear the spirit of the spring laughing, and in that moment, I would be able to breathe again. She would always ask me the same thing: 'Who are you?' I thought it was just a child's dream that never faded, but when I came to Rome for the first time, Marcius and I rode out into the country. That's when I recognized it. And now this divine shield, a king's shield, your kinsman's shield, found there? You and I could not be more drawn to the place if Apollo tied us to his chariot and dragged us there himself."

"Then let's go there."

"We cannot," he said. "Not now. The spirit rises with the dawn. That is when she is most active."

Amata set the simpulum back on the altar. "At dawn, then."

CHAPTER XX

The men who guarded the gates of Rome to the south of the city typically didn't see a lot of excitement in the early morning hours. While they kept their eyes open and their weapons ready, they still found the time to play a few games of dice and talk horses, to sharpen their knives and complain about life, the weather, and women. So when a pair of figures on horseback approached the gates to exit the city, only two guards broke away from their gossiping colleagues to meet them.

"*Salvete*, citizens," said one guard, making a cursory assessment of the man and his female companion, as well as the horses they rode on. The horses were superior, but the couple didn't seem to be packing anything suspicious out of Rome, so there was nothing to inspect. He was about to wave them through when his colleague interceded.

"Your Highness," said the second guard, bowing. He stood beside the king's horse, his eyes moving from Numa to the female rider with him. It was the priestess Amata. He bowed to her, and looked back up at the king. "Sir"—he struggled with how to ask about the king's business without directly asking about the king's business—"may we accompany you out of the city?"

"We are fine on our own, soldier. Open the gates for us."

The guard shifted worriedly on his feet. He took a second look at the unarmed king and his important companion, and then unfastened the leather belt and knife around his waist. He passed it up to Numa. "Please, Highness. Take this."

Numa reached down to accept the items. He secured the belt around his waist and adjusted the knife at his hip, then covered it with his cloak. "Thank you, soldier."

The guard bowed again. "May Mercury protect you, sir." He signaled for the men at the gates to open them, allowing the pair to leave the city.

Once outside the gates and trotting along the empty road well beyond the waking sounds of the city, Amata sensed the air around her change. It was eerily devoid of human sound or activity, but teeming with song and life as sparrows darted past her head and hawks flew over it. Swathed in a world of green, she felt like she was riding into a secret place. She often felt that way when she woke early. The world was different when she rose with the sun. It was like walking through a door that had just been opened and wandering around a magnificent place all alone. It felt like a privilege, as though the gods were showing her the world as they had first made it. Except this morning, she wasn't alone. Numa was with her, and she could tell by the way he held his face up to the sun that he felt something similar.

They rode without speaking until the sound of a softly gurgling spring joined the birdsong. The air seemed to change again as the green spring came into view: it was cooler, crisper, fresher. Numa dismounted his horse but did not bother to tether the animal to anything. Amata did the same, noting the expression of reverence on the king's face as he regarded the spring. He took a small terracotta vessel of oil from the satchel that hung from his horse, then walked to the spring's rocky boundary, beckoning for Amata to follow. She did.

"The elders who live in the nearby settlements say this spring is home to the nymph named Egeria," said Numa. He knelt down and poured a stream of oil into the water. "Whenever I sit down to write the pontifical books, I only drink her waters. The words and the rites come to me effortlessly that way." He rose and removed his cloak, letting it drop to the ground. He then reached out and removed Amata's cloak. "She can purify you, just as she has purified me."

Together, they removed their tunicas. Naked, Amata followed Numa into the spring's waters, gasping as she strode in to the waist. The waters were like ice.

"It is too cold," she said.

"Wait," Numa replied. "The heat will come."

She steadied her breathing and forced herself to stand in the center of the spring, face to face with the king. After several long moments of biting pain, the cold faded into an unusual heat, and then, a slight burning sensation. Her breathing became relaxed. Her body did too, immersed as it was in the nymph's powerful waters. The water soaked her skin, permeated her flesh and entered the flow of her blood, rising upward through her body to spill out of her eyes as tears.

"I wish to be reborn," she said to Numa, "as a virgin priestess of Vesta."

Numa withdrew the knife from his hip. "Blessed Egeria," he said, "watch us shear away this woman's sin." Raising his arms to Amata's head, he began to crop her hair, cutting away the long brown locks and letting them fall into the spring water.

Amata raised her hands to feel the strangeness of her cropped hair. Her head felt lighter, and she could feel the skin on the back of her neck in a way she never could before. Numa placed the knife back in its sheath and raised his arms again, this time holding the terracotta vessel above her and pouring oil over her head, anointing her body as she dropped her arms to submerge her hands in the cleansing water.

"Amata Silvia," he said, "from these purifying waters you are reborn as a virgin priestess of Vesta." He looked questioningly at her, and she nodded. "I take thee, Amata," he continued, a proud smile now forming on his face, "to be the Vestalis Maxima of Rome, and to perform the holy rites, which is proper for the high priestess to do for the Roman people and their king."

Amata wiped the oil from her eyes and followed Numa out of the water. Dripping wet and shivering from the cold, she dressed and mounted her horse, eager to return to the temple where she could warm herself by the goddess's sacred flame once again.

CHAPTER XXI

There were all kinds of slaves in Rome. There were body slaves who helped their masters and mistresses bathe, dress and set their hair. There were cooking slaves, sewer slaves, blacksmith slaves, brothel slaves, temple slaves, and slaves that tended to the fields and herds. There were skilled slaves who could read and write various languages, depending on where they were from and what their status had been in their native land. Some slaves were privately owned. Others were owned by Rome.

Most slaves had been taken from conquered cities, but some had sold themselves into servitude to pay off a debt or, sometimes, simply to have food in their bellies and a roof over their heads. In rarer cases, Roman fathers sold their children into slavery—it was a right that King Romulus had bestowed upon the male head of the family. After all, it could come in useful. If a man had five children but could only feed three, then selling two was better than letting all starve. Plus, if the two he sold were girls, he could sidestep the dowry requirement and probably come out ahead in the end.

The slave known as Cyra knew all of this, and all things being equal, thought herself quite lucky. As a laundry slave owned by Rome, she worked hard, but the food and living conditions were decent enough. And if one were able to make the right kind of connections or friendships, one could even find a way to have an even better life. That's what she had done. She had caught the eye of a free man, Theo, and that relationship had afforded her a chance at freedom...well, as much freedom as any woman who married could expect to have. She smiled when she thought of him. She wouldn't mind being his wife. Surely washing one man's tunicas was preferable to washing hundreds. And anyway, he was sweet. He would treat her well.

She knelt on the banks of the Tiber, upstream from where the sewer emptied into the river, and thrust her hands into the cold water, scrubbing the last traces of a stubborn stain off a large tunica. At first, she thought it was wine, but it wasn't. It was blood. She had learned to tell the difference in the way the stain came out, and in the way it discolored the water. Blood came off flaky. Wine didn't. She turned to the young man next to her, a slave also on his knees, and also scrubbing a bloody tunica in the river.

"What's going on?" she asked.

"It's the interrogations," he replied, drawing an arm over his sweating brow. "They're doing more of them."

"For the missing gold, you mean?"

"Yes. I hope they find the culprits soon. Blood is hard to get out. I'm wearing my knees to the bone here." He frowned unhappily and glanced over his shoulder to where rows of water-filled tubs lined the shore: a worker was standing in each tub, stomping the clothes within to clean them. "Why don't we take shifts like we used to? Why do we spend hours breaking our backs, scrubbing out stains in the river, while they get the easy job of stamping linen and wool that is barely soiled in the first place?"

"It's the new laundry guild," said Cyra. "The boss wants things to look more organized. He has to justify his increased pay somehow." She grunted with effort as she wrung out the tunica, then stood and carried it to one of the long clotheslines that extended between the trees. Another slave, this one in charge of hanging the clothes, took it from her and found a place for it along the line. He returned carrying a large wicker basket full of neatly folded clothes and passed it to her.

"Take these to the citadel," he said.

She balanced the heavy basket on her hip and began to make her way along the busy street to the Capitoline Hill. *If they are so concerned with efficiency*, she thought to herself, *then why do they not load fifty baskets in a donkey cart and have the whole lot sent over at once?* On second thought, it was good the boss hadn't figured that out. If her services were to become superfluous in the laundry, she would likely be sent to the brothel. She shuddered at the thought.

Reaching the base of the Capitoline, she stopped for inspection. Although the guards knew her—she made this same journey several times a day, every day—they regarded her as if they had never seen her before, asking her questions to confirm who she was and what her business on the citadel was, and going through every piece of clothing in her basket. It was as her friend had said. The city was redoubling its efforts to find out who was stealing from the treasury.

After being cleared at that checkpoint, she walked up the stairs of the Capitoline and turned toward the citadel, only to be stopped and scrutinized a second time. The guards waved her on. She proceeded to the laundry hut where she delivered the full basket of clothes and was given an empty one in its place. She turned to make the journey back, trying not to sigh as the guards at both top and bottom checkpoints peered into her basket, pulling on the wicker to make sure there was nothing hidden behind or below. One of the soldiers noted her impatient expression and tapped the blade of his dagger on the basket.

"They say it was a laundry basket that carried the founder to Rome," he said. "So you just never know."

"Yes, sir."

Rather than heading straight back to the river, Cyra lingered in the Forum, her eyes searching the passersby until she saw him—Theo. He saw her at the same time and ran up to her.

"I was waiting for you," he said. "Do you have time for lunch?"

"Yes," she said. "I will tell the boss it took longer to pass through the checkpoints. I wouldn't be lying."

Theo shifted his gaze to the guards behind her. "I see."

Theo went ahead to get them food and wine from a vendor while Cyra found their favorite bench and waited, setting her basket on the empty space beside her to save it for Theo. He returned with fresh bread, on top of which sat what looked to be some kind of delicacy.

"What is that?" she asked.

"Flamingo tongue. I tried one earlier. You will like it."

"Theo, you should not spend so much money on me," she said sincerely. "I am happy with bread and olives," she smiled, "and your company."

"Try it."

She bit into the costly treat. "Oh...it is delicious."

Theo laughed, but his high spirits fell at the sight of a slave—his eyes were swollen shut, and blood poured out of his nose—being dragged away from the base of the Capitoline, toward the Campus Martius where the interrogations were taking place.

"I've seen that man before," said Cyra, thinking. "Yes, he's a slave in the treasury. I've delivered clean laundry to him a few times."

Theo knew him too—it was Larce. His stomach suddenly contracting with cramps, he set his bread on the bench.

"Is there something wrong with the bread?" Cyra asked him, noting the look of distress on his face.

Theo shook his head. "No, I'm just full. I had a big breakfast. You can finish it." He stood. "I must get back to work."

"Oh, all right then. I will see you—" Cyra's shoulders slumped. He was already walking away, without kissing her on the cheek as he usually did, without even saying goodbye. She took his bread and bit into it, chewing as she watched him leave.

He hadn't cleared the first row of vendor stalls when a large man ran up to him: he was an odd-looking sort, bulky, with thinning hair and a desperate way about him. He gripped Theo by the shoulder, but Theo pushed his hand off and pulled him aside, away from the crowds. Cyra wished she could hear what they were saying. She stood up, craning her head this way and that to watch them. The big balding man looked distraught with fear. He extended an arm behind Theo, gesturing in the direction the guards had dragged away the treasury slave, and then put his hands on his head in angst as Theo tried to calm him down.

Cyra looked down at the scraps of the expensive flamingo tongue...and chuckled at the very thought. It was impossible. There was no way that Theo could be involved in something as criminal, as sensational, as the treasury theft. She finished her food and drink, picked up her basket, and headed back to her work along the Tiber.

And yet she couldn't quite shake the nagging feeling that something wasn't right. She scrubbed tunica after tunica, trying to remove her own suspicions in the process, but to no avail. With each tunica she handed off to dry in the slight wind, another doubt blew into her mind. Theo had been spending a lot on her lately. He had been dressing better, too. Even today, at lunch, she had noted his new sandals. Why would a man who worked in the sewer all day wear such fine sandals? Only someone who could afford to replace them as necessary would do that. And then there was his reaction to seeing the treasury slave...she couldn't stop thinking about it.

As the afternoon dimmed to early evening, Cyra was dismissed from work. Yet instead of returning to the slave barrack where she had a bed, she walked back to the Forum and all the way to the gates of the city.

"I can travel unaccompanied to the Viminal Hill," she told the guard, "on the authority of General Acrisius."

The guard reached out to inspect the wooden tag that hung from the collar around her neck. It bore the general's mark. He let her pass.

Although the road to the increasingly populous region of the Viminal Hill was normally only sporadically patrolled, this evening no fewer than five fully manned checkpoints were stationed along the route. Cyra had to stop at each one, showing the general's mark to hyper-alert guards before being allowed to continue on her way. The king was obviously redoubling his efforts to find the thieves.

Finally, she arrived, her body tired and her thoughts unsettled, at Theo's little hut. She let herself in. He was standing with his back to the door, facing the fireless hearth, and nearly jumped off his feet when she entered.

"Theo," she crossed the floor to take his hands. "What is wrong? You have not been yourself since lunch."

He wrapped his arms around her. "Everything is fine. You worry too much."

She rested her chin on his chest and looked up at him. They had only known each other for a short time, but it was easy to read his mood: the way his lips twitched almost imperceptibly, the nervous breaths that came out as shallow puffs, and the faraway look in his eyes. Something had him very distracted, very worried.

They moved to the bed and undressed, but despite their newness, he was unable to couple with her. He blamed fatigue, but Cyra knew the impotence was born of something more sinister. That was why, the moment he finally fell into a troubled sleep— it was more morning than night by that time—she quietly slid out of the bed and tiptoed to his satchel. By the lighted flame of an oil lamp, she untied the leather strap, but found nothing more troubling than a few iron tools and a set of four knucklebones. She left the tools in the satchel, but gripped the knucklebones in the palm of one hand and moved quietly to crouch behind a chair, taking the oil lamp with her for illumination.

Placing the knucklebones between her cupped hands, she shook the pieces softly, barely able to hear their gentle rattle. "Venus, is he a thief?" she asked in a whisper. And then she dropped them as quietly as she could on the floor. All four pieces landed on different sides.

She gasped. There was no doubt. The goddess had answered— *yes*.

Standing, she peered at Theo in the bed. He was asleep, though turning restlessly. Moving like a mouse in the night, her heart beating as rapidly and her motions as skittish, she began to search his hut. She looked under the cushion on the chair, inside the jugs and pots, and rummaged through the other animal-skin sacks that hung from the walls. Finding nothing, she scoured the rest of the home with her eyes, hesitating over the hearth in the hut's center. Theo had not started a fire last night, despite the bite of cold in the air. She knelt before it and burrowed her fingers into the cool ash...she felt something hard, nugget-like, and pulled it out.

It was dull and gray from ash, but once she blew on it, the gold sheen of its surface shone through. "Oh, Theo," she whispered to herself.

She dug through the ash and found another, just as gleaming and exhilarating as the first. She looked at Theo—he was mumbling, though in sleep. She knew what he was thinking. Hoping. He was hoping that the treasury slave would keep his mouth shut during interrogation, that the threat would pass, and he could keep stealing until he had enough to build a good life somewhere else. But he was naïve. Once, Cyra had been told to deliver a basket of wash-up cloths to the interrogation stable. She would never forget what she saw inside—the instruments, the blood, the grotesqueness of human torture. No man could endure that. No woman, either. She had to get as far away from it as possible.

She said a soft prayer for Theo, and then squeezed the gold in one hand, gathered her tunica, sandals, and the prophetic knucklebones, and soundlessly exited his hut.

CHAPTER XXII

Alba Longa

Amata had hoped to travel in and out of Alba Longa with a minimum of fuss and even less emotion. She had gone early to the Temple of Vesta on Mount Albanus to collect a few holy items from her personal store and to perform the rites that would allow Priestess Cloanthia to replace her as High Priestess of the Vestales Albanae. Ten years Amata's junior, Cloanthia had been in the last days of her six-month tenure to the goddess when her betrothed had been killed by a falling building stone. The couple had been a true love match, and Cloanthia had vowed to never wed another. Instead, she had committed herself to a lifetime of religious service.

Until very recently, a key difference between the priestesses Amata and Cloanthia had been their capacity for choice. Cloanthia had always been free to leave the order if she chose to, but it was only after the death of Romulus—her overseer, as Numa had once called him—that Amata had been given that choice. She too had chosen a religious life—though it would no longer be in Alba Longa, but in Rome.

It had been a bittersweet parting at the Temple of Vesta. The

priestesses and priests who served in the other temples on the sacred mountaintop had been surprised by Amata's decision, but
supportive of it. They knew, as Amata did, that the new high priestess of the Alban order was both pious and proficient. Many even felt
that, after years of playing a secondary role, Cloanthia deserved the
elevated status. The Alban order deserved it, too. A good change at
the top was like adding fresh kindling to a sedate fire.

Unfortunately, Amata suspected that Sextus would not see it
that way. She thought about visiting the royal palace and speaking to Penelope about it first, before informing the Alban king,
but she wasn't quite ready for that kind of confrontation just yet.
Instead, she returned home to the Silvian palace to put a few
things in order, well aware of her own procrastination.

Yet there was one thing she could not put off any longer. Full
of dread but also determination, she passed through the wing of
the palace that formerly served as the royal private quarters and
entered the king's sitting room. The large fireplace before which
she used to play while her father worked had not seen flames in
decades, though there was still a stack of firewood piled beside
it, the blade of an axe sticking out of the top log. Amata gripped
the tool by the handle and pried the blade out of the wood. She
left the king's private wing and returned to the statue-lined cor-
ridor, ignoring the curious looks of slaves as she passed by.

She kept walking until she reached a terracotta statue of Diana. Leaning the axe against the wall, Amata wrapped her hands
around the goddess's torso and dragged the statue to the side.
Catching her breath, she picked up the axe—and swung it, with
all her strength, at the wall behind where the statue had stood.

The blade sank through both the plaster of the false wall and
the wooden door behind it on the first strike, though it lodged in
the splintered wood so tightly that Amata had to pull hard to
wrest it free. She aimed the blade at the jagged hole and swung
the axe a second time. The hole grew bigger, making the blade
easier to withdraw. She swung repeatedly, until the floor was littered with chunks of plaster and wood. Finally, when the hole

was large enough for her to pass through, she dropped the axe. Without giving herself time to peek inside the room first, she squeezed through the hole, wood splinters snagging her dress, and stepped into the royal stateroom that she had ordered sealed off from the living world nearly thirty years earlier.

The air in the room felt and smelled stale, not in the same way as the tombs in the necropolis, but still stagnant. The sound of her heavy breathing echoed off the walls, as though the room, which had been still and silent for so long, found the sound of life to be an uncomfortable intrusion. Her eyes immediately moved to the high-backed chair that sat on a raised platform at the front of the luxurious room—her father's once throne. She could picture him upon it, holding audience with his advisers or meeting with the important men of Latium, men like Albus Julius and Mamilian of Tusculum, men to whom Nemeois had been generous but who had nonetheless turned their backs on him when Rhea Silvia had returned from the dead with her sons.

Slowly, Amata walked to the area of the floor that had once been covered in Amatus's blood. As the blood had pulsed out of his open throat, yet another man had turned his back to her family's plight—Proculus. Her brother's best friend. As Amatus's young body had flopped to the side, the life draining out of him faster even than the blood, Proculus had turned away. How quickly, how completely, he had abandoned his oldest friend in favor of his newest one.

Amatus! Amatus!

Amata shook her head, clearing the sound of her mother's screams from her ears. She glanced around the room: the carved mahogany chairs, the huge fireplace with the rosette designs around the fine edging, the tapestries, paintings, statues of gods and busts of kings. How amazing to think that such thin plaster could keep out Cronus. Time had not entered this room. Nothing had entered. And nothing had left.

That included the ghosts whom the plaster had sealed inside along with the lifeless fireplace and the voiceless statues. But if

Amata had been set free, did the ghosts not deserve to be set free as well? She glanced around the stateroom for a last time—it would be the last time—and departed through the void in the wall, leaving the ghosts free to do the same when they were ready.

Whenever Amata visited the palace of the Julii in Alba Longa, she was typically shown into the palace and greeted by her friend, Queen Penelope. They would visit in the dining room and later, when Sextus was finished whatever kingly business he was attending to, he would join them and they would take supper together, discussing whatever state or religious matter was pressing, or simply engaging in casual talk.

Today, Penelope had not come to welcome her. Instead, Amata had been shown to the courtyard and asked to wait for the royal couple as if she were an unscheduled caller and not a lifelong friend. She declined refreshments from the slaves. The day's tasks—first stepping down as high priestess from the temple, followed by hacking through the false wall in her home—had left her stomach in knots.

She sat on the edge of a large oval fountain in the colorful garden, dipping her fingers into the cool water and gazing up at a statue of a dolphin. Back when the palace was still the home of Albus Julius, there was a statue of Pegasus here. But after Albus had died and left the palace to the first Julian king—Sextus—the winged horse had been replaced by a dolphin, symbol of Venus, the goddess from whom both the Silvii and the Julii claimed descent.

Yet if the autocratic tone of Sextus's more recent messages to Amata were any indication, he seemed to have forgotten that the Silvii, not the Julii, were the true royal line. Without Romulus to remind him, and with no male Silvian heir to the Alban throne, perhaps such entitlement was inevitable. Or maybe the man was just getting old and choleric. Maybe his ego had yet to recover from the injury of his wife's betrayal, and anything to do with

Rome or Romulus now struck a sore spot that left him wanting to strike back.

Regardless, Sextus left her waiting long enough to annoy her but not quite insult her. At last, a slave ushered her into the palace, though instead of escorting her to the dining room for wine and conversation, took her directly to the king's meeting room. The small one. The one he used for receiving mere messengers and minor dignitaries. There, she sat on a chair and waited a little longer until the royal couple entered. Sextus proceeded to his throne at the front of the room, his wife at his side, while Amata stood before them.

So be it, thought Amata.

She bowed. "Your Highness, I have difficult news to share today."

"I know your news," said Sextus. "I heard it from one of the priests."

"I see."

"I was surprised you would inform the priests before your king."

"There is no insult in that, sir. My first duty is to the Vestal order." She folded her hands in front of her, adopting a more informal stance. "Sextus, it cannot be a total surprise. You know I have spent much of my time in Rome as of late. First, it was Romulus's disappearance, and now King Numa and everything he is doing with the Vestal order and the new religious college in Rome. To be honest, my decision to be a part of that was a sudden one. Had I known sooner, I would have told you sooner."

Sextus frowned. "Wait—you're going to serve as a Vestal priestess in Rome?"

Amata glanced from the king to the queen, back to the king. Obviously, whatever gossipy priest had divulged her resignation from the Alban order had stopped short of telling the whole story, perhaps fearful of the king's reaction.

"Yes," she said. "I am going to serve as High Priestess of Rome."

Sextus leaned back in his throne, his tongue gliding over his bottom lip in thought. Amata could feel his tension. So could Penelope. She looked nervously at her husband.

"Priestess Cloanthia is the new high priestess of the Vestales Albanae," Amata continued. "She is just as capable as I am, and her Trojan ancestry gives her merit. The Alban order will lose none of its esteem."

Sextus stood. "You should have sought my permission before making such a decision."

"The Alban priesthoods do not require royal permission for appointments," she said.

"I don't mean about Cloanthia. I mean about leaving. I am your king."

"You are not my king," replied Amata, careful to keep any trace of defensiveness out of her voice. It was simply a statement of fact. "Numa is my king now."

"Your palace is in my city," said Sextus, "so you are my subject."

Penelope put her hand on her husband's arm. "Sextus, please."

"I forfeit my ownership of the Silvian palace," said Amata. "I endow it, and my household of slaves, to you, Your Highnesses, to use as you see fit."

"Amata, please do not do this," implored Penelope. She looked at her husband. "My love, we have been friends too long for—"

Sextus ripped his arm out of Penelope's soft grip and shot her a cold, scornful look. "Now you will tell me how to rule?" he asked her. "Did Romulus teach you how to do that as well?"

Penelope looked away and wiped her eyes.

Sextus turned back to Amata. "Rome..." he ruminated. "Things won't go the way you think they will." He signaled to the guard waiting at the threshold of the meeting room. "Escort Priestess Amata to the gates."

Amata could hear the guard behind her move forward. She bowed to the king and queen of Alba Longa and left the meeting room. Ending a long friendship this way, on such bad terms...it was a sickening feeling. Yet as she walked out of the palace, keenly aware of the guard on her heels, she was surprised to feel the knots in her stomach loosen into relief.

CHAPTER XXIII

Rome

Proculus tiredly thrust his hands into a basin of clean water, sending clouds of red swirling into the clear liquid and instantly making him think of how badly he needed a cup of strong wine. He rubbed his hands together and the water grew even redder. Like his mood.

No matter how many people he and his men interrogated, no matter how many fingers they cut off or how many eyes they gouged out, they were still no closer to finding the treasury thieves. He'd had a glimmer of hope the day before when a slave who worked in the treasury seemed to crack after a single stab to the thigh; however, the wound had been ill-placed and he had bled out before he could talk. Proculus didn't let himself think about it too hard. If he did, he was likely to strangle the idiot interrogator.

His hands more or less clean, he splashed the red-tinged water on his face to wake himself up. A tap on his shoulder made him turn around. Statius was there, holding a fresh towel out to him. Proculus took it and patted his face dry.

"Anything?"

Statius motioned to the slight woman standing behind him. She was trembling and staring at her feet. "This one's a laundry slave. Goes in and out of the treasury." He grinned, and said in a whisper, "I think we have them, sir."

The towel dropped out of Proculus's hands. "Clear the stable!" he shouted. "Everybody out!"

The soldier-interrogators in the rows of stalls stopped in mid-torture and grabbed their subjects, variously carrying or dragging them out of the stable. When the building was empty of everyone but Proculus, Statius and the laundry slave, Statius eyed the woman.

"Tell the general what you told me," he demanded.

The girl turned to Proculus, though avoiding his eyes. "Sir, my name is Cyra and—"

"I don't care what your fucking name is," said Proculus. "What do you know?"

Cyra stopped herself from saying *I was just about to.* "Yes, sir," she said. "General Proculus, I swear I knew nothing about it, not until I found a couple gold pieces hidden under the ash in his hearth...his name is Theo, and he's in charge of the sewer."

"The sewer?"

"Yes, sir." She stared at the ground. "We were in the market when we saw a treasury slave being dragged away for interrogation, and Theo was really upset by it. And then, I saw him talking to another man—I'd seen him in the treasury, too—and they were arguing about something. They looked like they were panicking." She pressed her palms together pleadingly and forced herself to look up at the intimidating general. "I wanted to do the right thing, sir. I searched Theo's house after he fell asleep, and that's when I found the gold. I swear to the gods, I didn't know! As soon as I figured it out, I went straight to Commander Statius and told him."

"As soon as you found out?"

"Yes, sir. I was terrified that Theo would be caught and you'd think I was involved...I'm afraid of the interrogations...but I've told you everything I know, I promise!"

"Everything?"

"Yes, General."

"The sewers," pondered Proculus, then asked Cyra, "How do they get the gold out of the treasury building?"

"I don't know, sir."

"Where are they keeping it?"

"I don't know, sir. I only found the two pieces." Desperate to give him something, she put her hands to her chest and spoke quickly. "You could check the field behind his house. He's been out there a lot lately with a shovel. He said he was filling in rabbit holes, but maybe..."

Proculus raised his eyebrows, and jabbed at Cyra's forehead with a finger. "Oh, so there is more in there after all." He spoke to Statius. "String her up."

"What? No!" screamed Cyra. "I don't know anything else!"

Statius's vise-like grip closed around her forearm, instantly stopping the flow of blood and making her whole arm throb. Her heart pounded. This was every fear she had imagined, now coming true. Thoughts, regrets, flew through her mind. *I should've followed my instincts and run! I should've woken Theo and told him to gather what he'd stolen so we could run together...we could've taken the gold and fled to the sea, to a ship, but now it is too late!*

Desperate, she tried to pull out of Statius's grip, twisting her arm and collapsing onto the ground, but it was no use. Her body was a mere cloth doll in his hand, and it flopped wherever he wanted it to. And right now, he wanted it to flop from the heavy rope that hung down from the stable's roof.

Statius bound her wrists together tightly and leaned over to reach the slack rope by which he would hoist her body up. When his grip loosened, she slipped out of it and made a mad dash for the stable doors, only to reach the end of the rope and have her body jerk back like a runaway dog abruptly reaching the end of its leash. She fell to the ground. Statius sighed irritably and kicked her hard in the stomach. She gagged and vomited as he raised her body up by the wrists.

"Please, have mercy! I don't know anything else!"

Proculus thought. He was fairly certain the treasury slave the girl had mentioned was the same one who had died prematurely during yesterday's interrogations. And it would be easy to find this sewer worker named Theo. But what about the other man? Who else was involved?

"The man you saw arguing with Theo in the market. What's his name?" he asked Cyra.

"I don't know," she said gruntingly, tears streaming down her cheeks.

"What did he look like?"

"I don't remember..." her eyes widened in horror as Proculus pulled an iron stoker out of a burning brazier. "Wait! He was big. Really big. And balding."

"What else?"

"That's all I remember!" she cried.

Proculus pressed the red-hot point of the stoker against Cyra's right breast, directly over the nipple. She screeched in agony, her body convulsing as it hung helplessly. Her hands were bloated and blue from the pressure around her wrists, and blood from where the rope dug into her flesh dribbled down both extended arms.

"Think," the general encouraged her.

He removed the iron stoker from her breast and Cyra's head fell back on her shoulders. The sound of her guttural sobs hung in the thick, dusty air of the near-empty stable.

"I think..." she sputtered.

"Yes?" prompted Proculus.

"I think Theo was coupling with one of the Vestal sacerdotes."

"I don't care if he was fucking Juno in the bushes behind the temple!" shouted Proculus. He held the searing tip of the stoker in front her. "The gold, woman! Think! What else do you know about the damn gold?"

A current of sobs washed over her words. "Nothing, sir...nothing, I swear!"

Proculus faced Statius, finding the commander of the citadel nodding. "I know every man in the treasury by name," said Statius. "Big and balding. She's talking about Glaucio. A metalworker."

"Get him," said Proculus, "but keep it quiet. We don't want to scare anyone off before we find out who else is involved."

"Yes, General."

Proculus thrust the point of the stoker back into the flames of the brazier and regarded the weeping girl hanging before him. After all his interrogations, after the countless men he had sent out to investigate in any way they saw fit—and they had seen to some very painful ways—would the crime of the disappearing gold really be solved by this unremarkable city laundress? He almost felt bad for torturing her. Almost. He withdrew the stoker from the fire. This girl had a way of trickling information out just when it seemed she was empty. No matter. He had become very adept at draining every last drop of whatever a person had in them.

The Regia was full of people, though not uncomfortably so. In addition to the king, the Pontifex Maximus and the Vestalis Maxima, also in attendance were the head priests of Jupiter, Mars and Quirinus, the chief augur Aule and the high priestess of Ceres. They had all come to see the shield of Romulus—Numa called it the *divinum ancile*—that Gellius had found buried in the ground near the spring of Egeria, thrown down from the heavens by the founder himself.

The Flamen Martialis, the high priest of Mars, inspected the shield with particular keenness. Although now in his mid-fifties, he had been one of the first soldiers to staff Romulus's personal bodyguard in the early years of the city. Romulus had given him the nickname Adonis for his unusual good looks. The man had been ribbed incessantly for it by his fellow soldiers, but the nickname had stuck. He shook his head in disbelief, began to say something, and shook his head again. Finally, he took a seat opposite Amata and looked at Numa.

"It was his, all right," he said. "There is no doubt. Will you keep it here, Your Highness?"

"For now," replied Numa, "but Marcius is concerned it will be a target for thieves or an enemy trying to demoralize us. I will have to find a more secure location. The new temple to Mars seems a logical choice."

Adonis canted his head in thought, his gaze now back on the shield. "During the war with Velsos, Romulus feared the Etrusci would dispatch men to steal the Palladium. So he had a decoy made, a perfect copy, and kept that in the Aedes Vestae. I wasn't privy to where he hid the real one. General Proculus was probably the only one who knew."

Marcius vocalized a grunt of interest. "Why stop at one copy? We could make as many as we like." He extended his arm to Numa as an idea came to him. "There should be one for each of the twelve *dii consentes*. Eleven copies, plus the true relic."

Aule nodded, concurring. "That is an auspicious number considering the recent reforms to the calendar. Twelve months, twelve shields."

Numa looked at his scribe. "The Flamen Quirinalis will oversee the manufacture of the copies," he said, as the scribe wrote down his instructions on papyrus, "but the priesthood of Mars will be in charge of their safekeeping."

A slave bowed as he entered the room. The pontiffs looked up expectantly, hoping for wine, but unfortunately the man had come empty handed.

"Your Highness," said the slave, "Commander Statius is asking to speak with you."

"Tell him I'm meeting with my priests," replied Numa.

"He is insistent, sir. I don't think—"

Statius strode in like a strong wind, forcing the slave to stumble clumsily out of the larger man's way. "Your Highness," he said, "General Proculus is requesting your immediate presence in the

Campus Martius. A carriage is waiting for you."

"All right, Statius," said Numa, conceding to the soldier's persistence.

The king rose from his chair and left his priests to keep working while he trailed Statius out of the Regia, toward a horse-drawn carriage waiting a few steps away on the street. He was about to step into it when he noticed Amata had followed him out of the Regia.

"Is something the matter, Priestess?"

"No, sir. I had just wanted to speak to you about something in private."

"Then ride with me."

"Thank you, Your Highness."

Numa helped Amata into the carriage and stepped in after her. Once they were seated, Statius climbed into the front of the vehicle and began to drive the single brown-spotted horse through the Forum and toward the Campus Martius, though at a faster pace than Numa thought prudent.

"The *divinum ancile*," Numa reflected, gripping the edge of the carriage as its wheels hit a bump. "The more time I spend in its presence, the more certain I am of its significance. It is as much a guardian of Rome as Vesta's fire and the Palladium."

"The Palladium," said Amata. "That is what I wanted to speak to you about."

He grinned at her. "Do you know why I chose to store it out of view in the temple?"

"The sacerdos Lollia said it was to inflate the reverence that people have for it, but I suspect you have heard the legend of Ilus, the founder of Troy. When he first looked upon the Palladium after it fell from the heavens, he was blinded by its light, and so insisted it be stored out of sight." She returned his grin. "Not many people know that story anymore, but I think you are referencing it."

Numa looked approvingly at her. "It is that kind of history that must never be lost. That is why I'm assigning you your own scribe.

You will record the history and customs of the Vestales Albanae for the pontifical books, even as you create new laws and rites for the Roman order."

"It would be my honor," Amata replied, "although that makes what I must ask even more difficult. I did not leave Alba Longa on the best terms, at least not with King Sextus. He resents me for leaving the Alban order."

"And you want to return the Palladium to him as a gesture of goodwill."

"His claim to it has merit. Romulus should not have taken it from Alba Longa."

"I disagree," said Numa. "Since the fall of Troy, the Palladium has been in the stewardship of the Silvii. Aeneas, Ascanius, and then Romulus." He angled his head sympathetically. "I understand why you want to return it, and it's hard for me to deny you any request, but I can't allow it. Romulus wanted the relic to be in Rome, and it was his right to bring it here. There is a pact between kings, even between the living and the dead. I won't break it."

Amata found herself nodding. She almost wished she hadn't asked. "I understand."

"Besides," said Numa, "I don't know whether I'm in the mood to be charitable to Sextus. I received a messenger from Mamilian of Tusculum last night. According to him, Sextus has been actively petitioning the revered fathers of the Latium Confederation to condemn Rome's so-called illegal possession of the Palladium. He has also been openly ridiculing my religious reforms and slandering the Vestal order in particular. I'm sure the revered fathers know it's only because he resents your dedication to it, but still, I must do everything I can to protect the esteem of my new religious college. This isn't the time to forfeit religious relics. It would look weak."

"I had no idea," said Amata. "Sextus is a different man these days. A different king, too. He is losing alliances."

"He had the same overseer as you, Priestess. He knew that Romulus could have rightfully reclaimed the Alban throne at any point. That must have been a constant threat. Now that it's gone, we are seeing who he really is."

The carriage arrived in the bustle of the Campus Martius and weaved through the armament stations and troops of soldiers— some training, others eating, a few lying on the ground and trying to doze off for a few moments—all of whom stood at attention at the sight of the king. Statius took his passengers through all of it until they arrived at an oversized military tent, one sequestered from the others by an encompassing wooden rampart that gave it a bastion-like feel. A guard opened the gate to allow the carriage to enter. As it did, Amata noticed an emblem of Venus sewn into the heavy goatskin above the tent's closed flaps, immediately identifying it as the private headquarters of Rome's top military man, General Proculus Julius.

Statius stopped the carriage. He alighted and looked back to make sure the gate was closed. Numa noticed the commander's caution and for the first time felt some trepidation. Whatever Proculus was about to tell him, it had to be significant. He stepped down from the carriage and helped Amata do the same.

"Let's see what the general has for us," he said, and led her toward the tent, both of them following Statius.

Statius untied one flap just enough for the three of them to enter, Numa going first and the commander last. Once inside, the king took three headstrong strides before stopping abruptly at the sight of a severely beaten woman—bloody and gagged— bound to a chair. Next to her, also bound to a chair, was a very large balding man who looked like he had taken an even worse beating. Blood seeped from various parts of his body, running down the chair's legs in red rivulets to pool in four spreading spots on the floor.

Proculus was sitting on a chair across from the balding man, the general's legs resting on a stool, elbows on the armrests, staring at his prisoner over interlaced fingers. When the trio entered, he stood and bowed to Numa, then jutted his chin toward the battered man.

"Your Highness," he said, "there is one of your gold thieves. Glaucio. He's a metalworker in the treasury."

Numa put his hands on his head, his expression opening to joy. "Thank the gods!" He extended an arm out to Proculus, and the general clasped it congenially. "Good work, General!"

"Thank you, sir." Proculus moved to stand behind Cyra's chair. He put his hands on her shoulders, squeezing tightly enough that she whimpered. "But we should really be thanking this one. She gave us the first name—Theo, a sewer worker. He and Glaucio have come up with a profitable shit-and-sweep system, one just disgusting enough to avoid detection."

Taken aback, Numa stood with arms akimbo. "Theo...I know him. Is he in custody?"

"Not yet, sir, but we know where he lives. I've instructed my son Gaius to keep a discreet eye on him. He's the only one I can trust to keep it quiet. We don't want to alert anyone that we're on to them just yet."

"So right now, who all knows?" asked Numa.

"Other than Gaius, just the people in this tent," replied Proculus, gesturing to the king and Statius. His eyes briefly hesitated on Amata as if he hadn't noticed her before. He couldn't be blamed if he hadn't: she had stood quietly against the goatskin wall of the tent, watching it all unfold from a distance. Proculus gave Cyra's shoulders one more painful squeeze and moved to stand behind the male prisoner's chair, patting the top of his balding head as he would a dog. "Before word gets out, we need to see what else Glaucio here can cough up. There's no way it was just him and the sewer man."

Numa considered the man's injuries—the missing earlobes, the severed nose, the bloody nailbeds of his fingers—and nodded encouragingly. "Good."

Proculus stepped in front of the prisoner. He withdrew the dagger at his hip and thrust it into the man's shoulder hard enough that it went straight through his body, the tip sinking into the wooden back of the chair to pin the prisoner in an upright position. Glaucio gave a muffled scream from behind the soiled rag stuffed in his mouth and rolled his head back in agony.

"We're almost there, aren't we, Glaucio? Theft is a family business, isn't it? A man doesn't endure this much pain unless he's protecting family. Like his two brothers who work alongside him in the treasury." Glaucio made another muffled noise, but Proculus ignored him and spoke to the king. "There's no doubt his brothers are in on it, too. I suspect that's the extent of it, but we need to be sure."

"Gods," said Numa. "Four common city workers have managed to make a mockery of Rome's security on its own citadel? I don't know if I should be impressed or disappointed."

His words stoked the flames of an idea in Amata's mind. She glanced at Statius. He could be trusted. They would need him. She stepped forward. "You're right, Your Highness," she said. "It does seem wasteful to punish such trifling men for such a great crime against Rome," she paused before continuing, "especially when more powerful men—men who have committed even greater crimes against Rome—go unpunished."

Proculus extracted his blade from Glaucio's shoulder, holding Amata's gaze as her meaning grew clear. Was she really going to do this? He shook his head. "Amata…"

She pulled her eyes away from him and looked at the king. "Your Highness, you once asked me what really happened to Romulus," she said, moving closer to him. "I will tell you. He was murdered by a group of senators during an early morning meeting in the Curia. After they killed him, they dismembered his body and buried the pieces in different locations."

Numa felt his face flush with emotion—shock, sadness, outrage. He glanced around the tent and crossed the floor to pour a cup of water. Taking a long draw, he sat heavily in a chair. Proculus and Amata watched him, noting the way his hand gripped the cup with brewing rage.

"The senators…what are their names?" Numa's voice sounded different. Frightening. Even Proculus adopted a more deferential demeanor.

"Naevius, Pele, Carteius, Antonius," said the general, "also Senator Calvisius. He had brought his son Lucius to the meeting, and it was he who first attacked the king."

"Naevius," said Numa. "I don't know that name."

"He's dead," replied Proculus. "I killed him before you came to Rome."

"Did you also kill Senator Pele?"

"I am ashamed to say so, but no. He died in his sleep."

"You *should* be ashamed," said Numa. He took to his feet again and began to pace aimlessly, angrily, in the center of the large tent. "These regicides have sat across from me in the Curia. I have dined with them. I have honored the gods with them. Why did you not bring them to justice when you first found out?"

"The general was about to arrest them," said Amata. "I stopped him."

"Why?"

"Because I didn't spend over thirty years of my life in slavery for nothing," she said. "The death of my parents and my brother, all of it, it had to be a part of something bigger. If Romulus wasn't the divine son of Mars, if he didn't ascend to become the god Quirinus, then the Silvii will be forgotten." She spoke to the king in a way that struck Proculus as unusually intimate, but he didn't permit himself from lingering on the thought. "Numa," she continued, "why did you paint those scenes—Aeneas fleeing Troy, Rhea Silvia, the she-wolf—on the fence around the Capillata tree? Why did you build the hidden chamber for the Palladium in the temple? Why do you treat the *divinum ancile* with such honor? Because you know it, too. If Romulus was not special, then neither is Rome."

The king had stared rigidly ahead during her explanation, but the more he contemplated it, the more his expression relaxed. He looked at her. "What are you proposing?"

It was Proculus who answered. "Calvisius's fortune has dwindled in recent years. He's sold most of his slaves and land, and he has little to leave his family. He has the benefit of a good reputation, but his son? Not so much. He's been accused before of swindling. It's a small step from there to thievery."

"How would you prove it?" asked Numa.

"I'd keep it simple and make it fast," Proculus replied. "Plant some gold on their land, arrest them, and cut out their tongues. Execute them publicly alongside the actual thieves." He glanced at the two gagged and chair-bound prisoners: considering what they had overheard, their tongues would be out even sooner.

"How many men do you need to make it happen?" Numa asked Proculus.

"No more than the ones I have. Statius, Gaius and I can manage it."

"Then do it."

Numa took a last look at the gagged and bound pair of prisoners. For a moment, he looked as beaten as they did, but then his eyes glinted with optimism. "We have solved the treasury crime," he said. "It is a good day for Rome."

He exited the tent with Statius.

Amata regarded Proculus. "Telling him was the right thing to do."

"I know."

"Then why are you looking at me like that?"

"Because I know how you get when you're angry," he said. He walked to the laundress and pulled the gag out of her mouth. She retched, and a mouthful of sputum fell out to land on her chest. "And once this little one tells you what else she knows, you're going to be very angry."

CHAPTER XXIV

In the three years that Theo had lived in his little hut on the Viminal, only two people had ever visited him. The first was Petronia, and the second was Cyra. The patch of land he had found and claimed for himself was in an unpopular and therefore mostly unpopulated area well off the beaten path. Even if more people knew he lived there, no one wanted to see him badly enough to warrant marching through the wasp-filled grasses. But Theo didn't mind the lack of company or the isolation. Sure, he had to cart his supplies and water a bit farther, but at least he didn't have to seriously worry about anyone stealing his goat. Or, these days, his gold.

That's why he was immediately alarmed by the sight of two figures approaching his hut. From his position in the field behind it—he was burying a small pouch that held another few pieces of gold—he froze and watched the pair intently, slowly lowering himself to the ground and hoping the tall grasses would hide him from their view.

Go away, he willed them. *Just turn around and walk away, please!*

He parted the shoots of grass with his fingers and tried to get a better look at the two men. They were wearing simple tunicas, nothing fancy or official, with no weapons other than the single dagger that hung at one man's waist. So they weren't soldiers. He breathed a sigh of relief. But if they were not soldiers, then who were they? Maybe Glaucio and his brothers had finally decided to cut their risk and pay a couple thugs to kill him...but they didn't know where he lived. Whenever Theo left Rome, he was always careful to ensure no one was following him.

Maybe it is nothing sinister, he thought. *Maybe they are selling something, or maybe they are new neighbors...*

Yet there was something about one of them that nagged him as being familiar. He let his mind work through it, pulling up images and putting the pieces together, until the man's identity hit him like a rock falling from above—it was Commander Statius. His humble attire had made it hard to place him at first, but now there was no mistaking it. There was no denying it, either: Theo had been found out. Glaucio and his two brothers were probably having their guts ripped apart at this very moment.

He dropped his face into the dirt and whispered a prayer to the gods below.

"Father Pluto, do not come for me yet."

When he looked up again, a figure was moving toward him. But it wasn't the men. It was too short and its path was too meandering. It was his goat. Perturbed by the visitors, she had wandered into the field to find her master and complain. Theo made a soft hissing noise and waved his hand, trying to dissuade her from approaching, but it was no use. She pawed at the ground, irritated by his unusual behavior, and bleated loudly.

Theo dug his hand into the dirt, his fingers finding the small pouch he had just buried. He held onto it. And then he jumped to his feet and made a run for it.

"He's on the move!"

Theo wasn't sure whether it was Statius or his companion who had shouted, but it didn't matter. They had seen him, he knew they would, and he had no option but to run. He pushed himself like a racehorse, feeling his heart hammer in his chest and his leg muscles burn with the exertion. He didn't dare look back, not until he had made it to a line of trees. There, he risked it. Without stopping, he glanced over his right shoulder. Even in his panic state, he felt a mild flush of relief to see how much ground he had gained on them. His pursuers had at least ten years on him in the wrong direction.

Yet Statius had spent those ten years in constant military training, and it was about to show. After a few more moments, he seemed to appear out of nowhere on Theo's left—his elbow appeared out of nowhere, too, striking Theo in the nose and fracturing the bone instantly. Theo coughed out a mouthful of blood and stumbled to the side. He tried to catch himself but fell hard, landing on a jagged tree stump and feeling the thick wood splinters sink into his stomach like a bundle of spears. He screamed, though more from the horror of it than the pain. Strangely, he didn't feel any pain.

That changed when Statius and his companion each gripped him by a shoulder and pulled him off the stump, like a piece of human meat being pulled off a spit. This time, Theo's scream was one of agony. He looked down—at the blood seeping out of the holes in his tunica and his belly—and placed his hands over his wounds. He screamed again.

"Oh, keep it down," he heard a panting voice say. "I've seen worse."

The light disappeared and the air felt different, and although it took Theo a few pounding heartbeats to figure it out, he soon realized that a black hood had been thrown over his head. A string tightened around his neck to hold it in place. And then, for the second time, he felt the force of an impact against his head. After that, things got even darker.

※　※　※

Calvisius pushed a piece of tasteless bread into his mouth and threw the rest of the loaf onto the floor. His dog scampered over to retrieve it, but after an unimpressed sniff, left it lying where it was.

"Do you see that, Sempronia?" the senator asked his wife, who reclined on the adjacent couch. "Even the dog won't eat it. I should beat the cook."

"It's not his fault," she replied. "The grain rations are still on, you know that. If you want to blame someone, blame Ceres. It's her pestilence." She beckoned a young male slave who quickly refilled his master's cup with wine. "Drink more, husband," she said, holding out her own cup for the slave to fill. "It makes the bread taste better."

"Is that your excuse?"

"Oh, do shut up."

Calvisius snickered and leaned forward to kiss Sempronia on her lips. She pretended to slap his face, but pinched his cheek affectionately instead.

The slave carried the empty wine jug out of the room and then out of the house, leaving the empty vessel on the ground outside and proceeding to a nearby root cellar to collect a fresh one. He bent down to remove the wooden covering of the cellar. A dark shadow appeared above, and he looked up. His master's son, Lucius, was standing with his groin at the level of the slave's face. He smiled down at him.

"Finish whatever errand you're doing," he said. "Then come to my bedchamber."

"Yes, Domine."

The smile faded from Lucius's face at the sound of a curious ruckus coming from the thick trees located behind the cookhouse. A moment later, two slaves darted out of the trees wearing expressions of terror on their faces.

"That bloody wolf is back," said Lucius. He took a couple cautious steps toward the shelter of the main house as another slave burst from the trees. This time, the animal followed close behind—

not a wolf, though. A horse. A horse with a sword-wielding Roman soldier on its back. More horses and more soldiers followed.

Lucius held his ground as the first horse reached him. Its rider was General Proculus.

"General," said Lucius, forcing as much privileged indignation as he could into his voice, "you'd better have a damn good reason for this!"

Proculus dismounted his horse and advanced on Lucius with more ferocity than any wolf could have. He raised his sword and struck Lucius on the temple—the spoiled twit didn't even have the humility or sense to duck—and spat on his limp body before it even hit the ground. Reaching down, he gripped the back of Lucius's tunica and dragged him, unconscious, into the house as his soldiers rushed ahead to secure the area.

He arrived in Calvisius's dining room to find the soldiers had already knocked the senator to his knees. One soldier held the blade of his long sword against Calvisius's throat, while another restrained Sempronia by the forearm several steps away. As Proculus entered the home, callously towing Lucius's motionless body behind him, Sempronia let out an ear-shattering shriek and tried to break out of the soldier's grip.

"His head is bleeding! You killed him!"

Irritated, the soldier wrapped his arm around her neck and squeezed, forcing the breath out of her. She gulped for air. He released the pressure and her loud resistance subsided into quiet snivelling.

Proculus let go of Lucius's tunica and his body slumped down, his head hitting the floor with a solid thump that made the general grin. He glared at Calvisius.

"We've arrested your accomplices, Senator," he said. "The metalworkers who have been stealing the city's gold. They told us it was your idea." He held out his palm and a soldier moved to place a handful of gold nuggets in it. "They also told us where you've been hiding your share—behind the boards of a hunting stand in those trees to the south."

Calvisius glowered at Proculus but said nothing. Since the moment Lucius had stabbed the king in the back, since the morning he himself had ridden to the Esquiline with Romulus's mutilated torso stuffed under his toga like some kind of horrific fetus, he knew this day of reckoning would come. He was only surprised it had taken this long. Yet as his eyes shifted from his petrified wife to his unmoving son, his hate for Proculus found its voice.

"You've been waiting a long time for this, haven't you, General?" He laughed humorlessly. "Although to be honest, I don't know why you'd want to punish me. Shouldn't you reward me instead?" He shook his head, feigning bafflement. "I don't know how you lived with yourself all those years, prostrating yourself to him, taking lashes from him, no different than a slave forced to suck his—"

Proculus took two powerful strides forward. "Hold his head still," he barked to his soldiers. As they did, he withdrew his dagger and forced Calvisius's lower jaw downward. He thrust the blade inside and sliced indiscriminately as the senator wailed in anguish, chunks of red flesh falling out of his open mouth.

Sempronia couldn't help herself. She screamed.

The shrill sound broke through Lucius's unconsciousness. He began to groan and writhe on the floor, slowly coming to. But Proculus wasn't about to listen to the son echo the father. He left Calvisius to gag on the seeping red leftovers of his tongue and moved to kneel on Lucius's chest. The idiot was still so groggy that Proculus didn't even need the help of another man to open his mouth. As he sliced off Lucius's tongue, the best his victim could manage was to grunt feebly and slap at Proculus's arms in weak protest.

Proculus stood and tossed the end of Lucius's tongue across the room. It landed near a piece of bread.

"Take them out," he said to his men.

His soldiers hauled the two bloody, mute prisoners out of the house and toward their horses for the ride back into the city.

The solider who restrained Sempronia caught the general's attention. "Sir, what do you want me to do with her?" he asked.

"I'll have someone stay back with you. We'll keep her under house arrest for now." He looked around the fine space: the soldier had probably never been inside such a rich home. "Enjoy the place," he said. "Have some fun."

"Yes, sir. Thank you, sir." He hauled the distraught woman deeper into the house.

Proculus began to walk out of the room after his men. As he exited, he happened to notice a heavy black curtain covering a small alcove in the wall. It was an unusual color choice for a shrine, so he pulled back the curtain. It was indeed a shrine; however, instead of holding statues of the household gods and other holy items, it held only a single statue—Quirinus. Proculus looked down at the blood on the blade in his hand. He touched it with his fingers and then wiped it on the statue, coating its surface with the red lifeblood of the king's assassins.

※　※　※

"Wake up, Domina!"

Petronia sat up in bed with a start. She gaped at her slave, her hand flying to her chest. "Malla—oh no, did I sleep in?"

"No, Domina. It is still night, but there are men here. Soldiers. Get up."

Confused, Petronia pushed off the covers and got out of bed as Malla wrapped a blue wool shawl around her shoulders. It was the shawl that Paullus that had given her yesterday. He had given her a gift every day leading up to their wedding day.

This is the last gift I give to my betrothed, he had said to her. *The next, I give to my wife.*

Petronia clutched the fabric to her chest. "What are they doing here?" she whispered to Malla. "Priestess Amata has forbidden men from entering the sacerdotes' house without permission."

"I don't know," said Malla, "but I heard them asking for you."

"For me? By name? Why?"

"I don't know," replied Malla, clinging to her mistress's arm.

The two women heard deep voices coming from the other side of the weighted curtain that shuttered Petronia's private room from the rooms of the other sacerdotes. The curtain flew open, and Commander Statius stepped inside.

"You will not speak a word, Lady Petronia."

"Then I will speak for her," said Malla. "What is the matter? My mistress has done nothing to deserve this treatment!"

Statius glanced at a man over his shoulder, and the soldier stepped past him to grab Malla. The slave protested loudly, so he clamped his hand over her mouth and pulled her away.

Petronia felt lightheaded. Her thoughts were as tremulous as her body. What was she possibly being accused of? Her one fault had been her relationship with Theo, but even if that had been discovered, it would not warrant a midnight arrest by the commander of the citadel. It would be a private matter: Paullus would break off the engagement, Priestess Amata would eject her from the temple, and she would be sent back to Cures in disgrace. Not a desirable outcome, but certainly nothing that would have the city's soldiery showing up in her room.

She wanted to speak so badly. To demand that Statius tell her what was happening so that she could defend herself—whatever it was, they had it wrong!—but the commander's bellicose manner was an effective deterrent and she did not speak, other than to the gods, which she did with silent desperation in her head.

Protect me, Vesta Sancta! Intervene for me, Juno Mater!

"Let's go," said Statius.

The soldier at his side passed him a black piece of fabric, and the commander raised it over Petronia's head. Instinctively, her hands came up to resist. *No, not that!* Rough hands gripped hers, cranking both of her arms behind her body. A coarse rope wound around her wrists, quickly cutting off the circulation and making her hands feel grotesquely swollen, as if they were no longer part of her body. The black hood came down over her head to separate her from what little light there was by the oil lamps and even seeming to separate her from the world itself. She felt the carpeted floor of the house of the sacerdotes against her bare feet as the soldiers hauled her out of her room.

By now, the house of the sacerdotes was fully awake. Lollia stood in the threshold of her room and watched—hair messy, eyes wide with fear—as the soldiers dragged her friend along. She stepped forward, but felt a hand on her shoulder. The sacerdos Gegania was shaking her head vehemently.

"Don't, Lollia," she warned in a whisper.

"I will get Priestess Amata," Lollia whispered back. "She will help!"

"Don't be foolish," replied Gegania, still holding onto Lollia's shoulder. "Do you honestly think the high priestess doesn't know about this?"

Lollia put her hand on top of Gegania's and squeezed. She was right, of course. High Priestess Amata had only just been made Vestalis Maxima, and already things were changing. Whatever was happening to Petronia, it was foolish to get too close to it.

The soldiers departed the house of the sacerdotes with their prisoner.

The void of frightful silence they left behind made the house suddenly feel very different. The shaken young sacerdotes who lived in it suddenly felt different, too. Less insouciant. More vulnerable. Slowly, they emerged one by one from their rooms. As some wept and others prayed, they moved toward each other until they shared one large embrace. Yet no matter how long or how tightly they held on, they found little comfort.

CHAPTER XXV

It had been a long time since Rome had seen a mass execution. By the last years of his reign, Romulus had killed just about everyone who needed killing, and that had been enough to deter even the most self-confident of criminals from committing any major crimes. But the theft of the treasury gold was not just a major crime, it was a subversive one. While the overall amount of gold stolen had hardly threatened to bankrupt the city, it had threatened to do something far worse. It had threatened to undermine the sense of control, of authority and security, wielded by the state of Rome. Gold could always be recouped, but power and respect were much harder to regain once lost. Thus the mass public execution.

The high-profile nature of the prisoners' offense and the discovery of their scandalous sewer-based scheme—a scheme that many people privately admired for its simple ingenuity—had drawn a large crowd to the area of the Comitium where the five culprits were about to be summarily executed on the tribune. Adding to the sensationalism of the event was the fact that two of the five criminals really should have been above this kind of thing: Senator Calvisius and his son Lucius had been implicated in the plot. At first, that revelation had been a shock. Yet once news spread of just how far in debt Calvisius was, and how many times Lucius had tried to con gold from foreign newcomers to the city, their involvement became evident... or at least believable enough that no one was rushing the tribune to save them from an unfair fate.

The five condemned knelt as miserably as any human could at the front of the great speaker's platform, wrists tethered to the wood planks, tongueless mouths gagged for good measure, tunicas stained with dried and fresh blood. Behind each man, an execution slave waited patiently for the order, each gripping a thick length of rope and rehearsing their moves in their heads. Before them, sprawled out to watch the capital punishment, stood what seemed to be half the city.

This pleased Proculus and irritated him at the same time. It was fitting that so many eyes would watch the life squeezed out of Romulus's assassins, yet as he looked around, he saw many faces that should have been at work. Oh well. This wouldn't take long. He inspected the restraints of the prisoners: it wouldn't be the first time a criminal had managed to wriggle out of them and make a dash for freedom at the last moment. The restraints holding firm, he walked to the front of the tribune and addressed the crowd.

"By order of King Numa Pompilius, these five men, all citizens of Rome, have been found guilty of stealing gold from the treasury"—he held an arm out to the people—"and of stealing from you, honest citizens! For when these thieves were taking from Rome's coffers, they were taking from your purses as well!" The people shouted in boisterous agreement, just as Proculus knew they would. Executions always went better when the crowd had a vested interest. He lowered his arm. "By further order of King Numa Pompilius, all five of these thieves are to be put to death for their unpardonable crime against the people and the city of Rome!"

A series of pathetic, muffled sounds emanated from the row of kneeling captives. Glaucio and his two brothers vocalized in a rhythmic way that suggested they were praying rather than protesting. A practical lot, they seemed to have made their peace with the ways of providence. But not so with Calvisius and Lucius. Strident pleas of protest emanated from behind their gags, pleas made all the more incomprehensible by the fabric shoved halfway down their throats. The sound of their panic made Proculus smile.

The general nodded to the executioners: they moved as one, each wrapping his rope around the throat of his victim and pulling. The muffled prayers and protests instantly disappeared, replaced by grotesque airless gurgles. Yet there was no resistance, no flailing arms batting at the stranglers' hands, no fingers desperately trying to pry away the ropes—after all, the prisoners' wrists were still bound to the wooden surface of the tribune. They couldn't move. Some in the crowd began to wonder whether it had really been worth the wait.

Yet had they truly understood the depths of Proculus's wrath, they would never have doubted it. The general had anticipated the somewhat anticlimactic efficiency of this form of strangulation and had given each executioner his own instructions. Glaucio and his brothers were to be killed quickly, without fuss: *Pull hard and get it over with*, Proculus had told their stranglers.

In contrast, the stranglers in charge of sending Calvisius and son to the gates of Hades were to take things slow: *Make it last*, Proculus had instructed, *and give them time to look at each other.* The stranglers were also to use the ropes that Proculus had personally supplied—not only were they thick and hard, but he had personally inserted shards of broken terracotta into their weaves. The effect was everything the more sadistic spectators in the crowd could have hoped for. As the terracotta pierced the flesh of the pair's necks, streams of bright red arterial blood spurted out of their throats, some shoots spraying far enough to splatter the faces of those watching from below.

Proculus watched with mounting satisfaction. Every moment that Calvisius and Lucius suffered, he savored. Every time the father's bulging eyes absorbed the sight of his dying son, Proculus remembered the sight of Romulus's eyeless skull as he had pulled it from the sludge under a forgotten shrine in Vulsini. As the stranglers finally let their victims experience the relief of death, Proculus let himself experience the relief of vengeance. He glanced up at the top of the Palatine. Although he could not see her from his angle, he knew Amata was there, watching with Numa. He wondered whether she felt the same as he did. Hearing two thumps, he looked back to find the corpses of Calvisius and Lucius slumped over, wrists still anchored to the platform.

Yet the satisfaction of seeing their dead bodies was fleeting. Proculus could not cling to it, not when Carteius and Antonius were still alive.

For their part, Carteius and Antonius wondered how long they would stay that way. Morbidly compelled to attend the execution, the two remaining assassins had watched in horror as it unfolded. When the ropes had tightened around the necks of Calvisius and Lucius, they had felt their own airways restrict with a terror that urged their bodies to run...to stuff a few essentials into sacks, disguise themselves in rough tunicas, and flee. It was their only chance.

Four of Romulus's six assassins were now dead. Naevius had been the first, dying by his own hand. Pele had been next, passing away in his sleep. When Carteius and Antonius had learned of those deaths, they had still been able to fool themselves into believing they were legitimate. After all, Naevius did have problems with his wife. There wasn't a slave in their household she hadn't bedded, and the man was humiliated beyond endurance because of it. And Pele? He was old and increasingly infirm. He could easily have died in his sleep.

But now, there was no fooling themselves. No hiding from the truth. There was no way that Calvisius and Lucius had been involved in a plot to steal from treasury. It was ludicrous. And in

hindsight, the deaths of Naevius and Pele were just too coinci-
dental. Proculus knew everything, and he was exacting his
revenge with slow certainty.

The two men took a last look at the bodies of Calvisius and
Lucius on the tribune. They had clearly been tortured. If Proculus hadn't known they were involved in Romulus's assassination
before, he definitely knew now. Carteius and Antonius turned
away from the tribune. Staying in Rome one more day was suicide. They slunk out of the Forum, throats dry and tight, both of
them resolved to be galloping at full speed to the sea by sundown.

Although her vantage point atop the Palatine Hill had afforded
Amata a good view of the Forum and the executions on the tribune, the distance had at first made it a challenge to distinguish
Senator Calvisius and Lucius from the other three condemned
men. It had not taken her long to figure out who was who
though: three men had fallen fairly quickly, while two had endured a much longer death than strangulation would normally
involve. Proculus's personal touch, no doubt. As she and the king
watched slaves lug the five corpses off the platform, the crowd
already dispersing, Numa grew restless at her side.

"I want it over with," he said. "All of it."

"Proculus is likely at his tent by now," said Amata. "Should we go?"

"Yes."

They turned around and walked several paces to where
Numa's horse and Amata's lectica were waiting. The king
mounted and rode ahead while Amata let the porters carry her
across and then down the slope of the Palatine. Reaching the base
of the hill, she closed the curtains. The city was bustling with
people who had come out to witness the executions, and she
could hear their excited chatter as her lectica moved along the
road to the Campus Martius. From behind her curtain, the chatter eventually segued into shouted orders and the sound of

clashing weapons, and she knew she had arrived in the field of Mars.

The lectica slowed and she opened the curtain as the vehicle passed through the gate of Proculus's headquarters. The porters set down on a level patch of ground and Amata stepped out, glancing up at the Venus emblem above the tent flaps as Statius held one of them open for her. She passed through to find Numa and Proculus already inside.

The last time Amata had been inside this tent, there had been two prisoners gagged and bound to chairs—Glaucio and Cyra. Now, both of them were dead. They had been replaced by two new prisoners, also a man and a woman, both of whom wore black hoods over their heads and were bound to the same chairs as their unlucky predecessors. Amata pulled the black hood off the woman.

Petronia blinked rapidly against the sudden burst of light, grunting from behind her gag and throwing her head from side to side as if trying to elude an anticipated blow to the head. When none came, she calmed herself and looked at Amata. Her eyes flashed with recognition and she howled unintelligibly.

"Quiet!" commanded Amata.

Petronia fell silent. If she had thought Amata was there to save her, the cold tone in the high priestess's voice immediately quashed that hope. She choked out a sob as the king appeared in her field of view. Whatever was happening, it was even worse than she had imagined. Her eyes jumped around the tent to take in her surroundings, and she saw another hooded person tied to a chair on the other side of the enclosure. Proculus moved to the second prisoner's side and pulled off the hood, and Petronia could not stop another howl from rising from her throat.

She and Theo locked eyes, both shocked to see the other there, both helpless to speak for themselves or for each other. Petronia's heart ached—the young man's right eye was swollen shut, his nose was bent at an impossible angle, and he could have been gutted for the amount of blood that drenched the midsection of his shredded tunica. The thoughts in Petronia's mind tumbled over each other. Obviously, their relationship had been discovered...but even so, why such severe castigation? She was not the first young woman to have had relations during her tenure to the goddess, and Theo was not the first man to have coupled with a sacerdos.

Amata stood before her, studying her. Finally, the priestess reached out to pull the thick fabric gag out of her mouth and stood back as Petronia retched uncontrollably for several long moments.

"I was kind to you," said Amata. "Generous."

"Priestess," sputtered Petronia, "I am so sorry! Please, forgive me!"

"For what, exactly?" asked Amata. "There are so many things that need forgiving. There are the lies you told me. There is the way you humiliated me. I was good to you, Petronia. I arranged for you to marry an exceptional man, the son of my dear friends. Can you imagine how mortifying it was to tell them I had so wildly misjudged you? That the girl I said was pure had corrupted her body by coupling with a sewer worker, even while betrothed to their son? That the girl I said was loyal beyond measure had lied to me and to them?"

"I was with Theo before my engagement to Paullus, Priestess!" Petronia looked at Theo, her stomach sinking at the sight of his brokenness. "He is not to blame, Priestess, not for anything. And I broke it off with him as soon as—"

"I have given years of my life to the chaste service of the goddess, Petronia. And you could not give mere months?" Amata had barely spoken the words when she privately rethought them. She had not been quite as chaste as that.

"It was unforgiveable, Priestess. I meant no disrespect to you or to Mother Vesta, I swear it!"

The high priestess scoffed. Realizing she was still holding the soiled gag, she let it drop to the floor. "I am the Vestalis Maxima of Rome. I have taken a vow to reform the Vestal order in this city and to raise it above any other priesthood. And yet, within days of taking my sacred office, I learn the senior sacerdos has denigrated not just herself, but also the temple. You are a second Tarpeia! But I will not let you bring shame and scandal upon the order as she did."

"That is the last thing I want to do, Priestess!" cried Petronia. "The goddess has been good to me, and you have been like a—" she stopped in mid-sentence as she saw Proculus unsheathe his dagger and press the blade against Theo's neck. The young man squeezed his eyes closed and moaned. "Wait!" shouted Petronia. "Don't kill him, I beg you!"

"You can save him," said Amata. She moved closer to Petronia and used the edge of her shawl to wipe the tears from the bound woman's eyes. "It is within your power to save his life, and your own. All you have to do is speak a few words that we put in your mouth."

CHAPTER XXVI

T he prevailing mood among the senators in the Curia was one of satisfaction. The treasury crime had been solved, and those responsible for it were dead. Sure, there were some vestiges of trepidation—after all, they had witnessed one of their own strangled to death only steps away from where they now convened—but it had been his own doing. His own undoing.

Nonetheless, there were disconcerting rumors that more senatorial drama was to come, rumors that grew into certainty as the Pontifex Maximus Marcius passed through the columned portico of the Curia to enter the assembly space with two women: the Vestalis Maxima Amata, and the senior Vestal sacerdos, Lady Petronia. All three both bowed to the seated king and stood by the altar in the center of the temple. Marcius drizzled a libation of oil into the sacred flames as the elderly senator Oppius invited him to speak before the house.

"Esteemed senators," said Marcius, addressing the entire body, "by the authority of royal decree, and with the assent of the holy collegium and your own majority vote, Rome's religious institutions, practices, and laws have all recently seen great reform.

Perhaps no institution has seen greater reform than the Vestal
order, first under the gentle guidance of Priestess Amata, and
now under her official command as Vestalis Maxima of Rome."
He paused as a lively round of approving cheers rose and fell.
"Esteemed senators, both myself and High Priestess Amata agree
that any violation of our new religious laws must be dealt with
swiftly and severely. We must show unyielding will and set an
example for those who would undermine the great work we have
done. The *pax deorum*, that peaceful pact we have forged with
the gods of Rome, must be upheld at all costs. To dishonor the
gods, to break religious law, is tantamount to treason, for such
actions threaten the security of Rome itself."

"We are all in agreement on that, Pontifex," said Senator Claudius, "but why are there women in the Curia?"

"Colleagues and fellow citizens," said Marcius, speaking to the
assembly rather than just Claudius. "The burden of upholding
the pax deorum falls upon us as the holy men and the wise men
of Rome." He motioned to the women at his side. "Yet under our
new laws, it is permissible for a Vestal sacerdos to give testimony
before the Senate. The venerable nature of that appointment war-
rants such privilege. Accordingly, the sacerdos Petronia will now
speak on a matter of great importance."

The Curia fell silent as Petronia looked at the faces around
her. The faces of old men. Judgmental old men. She knew many
of them. Some had flirted with her at festivals, after sacrifices, or
in the quiet corners of temples, while others had simply let their
eyes move over her while she performed the sacred rites. The
idea that she would have to confess her sin to such hypocrites...an
image of Theo's broken face and body flashed through her mind.
His life, and her own, depended on what she did here today. She
glanced at Amata but the high priestess's face was stone, so Petronia swallowed her indignation, licked her dry lips and spoke.

"Honored fathers of Rome," she began, "I stand before you
with shame in my heart, for I have dishonored my station as a
sacerdos. I have not served the goddess as a virginal maiden, but

have coupled with men during my tenure." She held up her palms, as she had been told to do. "I have nourished the sacred fire with impure hands, and for that I beg for your forgiveness." She laced her fingers together and raised her head. "But sirs, I did not commit these sins against Rome alone. My first conspirator is not known to you. He is a mere sewer worker, and I confess that my feelings for him were true." She ignored the grumbles of disapproval. "Honored fathers, he was not the only one, and I am compelled to tell you everything. I am a poor woman, with only a borrowed slave in my service. Shortly after a sacrifice to Ceres, I was approached by Senators Carteius and Antonius—"

A low clamor of surprised utterances interrupted her. The senators in attendance all looked at the spots where the two aforementioned senators usually sat, suddenly noting their absence. Petronia looked to Amata.

"Keep talking," mouthed the high priestess.

"Senators Carteius and Antonius approached me," Petronia began again, "and knowing my impoverished state, offered me silver in exchange for...in exchange for my favors." The clamor rose. "Sirs, I did not initiate this sacrilege, but I was in no position to oppose either, such was my poverty."

Senator Occius stood. "Poverty? Rome was feeding you, girl! Rome was sheltering you. What more did you need?"

"Wait," said Senator Claudius. He stood as well, but addressed Marcius. "Senators Carteius and Antonius have been distinguished members of this council for years. Where is the proof of their wrongdoing? If this girl is so poor, perhaps she is receiving payment for slandering them here today."

"From who?" asked another senator.

"I don't know," replied Claudius. "Senators Carteius and Antonius have their enemies and debtors, as many of us do. Perhaps they have—"

Marcius interrupted him. "The proof of their wrongdoing is beyond doubt. General Proculus and Commander Statius have interviewed the guards stationed at the gate, as well as those posted along the road to the Viminal. As some of you know, Senator Carteius has a villa on the Viminal. The sewer worker in question also has a home there. These guards have confirmed our suspicions. Lady Petronia often departed for the Viminal shortly after her colluders. There is also the testimony of a Lady Helena, a friend of Lady Petronia. She told the commander that the sacerdos visited often, though only for very brief periods of time. It was the commander's finding that Lady Petronia was using this friendship as an excuse to visit her colluders."

Senator Claudius chewed his lip, considering this. "Where are Senators Carteius and Antonius now? When will we hear testimony from them?"

Marcius gave a signal to a priest standing by the entrance to the temple. The priest in turn relayed a hushed instruction to someone else, and General Proculus strode into the Curia.

"With the permission of the Senate, General Proculus will speak," said Marcius.

"You are permitted, General," said Oppius. "Tell us what you know of this."

"Senators Carteius and Antonius are in custody," he said. "They learned of the accusations against them yesterday and immediately fled Rome. Luckily, my men were able to apprehend them just south of the city. They have been interrogated and have confessed to their crimes."

"Crimes?" Senator Rasinius, one of the men who had unsuccessfully run in the regal election, took to his feet. "All of this is scandalous to be sure," he said in a droll voice, "but criminal? Hardly."

"It is criminal now," said King Numa. It was the first he had spoken since the assembly had begun, and the gravity in his voice made those senators who were on their feet obediently take their seats. It was the king's turn to stand, which he did. "Vesta is Rome's protector. An offense against her puts all of Rome at risk." As the senators watched, captivated, he moved from his seat toward the central altar and poured a libation into the flames. He turned back to the assembly. "What is Rome?" he asked, spearing the question toward every man present. "Is it the tyrant of Latium? Are you content with that? Because I am not. When Father Quirinus ascended to the heavens, he did so with these words— 'Tell my people that their destiny is to conquer the whole world with warfare and piety, and to thus be the Caput Mundi, the head of the world!'" He clenched his fists. "Do you think we can achieve that destiny when we openly mock the gods? When I came to Rome, this city was only respected and feared for one thing—its merciless capacity for war. But if we are to fulfill the founder's vision, Rome must be respected and feared for its merciless devotion to the gods. If our city is to be the head of the world, the city of the eternal gods"—he shook a clenched fist at the assembly—"then we'd better bloody start acting like it!"

A shout of "Hear hear!" went up.

"Rome makes its own laws and its own punishments," Numa declared, as more shouts of assent began to call out. He could feel Rome's patriotism stirring in the Senate: this was his time to sew it into the city's fabric, and to bind that patriotism with an implacable piety that would elevate Rome above every other city, every other kingdom. If he did not, men like Sextus would always feel emboldened to ridicule. He stepped menacingly toward Petronia. "It is our piety, and our punishments for impiety, that will safeguard Rome and show the world who we are!"

Petronia shrunk back from the king. As the calls for justice rang out around her with increasing fervency, she turned to Amata.

"High Priestess," she whispered, "I did what you said."

"You did well, Petronia," Amata replied.

Numa motioned for calm. "The sacerdos Petronia is hereby placed under the authority of the Pontifex Maximus and the Vestalis Maxima," he announced. "You will see to it, General Proculus."

"As you wish, Highness." The general bowed to the king and led Amata and Petronia out of the Curia.

As Petronia passed through the columns of the portico, she noticed a sacrificial bull calf draped over the surface of a stone altar. Blood dripped from its nose and mouth. A grim sense of doom crept up her spine...such a helpless creature, left to the knives of priests and senators...she turned away, but the sense of doom only surged as she spotted a frantic Aule running toward her.

"Petronia!" he exclaimed, "you foolish girl! What did you tell them?"

She reached out to him—how desperately she needed the comfort of a friend—but Proculus forcibly injected himself between the two of them. "This is none of your concern, Sacerdos," he said. Unbelievably, Aule raised a hand to strike the general, but Proculus effortlessly gripped the elderly man's arm and held it steady. "Settle down, old friend."

The augur glared at the high priestess. "She is a child, Amata," he uttered, "just as you once were. You have thrown her to the wolves."

Amata turned away from him. She followed Proculus and his prisoner away from the Comitium, leaving the aggrieved augur behind. Petronia was no child. As for the rest—well, she couldn't really deny the rest.

CHAPTER XXVII

The morning seemed unusually quiet to Amata as she neared the Temple of Vesta. The sky was awash with an orange glow and the sun was pleasantly warm, but unlike most mornings, only a few birds darted overhead, and those were mostly mute. It was as though even the sparrows could sense that some kind of change was coming and had thus flown beyond the city walls to look for their breakfast seeds.

Amata opened the door and entered the warmth of the sanctum. The sacred fire burned robustly within the bronze bowl on the stone altar, and thin clouds of smoke rose up to escape through the oculus. Loud snaps and cracks echoed off the encircling wall as fiery tongues licked dry wood, nourishing the spirit of the goddess and sending bursts of dazzling red embers into the air with a series of emphatic pops. Vesta wanted to be heard this morning, and her high priestess would make sure that she was.

Nine sacerdotes stood with their backs against the circular wall, heads down, hands folded demurely in front of them. They were still shaken by the alarming events of the past few days. First, there was Commander Statius's midnight intrusion into their home and the shocking arrest of Petronia. Then there was the mass execution on the tribune. And only yesterday, there was the urgent sitting of the Senate and the news that Petronia and three men had been charged with religious offences and were currently being held in the Campus Martius. There was no word of when they would be released or what their punishment might be.

The high priestess moved to the fire and retrieved a simpulum from the altar. She poured a libation of oil into the vocal flames. "*Vesta Mater, nos audi.*" Stepping away from the sacred hearth, she put her hands behind her back and leaned against the wall, speaking to the sacerdotes. "Had I been my father's only child," she began, "and had he not been overthrown by Romulus, I would have inherited the crown. In Alba Longa, and in some other kingdoms in Latium, there is precedent for a king to name his daughter the crown princess if he has no son. Had circumstances been different, I might have been the queen of Alba Longa." Her expression grew pensive. "And yet had I married, my husband would have become king and I would have been reduced to his consort. Regardless of whether the man I married was a foreign prince, or whether he had no greatness in his bloodline whatsoever, I would have been expected to defer to his authority. He would make the law. He would control the temples and the army. The people of Alba Longa and the rulers of other cities would bow to him before me. Do you know why that is?"

The newest sacerdos, Gegania, broke the tense silence. "Because men are stronger," she said, "and more capable to rule."

"The queens of Egypt and Phoenicia, and of the Amazons, prove otherwise," said Amata. "It is not a matter of capability. It is a matter of perception. Had I as Queen Amata married a man, I would have been perceived as less than my husband, but also less than I was before I married him. I would have been reduced from monarch to mundane. I would have been profaned. There is only one way that I could have remained powerful and venerated by my subjects—by remaining a virgin queen. That is why, from this day forward, our sacerdotes will be called the Vestal

Virgins of Rome." She moved to stand before the row of young women. "The order is changing, but none of you will be compelled to change with it. You are free to leave." She leveled her gaze at a group of four sacerdotes, those she had found to be particularly lax in their duties. "You can go now."

It was more an order than an offer, and the four women slunk out of the temple. That left five—Lollia, Claudia, Aemelia, Elissa and Gegania.

Amata looked into the fire. "The priests say that both Apollo and Neptune wanted to marry Vesta. The goddess refused, wishing to remain the virgin of the hearthfire instead, such is the dignity of that status. That is why the Vestal Virgins will be held in the highest of esteem, and their order will be one of the most important and influential in the religious collegium. Vestal priestesses will be subordinate to no one but the Pontifex Maximus. They will lead privileged lives and will be the most respected women in all of Latium. But like any position of reverence, theirs will demand a certain amount of sacrifice. If it did not, the people would not revere it, would they? People never exalt the ordinary."

"What kind of sacrifice, High Priestess?" asked Aemelia.

"Time," replied Amata. "Years. Thirty of them."

Lollia inhaled sharply. "Thirty years? Priestess, I will be over fifty years old, how will—"

Amata smiled. "Not thirty years for any of you," she said. "From now on, novice Vestals will join the order as young girls, just as I did. After thirty years of pure service to the goddess, they will be free to leave the order if they choose. As for any of you who choose to stay and help me train the novices in the new ways, you will be expected to stay for ten years."

"Ten years..." Claudia thought aloud. "I will be thirty-two years old."

"And you will be a rich thirty two," said Amata, "since Vestals will be handsomely rewarded for their sacrifice. Gold, property, slaves. Vestals will also be independent, free to manage their own

wealth, and especially free of their father's legal control. A priestess who leaves the order will still be young enough to marry and
even have children, but it will be up to her whether she does or
not. If she does, she will choose her own husband." Amata moved
back to the fire and placed a piece of wood in the flames. "For
too long, women like Petronia have treated the goddess's sacred
house like a brothel. They have served their time with one hand
in the fire and the other trying to grab on to a husband. I understand why. A woman needs a husband to survive. Yet that
behavior has been an insult to Vesta. It has been an insult to you,
too. The new Vestal order offers freedom. The freedom that
comes with wealth and status. If you stay with the order after
your prescribed years of service, you will enjoy a life of comfort
and dignity as long as you are alive. If you leave, you will go on
to have a life of choice." She took an iron stoker and absently
stirred the ash at the bottom of the fire. "Believe me, I have come
to know how important choice is, and I vow that every Vestal
who comes after me will have it."

"After thirty years," said Elissa.

Amata set down the stoker. "Think about it," she said. "Go talk
to people on the street and in the fields. Find the oldest woman
you can, and ask her how much choice she has truly had in her
life. Then come back to me with your answers."

She smiled warmly at the sacerdotes and exited the temple,
leaving them to tend the unusually loud flames of the sacred fire
and debate their futures.

Gegania was the first to accept a ten-year tenure of service at the
temple, thus committing a decade of her life to training the novice Vestal Virgins of the new order. The same day she accepted,
King Numa made her father a senator of Rome. It was an appointment the man had been fruitlessly working toward for
years, although he had been repeatedly refused as he did not own

sufficient wealth or land. The king quickly rectified that formality by granting him legal ownership of all the lands and assets formerly owned by the late Senator Calvisius.

Aemelia was the next to accept. Later that same day, her father was given stewardship of a profitable stone quarry outside the city. Her cousin, who was in custody for drunkenly murdering a neighbor's most-prized slave, was freed. The city of Rome generously compensated the neighbor for the loss of property, and the matter was put to rest.

Soon after, Claudia and Elissa accepted. By the end of the day, both of their families had received special favors that made them richer and more influential. The pattern became clear as spring water, and soon every noble family who had formerly thought their daughter a burden now wondered whether she, not the son, might be the more profitable offspring. Soon, Amata and Marcius were inundated with requests from fathers wishing to advance their young daughters as novice Vestal Virgins.

Of course, a girl first had to meet the basic criteria. She had to be born of living parents, preferably wealthy nobles, but girls with notable lineage—such as a Gegania's Trojan heritage—were also candidates. She had to be free of any birth defects. Perhaps most importantly, she had to demonstrate a high level of intelligence: Vestal Virgins would be taught to read and write, and would be expected to perform vital religious rituals with diligence. They would also be trained in diplomacy, as their elevated positions made them representatives of Rome. These girls would grow into women who would mix and mingle with dignitaries—friend and foe alike—and who would act not just on behalf of the religious college, but also on behalf of the Senate, the Roman people, and the king himself.

For five full days, the Vestalis Maxima and the Pontifex Maximus interviewed girls and their families in the Regia. At the end of each day, they met with King Numa to discuss the strengths of each candidate. Although it was decided that, in the future, a lottery system would be implemented to select novices from a pool of qualified candidates, Numa wished to take special care with this first group. While he took Amata and Marcius's recommendations under advisement, he insisted on meeting each girl personally and choosing the final novices himself.

The first girl he chose was Canuleia, the ten-year-old granddaughter of Senator Canuleius. She was on the older end of what Amata felt comfortable with, but she was fiercely intelligent and practical minded, with an acumen for religious matters that seemed beyond her years. She struck Amata as the kind of girl who would wrestle a sacrificial bull to the ground if it gave her any trouble. She also seemed to understand the gravity of the undertaking, and was eager to accept it.

The second girl was Tullia, the daughter of Hostus Hostilius. Younger and sweet faced, she had a softness that Amata knew would endear her to the people of Rome. She also seemed to have Numa wrapped around her finger, and the high priestess had to twice remind the king to not show favorites.

Nine more regal appointments followed, bringing the number of novices to eleven. Yet there was one more interview to conduct: the candidate was Veneneia, the daughter of Gaius Julius and the granddaughter of Valia and Proculus. Rather than holding this interview at the Regia, Valia had invited Amata and Marcius to their home for supper. Amata had asked the Vestal Gegania to join them at the last minute. They had no sooner arrived than Amata privately congratulated herself for following her instincts. Like everyone else who had beheld Priestess Gegania in recent days, Veneneia seemed dazzled by her.

At nineteen years old, Gegania had absorbed Amata's teachings and was the model Vestal Virgin, effortlessly incorporating elements of the old Vestales Albanae with the new order of *Virgines Vestales Romae*. Like all of the Vestals, and following Amata's instructions, she wore an elegant snow-white *stola*. Beneath her white veil and the red and white woolen ribbons of a consecrated priestess—the colors symbolized a Vestal's dedication to the sacred fire and her own purity—Gegania wore her hair in the traditional braided style of the virginal bride-to-be, a style that spoke to her unique status as both daughter and bride of Rome. The vibrancy with which she carried herself and represented the order, and the example she set for the other priestesses, was in itself elevating the prestige of the Vestals. Amata could sense the young woman's natural affinity for the role and especially the reverence she inspired in others. It was humbling on a personal level—Amata was used to receiving deference alone—but she made her peace with it and used Priestess Gegania's popularity to increase the popularity of the order.

Veneneia's mother, Attia, sat beside her young daughter and spoke to Amata. "Will she live in the house of the sacerdotes?"

"Yes," said Amata. "The king is expanding the house even more, so it will be very comfortable. We can appoint her a body slave, or you can send someone from your household, someone she is already comfortable with."

"Can we visit her whenever we want?"

"We will have regular visiting days for family," said Amata, "and many special functions, but it is important that the girls see the House of the Vestals as their home and their fellow priestesses as family. They need to grow up together as sisters. That is the only way they will learn to work together and protect one another."

Attia was about to ask what the high priestess meant by "protect one another" when Proculus sat down heavily beside her, causing the couch's cushion to cave toward him. Attia straightened herself, ignored the wine on her father-in-law's breath, and stroked her daughter's hair. "Six years old," she said. "Why so young?"

"It is for her own benefit," said Amata. "It ensures her focus is on her duties and not..."

She was thinking of how to tactfully express the reasoning when Marcius spoke. What he lacked in tactfulness, he made up for in straightforwardness.

"Children who are indoctrinated into religious teachings at an early age are more devout," he said. "They are less likely to succumb to sexual temptation and more likely to maintain their vows. And as the high priestess has said, a young age of induction allows a Vestal to leave the order while she is still young enough to enjoy the wealth and connections she has spent three decades cultivating."

"Why thirty years?" asked Attia. "Why so long?"

"Other religious postings are for life," Marcius replied. "Even our soldiers are now expected to serve for decades. But mostly, it's a matter of constancy. Vesta's fire is eternal. It's a constant in the lives of Romans, and it's important that the Vestal priestesses are a constant in their lives, too. The people will find comfort in that. Priestesses will also be expected to form their own friendships and alliances—these will be for Rome's benefit and their own—so they must be enduring."

Proculus reached for a baked bird wing and spoke while he ate. "Thirty years," he looked at Amata as he chewed. "That's how many cities comprise the confederation in Latium. It's also the number of citizen units Romulus first divided Rome into."

"That is correct, sir," offered Priestess Gegania. "It is an auspicious number. It is also the number of piglets birthed by the white sow who guided Aeneas to Lavinium, and that foretold the founding of Alba Longa." She smiled warmly at Veneneia. "See? We are already sisters in history, for my ancestors were with yours in Troy."

Veneneia smiled back, shyly at first, then more boldly. "I like your veil."

"Thank you, sister."

"What will I do at the temple?" Veneneia asked.

"You will spend a long time—ten years!—being taught by senior priestesses like me," Gegania answered enthusiastically. "For the next ten, you will care for the sacred fire and help perform all the public rituals and sacrifices in Rome. You will be very important, and everyone will look up to you. For the last ten years, you will be like me, and you will teach little girls like you"—she poked Veneneia in the stomach, and the girl laughed—"how to do what you have learned to do."

The girl grinned and looked at her parents.

"Gaius," said Amata. "Attia. We have more candidates than we have room for right now. If you are not comfortable with this..."

"I'm not concerned about her care," said Gaius. "I trust you, Priestess. But I have to wonder whether this is best for the Julii. I've heard about all the favors flying out of the Regia after a priestess is appointed, but my father is a general and a senator in Rome, and my kinsman is the king of Alba Longa. Attia and I have even thought about moving there. So you see, my family already has influence in Latium. Veneneia may better serve our family through marriage."

Proculus looked askance at his son. "Don't be naïve, Gaius. A lot can happen in thirty years. With a daughter in the Vestal order, the Julii will always have a position of prestige in Rome. We'll always have a direct connection to the king and preferential treatment in the Senate. And even if it weren't the smart thing to do, which it is, our Trojan ancestry requires us to honor the sacred hearthfire."

Something in Proculus's voice—the solemnity, the unexpected respect for their shared lineage—made Amata look to him. She had not expected Proculus to support her, nor to show any concern for the new Vestal order. He noticed her stare, but avoided it and bit into the last of the meat on the bird wing.

Valia looked affectionately at her granddaughter, and then at Attia. "It may be a better life for her than marriage."

Proculus turned too quickly to his wife, an indignant look on his face. An awkward silence hung in the air. Proculus broke it by tossing the remnants of the bird wing onto the table and marching out of the room. In the even more awkward silence that followed, Amata stood. To the surprise of all, she went after Proculus, following him behind a heavy curtain into a kitchen space.

She shook her head in frustration. "These drunken, infantile outbursts," she whispered, "for the sake of Rome, they need to stop. You are the king's top general. We are close to our vengeance. And yet you still—"

"It happened so fast."

"What did?"

"Amatus." He let the name—the one they never spoke, but was always between them—linger in its own space for a few moments. He reached for a jug of wine on a table, filled his cup and drank. "Romulus wouldn't have killed him. I made sure he knew that Amatus and I were friends. I told him that we grew up together, that he was my closest friend...and he was." He turned away so Amata could not see, and wiped away a tear. "It was Remus—that's what I wasn't ready for. His impulsiveness. But Amata..." he paused, and swallowed the rest of the wine in his cup before again facing her. "I avenged Amatus."

Amata felt her breathing change with the admission. "How?" she whispered.

He sniggered. "All that fancy tutelage from Nikandros, and you've never figured it out." He poured another cup of wine.

"Put it down!" Amata said in a hushed shout. "Tell me!"

He set the wine cup on the table, speaking as he stared into the red liquid. "Back when the *ignis mirabilis* still burned in the Forum. I bribed a man to extinguish it. He was a kinsman of a soldier named Luperco, who at the time was Remus's right-hand man. I knew it would look like Remus ordered the sabotage."

"You"—Amata shook her head—"you extinguished the goddess's divine flame?"

"I did more than that," said Proculus, his voice somewhere between defensive and proud. "I got Remus's head on a spike," he looked back at her, "and I made sure the person who put it there was someone he cared about. I wanted him to feel the same betrayal that Amatus did." The defensiveness in his voice grew as he anticipated her thoughts. "And no, I never regretted it. Romulus was looking for an excuse to do it, so I gave him one."

Proculus waited for her to speak. He waited for the judgment, the moralizing.

"Good," she said simply.

She turned and left, returning to the gathering with Proculus following close behind. As she sat back down on her couch, Proculus sat next to Valia. Her eyes were apologetic, and he smiled at her, also apologizing.

Yet the drama was not over. Conversation had not yet begun again when a slave hurried into the room and bowed before Proculus.

"Domine, there is a woman here. She says she is the queen of Alba Longa," he said. "I would not believe it, sir, but there are soldiers with her."

Proculus rose and marched through his house, his guests jumping to their feet to follow.

They all arrived at the open door to find Queen Penelope there. An Alban soldier had his arm around her waist to support her. A number of Roman soldiers stood close by, their eyes locked on the foreign soldier. The queen was conscious and lucid, but clearly traumatized. She looked as though she had weathered a violent storm—battered, exhausted, and emotional. Amata rushed to her and put her hands on either side of her face.

"Penelope! Gods, what has happened?"

Penelope wrapped her arms around Amata and began to weep. "I told him it would happen," she cried. "Amata, they broke through the guards, through the gates...they stormed our home! They hanged him in our dining room!"

Proculus pulled the two women apart and forced Penelope to face him. "Are you saying they hanged Sextus? Who did it?"

"They stabbed him first!" Penelope shouted, her voice panic-stricken. "Then they hanged him!" She drew in a faltering breath. "Lucius Cluilius proclaimed himself King of Alba Longa. His son, Gaius, was about to kill me as well, but my guards fought him off and I managed to run away and hide. But they have ordered my death." She pushed past Proculus, back to Amata. "You must ask King Numa to protect me. I ask Rome for sanctuary."

"Of course," said Amata. "Penelope, try to calm down. You are safe now."

The high priestess led the fallen queen to the nearest couch to sit down. The women surrounded her to offer what comfort they could, while Proculus took Gaius aside. The astonishing news that their kinsman had been deposed as king had quickly sobered his mind and body.

"You know what this means, don't you, son?" he asked Gaius. "It isn't just the Silvii who are finished in Alba Longa. Now, the Julii are finished there, too."

Both father and son looked at little Veneneia as she cautiously slipped into the room, her eyes growing wide with confusion and concern. The Vestal Gegania took her by the hand and led her outside, presumably away from the commotion.

Don't be naïve, Gaius. A lot can happen in thirty years.

It hadn't taken thirty years. It had barely taken thirty drops of a water clock.

"She will join the Vestal order," said Gaius. He pictured Sextus hanging by the neck from a beam in his dining room. "You are right, Father. The future of the Julii is in Rome."

CHAPTER XXVIII

In the founding years of Rome, when sacerdotes of Vesta were among the only women in the city, Romulus had assigned guards to each one. After the death of the traitor Tarpeia, it was only the rare sacerdos—perhaps a wealthy or noble one—who was appointed a guard or two. There were more women in the city by that time, so there was less risk. But mostly, the laxity was born of apathy. The early work that Priestess Rhea Silvia had done to dignify the keeping of the *ignis mirabilis* in her son's city had been lost.

High Priestess Amata Silvia had changed all of that. On the authority of King Numa and the Senate, under the oversight of the Pontifex Maximus Marcius, and with the full support of the religious college of Rome, she had recently taken steps to end decades of disesteem by creating the official Roman order of Vestal Virgins. These stately and sacrosanct priestesses were Rome's new guardians, and they would tend the city's hearthfire with a type of untouchable allure and sacred secrecy that immediately commanded reverence.

Word of this new order was spreading throughout and beyond Rome. The chaste, white-veiled women were as enigmatic

as the holy fire that burned within the sanctum of the Temple of
Vesta, a sanctum that no man other than the Pontifex Maximus
could enter, and he only with the permission of a Vestal Virgin.
The women who tended to the sacred flame were deemed inviolate—they could not be touched without their consent, on pain
of death for the transgressor. A pair of stern-faced guards now
attended each priestess wherever she went, their hands on the
hilts of their daggers, unhesitatingly ready to kill any person who
threatened their charge.

Rumors were spreading, too, reports and stories that only amplified the public's fascination with this new portentous order of
priestesses. Some were based in truth, while others were awe-inspired fiction.

*The Vestals can grant sanctuary—I heard that Queen Penelope
of Alba Longa begged the Vestalis Maxima for refuge!*

*I heard that Priestess Gegania prayed to Vesta, and Senator
Livius's runaway slaves were fixed to the earth and captured!*

*They can predict the future...they know how to read the flames
and ash like oracles!*

Yet what truly inspired reverent awe for the order, as Amata
had known it would, was the new vow of chastity.

*They will take a thirty-year vow of chastity! Can you imagine
such sacrifice? Vesta will safeguard our city forever because of it!*

Before, a woman who saw a sacerdos on the street would pay
her no heed, and a man might even wink at her. Now, at the sight
of a Vestal Virgin, women and men alike stepped back and lowered themselves to their knees, heads bowed and palms held up
in hopes of receiving a blessing from one of the immaculate
priestesses of their powerful protector goddess.

All of this was why the crowd currently gathered in the Forum
was, at the moment, more focused on the Vestals who stood
upon the great tribune—High Priestess Amata and the priestesses Gegania and Aemelia—than on the king. They were also
focused on the twelve young girls who had been chosen to enter
the order as novices: they were dressed in white tunicas, long hair

tidily pinned up into buns, and they stood on the grand platform with more poise than one would expect from girls so young. Although they would not be officially initiated into the order for another few days, their training had already begun.

Of the five women who Amata had invited to stay on as senior priestesses and help train this first group of young novices, only Lollia had declined. That was all right with Amata. Lollia had known of Petronia's sacrilege, and while she had not enabled it, she had not reported it, either. If she had to lose one, Lollia should be the one to go. The other two who had stayed on, Claudia and Elissa, were currently on watch in the temple. That too was all right. They would soon learn today's lesson: Rome and the new order of Vestal Virgins would not tolerate sacrilege. Only the purest hands could nourish Vesta's sacred fire in the temple. The goddess and the laws of Rome would have it no other way.

But the sacerdos Petronia had broken those laws. Soon after being dragged out of the House of the Vestals in the middle of the night by Commander Statius, the Pontifex Maximus had found her guilty of coupling with at least three men during her tenure. These men—the noble senators Carteius and Antonius, as well as a lowly sewer worker named Theo—were also in custody.

How would she be reprimanded? How would the men be admonished? The people amassed in the Forum were there to find out those answers. Sure, they had just recently witnessed the high drama of a mass execution, but this public scolding was the result of illicit relations. And wasn't that much more interesting than mere thievery?

Speculation was rampant.

"The senators will be forced to forfeit a quarter of their lands to Rome!" said a vendor.

"They deserve it, those dirty old men!" his wife replied.

"Lady Petronia will be sent to the brothels!" someone else predicted.

"No, she won't," sneered his companion. "They'll just send her packing."

No one bothered to speculate on how the sewer worker would be disciplined. He wasn't important enough. Anyway, he already worked in shit—wasn't that punishment enough?

A horn blew, and those citizens who were prominent enough to have a seat before or alongside the tribune took to it. That included most of the city's priesthood, magistrates, senators and top soldiers, as well as Rome's old guard and their wives. Senator Gellius and Safinia were also there, along with their son Paullus, who had obvious reason to hope the penalty leveled against the three men would be enough to help him recoup some of his dignity.

King Numa ascended the tribune. He wore a white toga with a wide purple stripe on its border. On his head sat a gold crown of oak leaves, and on his arm was the *divinum ancile*. As he strode to position himself in the center of the speaker's platform to address his subjects, it occurred to him that this was his first time on the tribune since the day he had been named king. The day he had flung a firebowl into the riotous crowd to get their attention. He had thrown his crown and cloak into the mob, too. How naïve that performance seemed to him now.

"Friends and citizens," he said, "behold the shield of Romulus, thrown down from the heavens as a message, a sign, that we must defend our peaceful pact with the gods against all who threaten it! Make no mistake, citizens—a willful violation of the pax deorum is treason. Without the protection of our gods, our city walls would be breached in a day. Without the guardianship of Mother Vesta, who resides in the sacred fire in the temple and in the hearthfire of every home, our children would not be destined to rule the world, but rather to toil as the slaves of those who would rule us!" He passed the shield to a soldier, and then held out his arms. "In accordance with the new laws of Rome, the Pontifex Maximus has ruled that the sacerdos Petronia is guilty of the crime of *incestum*. She has polluted her body by coupling with men during her service to the purest of fires. Three Roman citizens—Carteius, Antonius and Theo—have been found guilty of corrupting her. All four of these criminals are traitors to Rome!"

The crowd had been so riveted by Numa's atypically severe speech that they didn't notice the rattling of the approaching horse-drawn prison cart until the vehicle was nearly beside the tribune. Statius and three of his burliest men hauled out the three male prisoners, and a current of disbelieving gasps swept through the crowd at their condition. The faces of both senators and the sewer worker were caked in red, as were their tunicas, neck to hem, the bloody aftermath of their tongues being sliced off.

The soldiers dragged the prisoners to three wooden scourging poles that stood in front of the tribune. While each soldier secured his man to a pole, each criminal's back to the crowd, Numa spoke again.

"In consultation with the high priests of Jupiter, Mars, Quirinus and Vesta, these men will be executed for their crimes."

The mood in the Forum changed palpably. The attitude of reserved amusement that many people had arrived with—it would be satisfying to see the lofty senators knocked down a notch or two—disappeared. Even critics of Carteius and Antonius frowned in unnerved surprise. Yes, their behavior was sacrilegious. Yes, it threatened the pax deorum. But the two senators were not the worst of the bunch, and they had actually done a lot of good for Rome over the years. As for the young sewer worker who was currently being tethered to a pole, voiceless and mutilated, even the most unforgiving among them felt a twinge of uncertainty. He hadn't killed anyone, and they all knew what Petronia looked like...the boy was only human.

The king glanced an order at Proculus, who was standing at attention on the tribune. The general jogged off the platform and unsheathed his dagger as he marched up to Carteius, whose wrists were secured, high over his head, to the scourging pole. Proculus thrust the point of his dagger into the fabric of the senator's tunica, cutting it off him in shreds, exposing his nakedness and slashing carelessly enough to carve into flesh. Carteius sputtered out a sob and pressed his genitals into the pole, doing what he could to preserve his dignity, but knowing his entire backside was helplessly exposed to the gawking crowd.

Proculus placed his mouth close to the man's ear. "Do you see that king on the tribune, Carteius? That is the not the king who condemns you today." He took a step back, spat on the man's naked body, and moved to Antonius. Lacerating that man's tunica and flesh with even less care, he exposed the senator's nakedness and whispered into his ear. "If I see you in Hades, Antonius," he said, "I'll do this all over again."

Finally, he moved to Theo. He sliced off the young man's tunica as if the action were an afterthought. Instead of instinctively moving to cover his genitals like the two older men, Theo only stood dumbly at his pole, staring up at the faces on the tribune. He blinked up at the king, and then met eyes with the Vestalis Maxima.

Amata's eyes shifted from the prisoner to the Vestals and novices who stood on the tribune with her. The two senior Vestals were doing a noble job of disguising their shock, but a couple of the novices looked as though they might start to cry. Amata tapped them on the shoulder and put her finger to her lips to shush them. They nodded and steeled themselves.

Standing several steps in front of the three scourging poles, hands on his hips, Proculus whistled and three soldiers, each of whom gripped a *flagrum*, took his position behind a prisoner. Proculus had thought about having execution slaves dispense this punishment, but none of them were skilled enough with a flagrum to get it right. The last thing he needed was the spectacle of a clumsy executioner lashing himself, his fellow executioners, or even spectators.

"*Agite!*" shouted the general, ordering the soldiers to begin.

This trio of soldiers had spent countless hours training to work as a team and it showed. They pulled back their arms in unison and snapped their flagrums forward, sending the biting tentacles forward at lightning speed to slice into the flesh of the men's bare backs and buttocks.

No doubt, the prisoners had thought about how much the scourging might hurt. No doubt, they had anticipated great pain. Nonetheless, they had underestimated it. Seconds after the snap of the lash, the two senators wailed—they wailed in a way that only tongueless men could wail, deep and guttural, writhing in pain against their poles. Only Theo remained mute, though his body went limp, overwhelmed by the paralyzing sting.

The soldiers coordinated another perfectly timed lash. Then another.

Soon, the three figures who hung from the scourging poles looked less like men and more like butchered slabs of fresh meat hanging from hooks in the market. Their backs and buttocks bore deep red gashes, from which streamed thick red flows of blood that moved like lava down their bodies, as if scorching what was left of their flesh.

After the twentieth lash, Proculus shouted for his men to stop. Carteius and Antonius were dipping in and out of consciousness, and the general was not about to take any chances. He wanted them fully awake for what would come next. He nodded an order to the soldiers and they each moved to one of the bloody prisoners and untied their hands. Theo and Carteius were in stupefied states and only stood swaying on their feet, but Antonius seemed to regain some of his wits. He looked up at the king on the tribune and emitted a tongueless plea for mercy. Proculus thought about knocking him on the side of the head to shut him up, but couldn't bring himself to do it. The sounds of the bastard's tortured vocalizations were just too satisfying.

"Move!" he commanded.

The crowd watched, transfixed by the cruelty and the suffering, as the soldiers took hold of the naked, blood-coated men and dragged them away from the tribune, toward the Capitoline. A collective murmur of subdued excitement moved through the gathering. They knew where the soldiers were taking them. After all, the king had said it himself—they were traitors to Rome.

Proculus followed behind as the soldiers hauled the men up

the east side of the Capitoline—they had to stop more than once to kick a fallen man to his feet again—and then across the hilltop to the plateau of the Tarpeian Rock. The spectators in the crowd jostled for position, for a good vantage point from which to see the final phase of the execution carried out. Their murmurs settled into expectant silence as they waited.

The sewer worker was thrown down first. It was an unremarkable fall, really. He didn't hit anything on the way down, he didn't scream, he didn't flail his limbs, and he didn't make much of a sound upon impact. Perhaps Senators Carteius and Antonius would be more spirited. Everyone waited. The common people, the merchants, the senators, the soldiers, the priests, the Vestals on the tribune and even the king—they all waited. They did not have to wait long.

An echoing, pleading cry of protest sounded in the air as the bodies of the two traitorous senators flew down from the top of the cliff. In an almost comical display of terror, the pair of condemned men clung to each other as they descended into freefall, but the force of the fall soon tore them apart. One of them struck the cliff's rocky face and sent a shower of rocks cascading down its slope. Their naked bodies plummeted through the insubstantial air, arms grasping at nothing and legs fruitlessly seeking footing. They landed with audible thuds at the base of the cliff, the spine-tingling sounds soon dissolving into the still, quiet air.

King Numa looked in the direction of the three bloodied corpses at the bottom of the Tarpeian Rock. He let the silence linger, then broke it with a sudden shout that brought the focus back to the tribune. Back to him. "Romans!" he said. "The men we have sent to Hades today, men who were weak in character, have taught us how to be strong! Their sins have taught us how to honor the gods!" He looked out over his subjects. "Every man here today, no matter how rich or poor, will remember the lesson these men have taught us with their lives. The Vestal Virgins are inviolate. They dedicate their youth to Rome. They toil tirelessly to keep the goddess's favor for your safety and the safety of your families. Disrespect them, and you disrespect every man, woman and child in Rome. Disrespect them, and you will soon find yourself the teacher and not the student."

The Capitoline Hill was unusually quiet. In light of the day's executions, the workers who melted, cut and noisily hammered precious metals in the mint portion of the Temple of Juno had been dismissed, as had most of the subordinate or novice priests. The citadel guards had been ordered to convey messages by foot instead of shouting them to each other across distances.

High Priestess Amata led her priestesses and novices up the slope of the Capitoline, continuing across the hilltop until they reached the stone altar that stood just outside the great Temple of Jupiter. A fire burned on top of the altar, but Amata did not have time to make an offering, for they had no sooner arrived than the Pontifex Maximus and the high priest of Jupiter emerged from the temple, each man holding one of Petronia's arms as they dragged her limp body along.

Petronia bore the evidence of a brutal lashing. White strips of her torn tunica lay over the red blood that coated her back and legs, reminding Amata of the red and white ribbons that lay under her own veil. Her hands were bound in front of her and she was gagged: when she saw Amata, she squeezed her eyes closed and dropped her head down in something between defeat and exhaustion. The Vestals Gegania and Aemelia looked away, and one of the novices whimpered.

The two priests dragged Petronia toward a man-sized wooden box that lay on the ground.

"Get in, girl," ordered the priest of Jupiter.

The shock of the command imbued her with sudden strength, and Petronia screamed from behind her gag, digging her bare feet into the ground and trying to twist away from the two men. It took them little effort to force her into the box. As the two of them held her down, a pair of soldiers dutifully placed a heavy wood lid over the box and nailed it shut. That done, they carried the box to a horse-drawn cart that stood several steps away. As the Vestals and novices watched, they carelessly threw it into the back.

Priestess Gegania whispered in Amata's ear. "High Priestess, should the girls really be seeing this?"

"We should all be seeing this," Amata replied, and Gegania nodded obediently.

Amata directed the priestesses and novices to a small caravan of horse-drawn carriages that awaited them, a driver ready in each one. The women and girls climbed in. As the priests rode away with the disgraced and crated sacerdos, they followed behind, traveling down the Capitoline and then riding to the northeast of the city.

"High Priestess, where are we going?" asked the young Canuleia.

"You will know when we get there," replied Amata.

The girl was not offended by the answer. "All right, High Priestess."

This one is a dutiful sort, thought Amata. *Numa was wise to select her first.*

Before long, the procession had traveled past the homes that lined the Quirinal Hill to arrive at a lonely field. There were no shrines—not even a modest roadside one—and no flowers, nothing but a scattering of trees here and there, and those looking as unhealthy and desolate as the land itself.

The somber convoy stopped near a disrupted patch of earth. As the Pontifex Marcius ordered the soldiers to carry the box toward it, Amata and the others stepped out of their carriages to follow, Amata carrying a basket that she had brought with her. The soldiers set the box down near a square plank of wood on the ground. The box swayed back and forth as Petronia struggled within, kicking the sides and emitting muted wails of panic.

The high priest of Jupiter beckoned the Vestals and novices to come closer. When they were gathered round, he bent down and lifted the plank of wood to reveal that it had been covering a deep hole, a black void, from which escaped a stale stench that was strong enough to make one of the girls cough.

The Pontifex Maximus stood before the priestesses and novices. "They call this place the *Campus Proditoris*," he said. "Traitor's field. This is where King Romulus buried the bones of the traitorous Vestal priestess Tarpeia. From this day forward, any Vestal Virgin who breaks her vow of chaste service to the goddess will be forced to descend into this pit and left to die."

Amata studied the girls. Some looked horrified, but others were more resolved. They had been told—warned—that the punishment for breaking the vow of chastity, the punishment they would witness Petronia suffer today, would be more severe than any of them could imagine.

Yet it was not an arbitrary punishment. Numa and Amata had considered various sanctions—from exile to a painless execution—but none seemed severe enough to fit the crime of incestum or to deter a particularly headstrong or impetuous Vestal from committing it. In the end, they had decided on capital punishment. As for exactly how to carry it out, Numa had asked Amata a simple question: *What is the worst death you can imagine?*

The answer had come easily to Amata: *Being entombed alive and left to die...like my father was.*

"You may think we are harsh to show you this," Amata said, and touched the top of little Veneneia's head, "but we do this because we care about you and your safety. You need to see for yourselves what will happen if you do not honor your vows to the goddess and to Rome. You are only girls and so you may think it will be easy to keep your vows, but one day you will be women, and it may not be so easy. Men will look at you and desire you, and you may be tempted." She blinked away a sudden mental image of her and Numa standing by the Spring of Juturna in the torchlight, and looked around at the bleak landscape. "Remember this evil field, girls. I pray this is the only time in your lives that you will ever see it."

The Pontifex Maximus and the high priest of Jupiter moved to the box that imprisoned Petronia and wrenched off the lid. Her legs flew up kicking, but they lifted her out with as little effort as they had put her in, and lugged her toward the open pit. Again, she dug her bare feet into the ground and resisted, her screeches growing louder as the ghastly realization settled upon her.

The priest of Jupiter bent down and reached into the pit, feeling around for the rickety ladder that descended into its depths. Finding it, he stood and unbound Petronia's wrists. Taking advantage of the sudden freedom, she quickly reached up and ripped off her gag, immediately looking to Amata.

"Priestess, I beg for mercy!"

"Climb down," said Marcius, "or we'll just have to push you down. That will only make it worse, won't it?"

Seeing no signs of sympathy in Amata or the priests, Petronia's eyes jumped to Gegania and Aemelia, her friends and the sacerdotes she had served with in the temple, but they too looked at her without emotion. Her eyes moved past them to survey the barren field in desperate hope of seeing someone. Amata knew who she was hoping to see—Aule. Her sole advocate. But Numa had ordered the augur to remain in his home, forbidding him from witnessing Petronia's lashing or live burial. He had even posted guards outside Aule's home to make sure he obeyed.

"No one is coming, Petronia," said Amata. "Take what dignity you have and descend with it. The gods of the underworld will respect you for it."

Petronia spun around and tried to bolt, but Marcius wrapped his arms around her waist and, in a display of unexpected strength, dangled her over the open pit. He let go and she fell downward, though managing in her panic to catch a rung of the old ladder at the last moment. She held on for her life.

"Help me! Someone help me!"

Marcius bent down and pried her fingers off the rung. Petronia fell again, this time all the way to the bottom. The Pontifex pulled up the ladder before she could grab it again.

Amata knelt at the edge of the pit and looked down. Far below, she could just make out the form of the wounded sacerdos struggling to stand. Amata's eyes adjusted to the darkness and, despite herself, she felt a pang of sympathy. Petronia stood but took a shuddering step backward as if retreating from something ghoulish that only she could see—was it the bones of Tarpeia?—and then looked up with wide eyes, eyes that were filled with a terrible awareness. They stared up at Amata, hungry for light and frantically trying to consume the last morsels of the living world above.

"Don't do it, Amata," said Petronia, just loud enough for the two of them to hear. "Don't leave me to die like this..."

Amata sensed her sympathy rise, but she tamped it with the bitter knowledge of just how close Petronia's wanton sacrilege had come to tearing down everything she and Numa had built for Vesta in Rome.

She and the king had revived the embers of what Romulus and Rhea Silvia had first envisioned for the sacred fire: the new temple, the House of the Vestals, the fine structures in the *area sacra Vestae*, and a respected and prestigious Vestal order to honor the goddess and represent Rome. But Petronia's behavior could have torn it all down with scandal. The last traces of Amata's sympathy morphed into spite. And yet, in that selfsame moment, she heard Nikandros's voice in her head: *We reserve the greatest hate for those who are most like us.*

The high priestess reached for the basket on the ground beside her. She lowered it into the darkness and let go. Petronia caught it in her arms.

Inside the basket were a loaf of bread, a jug of water, a vessel of oil for libation, and a small oil lamp lighted with a flame from the sacred hearth. Amata had not understood the purpose of giving these to someone so doomed, but the Pontifex Maximus had insisted. *Strictly speaking*, he had said, *it is a crime against the gods to kill a sacerdos.*

So they wouldn't kill Petronia. Not exactly. They would give her enough food and water to survive for a time. If the goddess wished for her sacerdos to live, she had the power to save her.

Marcius extended a hand to Amata and pulled her to her feet. The priest of Jupiter retrieved the square wood plank and dropped it over the hole with a dusty thud, covering the pit. Petronia did not scream—or if she did, they could not hear her—but somehow the silence was even more disturbing, so Amata led the priestesses and novices back to the carriages. They climbed in without speaking, while Amata turned back to look at the covered pit. She knew she had done the right thing...but still. Seeing her unease, Marcius approached.

"When Numa and I were younger men," he said, "we traveled to Eleusis in Greece."

"For the mysteries?" asked Amata.

He nodded. "They happen underground, you know. And while all who experience the Eleusinian Mysteries are sworn to secrecy, I can tell you that this"—he pointed to the pit—"is Petronia's opportunity for rebirth. That is why Numa insisted she be put into the ground instead of into a stone tomb, as you suggested. He is giving her a chance to be reborn, like a new seed taking root below the earth."

Amata considered this. For a passing moment, the Pontifex looked as though he might touch her, perhaps console her, but such gestures were inconsistent with his nature, so he merely nodded encouragingly and stepped into his carriage.

Following behind, Amata climbed into a separate carriage to sit with a group of novices and the Vestal Aemelia. Gegania was in another carriage with the remaining girls. The procession began to make its way back to Rome.

Amata did not look back again. What was there to see? There was nothing behind her but a barren field and a plank of wood covering a deep hole in the ground. Ahead of her was Rome. The future. Marcius was right. Petronia's live burial, and that of any Vestal who might commit the same sacrilege, did offer a type of rebirth—a rebirth of purpose, and a renewed commitment not just to the pure service of Vesta, but to all the gods, and to Rome itself.

Rome, the new Troy. Amata thought of Aeneas's flight as his city burned down around him. She would never let that happen to Rome. The king, the priests, the soldiers, the senators and the citizens of Rome would never let that happen. Fire would not destroy their city. Fire would sustain it forever.

EPILOGUE

T he morning air in the area of the Forum that was sacred to
Vesta was sweet and full of song. Gone were the stench of
the sewer and the shouts of workers, replaced by the mild
scent of incense and the joyful sound of the early birds as their
song rose like a chorus from the well-treed sanctuary of Vesta's
grove. There was the sound of people, too—happy chatter and
congratulations. Someone was playing a *cithara*.

The Temple of Vesta had been scrubbed clean and garlands of laurel had been wrapped around its wooden columns. Sacrificial tripods
stood around its perimeter and a fire burned atop each one. Pretty
city slaves carried baskets of freshly baked, ribbon-wrapped loaves of
bread, offering them to the people who had gathered around the temple to celebrate the official initiation of the first novices into the
Roman order of Vestal Virgins. After the punishment of the unchaste
sacerdos Petronia, the pestilence had abated and Numa had opened
the reserves of grain. Yet another reason to honor the immaculate
priestesses whose devotion kept the city safe and fed.

Amata, who now lived in the House of the Vestals rather than on
the Palatine, dressed with the assistance of a slave. The occasion

called for formal attire, and she needed help with the more elaborate headdress of the Vestalis Maxima, as well as her stately stola and palla. After receiving the final approval of her slave—she had been trained to properly dress her important mistress—Amata exited the house to step onto the street outside. Two red-cloaked guards stepped forward to take their place on either side of her, while an impressive pair of *lictors* walked ahead, leading her through the crowds to the temple.

As she walked along, people knelt and tossed flower petals before her feet. She saw familiar smiling faces amongst the gathering, including the families of those girls being initiated into the order today—Hostus and Lucia, Gaius and Attia, Proculus and Valia—and saw many people she didn't know as well. Many of them held gifts for the novices. Parents brought puppies and dolls, while merchants and dignitaries trying to impress brought gold bracelets and expensive fabrics. They would have the opportunity to give these presents to the novices after the initiation ceremony, which itself would be held inside the sanctity and secrecy of the temple.

Reaching the entrance to the sanctum, Amata glanced up at the statue of Vesta that stood near the oculus in the domed roof. It too had been freshly cleaned and shone in the sunlight as though approving of the happy occasion. And yet, the happiness had an undercurrent of something else. Everyone knew how Petronia had died—if, now four days later, she had in fact died. Perhaps she was still clinging to the last of life, underground, in what the people had taken to calling the *Campus Sceleratus*. The Evil Field. Regardless, the respect that Romans now had for their Vestal order was tinged with a shade of danger that only seemed to increase the regard they felt for it, and for the commitment these young girls were making today.

Amata opened the door and stepped inside. The Vestals Gegania and Aemelia stood by the sacred hearth as the Pontifex Maximus Marcius inspected the row of novices. The girls were dressed in white tunicas, long hair reaching down their backs, feet bare. Amata walked to the hearth and lifted a sacred wafer made of salted flour off a terracotta plate, crumbling the offering into the *viva flamma*, the living flame of the goddess. She had created the recipe for the purified offering herself, and ovens were currently being built in the House of the Vestals so the priestesses could oversee their production.

The Pontifex Maximus said a prayer and handed Amata a sacrificial knife. The high priestess moved to little Veneneia.

"Tell me if I'm pulling too hard," she said. The girl nodded, but did not flinch as Amata cropped off the novice's long locks of hair, letting them fall to the floor of the temple. "When we are done here," Amata continued, "you can hang your hair from the Capillata tree. And I shouldn't tell you, but there are many people outside waiting to give you presents." The thought of that distracted the young girl from the cropping and she grinned, not even seeming to notice the thin stream of anointing oil the Pontifex poured on her head.

Amata put her hand on Veneneia's shoulder and directed her to a washbasin full of water from the spring of Egeria. The girl put her hands in the purifying water, thereby cleansing the hands that would watch and nourish Vesta's fire.

Amata remembered the day that she and Numa had stood together in the powerful waters of the spring of Egeria , the day the king had purified her so that she could again serve the immaculate goddess. As she watched the ceremonial rites of the novices' initiation, she saw her own experience reflected in them. That was Numa's doing. He had insisted on modeling this ceremony on hers. She had been touched by that, and it made what was happening around her even more meaningful.

Gegania passed her a white veil, and Amata placed it upon Veneneia's head. As she did, the Pontifex Maximus knelt on the floor before the novice and took her tiny hands in his own. It was now time for him to speak the words that would welcome her into the Vestal order.

"I take thee, Amata, as one who has met the requirements of

law, to be a priestess of Vesta, and to perform the holy rites which is proper for the Vestal priestesses to do for the Roman people."

It was the verbal formula that Amata, Marcius and Numa had agreed upon—though with one alteration that Amata had not been consulted on and that took her by complete surprise. Rather than speaking the girl's own name, the Pontifex spoke hers. *Amata.* It meant *beloved one.* It also meant that, from this day forward, throughout the centuries that the goddess's sacred fire would burn in the temple, every novice initiated into the Vestal order would speak her name. The name of a Silvian.

NOTE OF INTEREST

*Sacerdotem Vestalem, quae sacra faciat quae ius siet sac-
erdotem Vestalem facere pro populo Romano Quiritibus,
uti quae optima lege fuit, ita te, Amata, capio.*

(I take thee, Beloved One, as one who has met the requirements of law, to be a priestess of Vesta, and to
perform the holy rites, which is proper for the Vestal
priestesses to do for the Roman people.)

According to the 2nd century CE Roman historian Aulus Gellius,
who is referencing a passage in Fabius Pictor's lost c. 200 BCE
History, these were the words spoken by the chief pontiff when a
Vestal was first "taken" to serve the goddess. Gellius cites the tra-
ditional belief that the first Vestal to be taken was named Amata.
Amata, in Latin, also means *beloved one.*

The First Vestals of Rome

Book I – RHEA SILVIA

Book II – TARPEIA

Book III – AMATA

Thank you for reading.

To see the author's other books on Vesta and the Vestal Virgins, please visit DebraMayMacleod.com.

You'll also find a wealth of supporting content on the author's website: articles, ancient history, videos, a gallery of images (including artifacts and coins either found in Debra's novels or which inspired certain elements in them), and much more.